Selected Chinese Short Stories of the Tang and Song Dynasties

Written by Yuan Zhen and others
Translated by Yang Xianyi
Gladys Yang
Huang Jun

Foreign Languages Press Beijing

First Edition 2001

Publisher's Note

This book has been translated from Chinese by Yang Xianyi and Gladys Yang jointly (stories 2, 4, 5, 6, 7, 10, 11, 13) and by Huang Jun (the fourteen others).

Home Page:
   http://www.flp.com.cn
E-mail Addresses:
   Info@flp.com.cn
   Sales@flp.com.cn

ISBN 7-119-02098-6
©Foreign Languages Press, Beijing, China, 2001
Published by Foreign Languages Press
24 Baiwanzhuang Road, Beijing 100037, China
Distributed by China International Book Trading Corporation
35 Chegongzhuang Xilu, Beijing 100044, China
P.O. Box 399, Beijing, China

Printed in the People's Republic of China

Contents

Foreword

The Tang Dynasty (618-907) and the Song (960-1279) witnessed the flourishing of short stories in China. The short story can be found in embryo form in China during the Six Dynasties Period (220-589), when a number of interesting anecdotes and weird tales appeared. While tales in the Six Dynasties Period were all stories of ghosts and spirits or fragmentary narrations of events, short stories in the Tang and Song dynasties differed from them in drawing their themes from people and events of the times, in being highly imaginative, having closely knit plots, a wealth of detail and clear-cut images of the characters. It is no exaggeration to say that the emergence of Tang and Song short stories showed that writers in China had begun to write stories consciously and also marked the coming of age of story writing in China.

The 22 short stories, 14 of the Tang Dynasty and eight of the Song, in this collection are a fair sample of earlier short stories in China. Short stories of this kind often involve supernatural events, adventures, political themes, Buddhist or Taoist preachments, or love between men and women. They reflect the thoughts and aspirations of the common people and are, in fact, consummate works of art imbued with all the vitality of their times.

1. The Runaway Spirit of Qian Niang

Chen Xuanyou

Having a limited knowledge of science, ancient people in China believed that there was a spirit separable from the body it controlled, and so tales of the spirit detached from its body, and acting independently were passed down from the dawn of civilization. It was not until the Tang Dynasty, however, that intricate stories like "The Runaway Spirit of Qian Niang" appeared in writing. Qian Niang (Elegant Girl) and Wang Zhou have been in love with each other since childhood but, despite earlier promises, Zhang Yi, the girl's father, decides to have her marry a more promising suitor. Qian Niang's spirit left her body to join her sweetheart Wang Zhou, but could not help missing her own parents and finally returned to her body at home.

Although the story is just fantasy, the description of the conflict between Qian Niang's pure love for Wang Zhou and her affection for her own parents is quite touching. Later, The Runaway Spirit of the Elegant Girl, *an opera by Zheng Guangzu in the Yuan Dynasty (1271-1368), was derived from this story, and legends like* The Peony Pavilion *by Tang Xianzu in the Ming Dynasty (1368-1644) were clearly variants of this strain.*

The story first appeared as Chapter 358 in Taiping Miscellany. *Nothing is known about the author's life, but we can tell from his work that he must live at the time of Emperors Daizong (762-779) and Dezong (780-805) of the Tang Dynasty.*

In the third year (692) of the Tianshou period, Zhang Yi of Qinghe Prefecture moved with his family to Hengzhou to become a magistrate there. He was not a very outgoing man, and had few close friends. He had no son but two daughters. The elder died young, while the younger, Qian Niang, blossomed into a serene beauty. Zhang had a nephew called Wang Zhou, from Taiyuan City, living in the house. Clever and handsome, the boy behaved so well that Zhang said on more than one occasion that at some time in the future he would give his daughter to him in marriage.

When the boy and girl grew up, they fell secretly in love with each other. However, when a promising young man who was a candidate for a new office asked Zhang Yi for his daughter's hand, Zhang consented. Qian Niang was mortified and Wang Zhou in a rage. The young man decided to leave for the capital on the excuse of an official transfer. Zhang Yi had no reason to stop him, and sent him off with many gifts.

With untold grief and indignation, Wang Zhou bade Zhang and his darling farewell and boarded a boat. In the twilight, the boat travelled some distance from the valley. Wang was tossing in bed when suddenly he heard someone tottering along the shore and boarding his boat. To his great surprise, he found Qian Niang barefoot, her shoes and stockings having been lost on the way. Joyfully taking her hand, Wang asked her how she had come.

"Darling, you have always loved me so much that I dream of you every night in my sleep. Now my father has shattered my dreams, but I know that your heart will always remain true, and so I have risked my life to come and join you," the girl said. Beside himself with joy, Wang Zhou hid the girl in the boat and vanished in the dark. Within a few months, they were in Sichuan.

During the next five years, they had two sons, and had no communication with Zhang Yi at all. However, Qian Niang could not help missing her parents. One day she said sobbing to her husband, "To be loyal to you, I desperately left my parents to join you. It has been five years now since I turned my back on them. How could I go on living like this for ever?"

"All right, my darling, let's go back then. Don't grieve any more," Wang said. And they returned together to Hengzhou.

On arrival, Wang Zhou went alone to Zhang

5

Yi's house, to apologize for eloping with Zhang's daughter without his blessing. "What nonsense. Qian Niang has been lying ill in bed ever since you left," Zhang exclaimed.

"But she is in the boat!" Wang said.

Astounded, Zhang sent a servant to the boat to check for him. Sure enough, the servant found Qian Niang in the boat. On seeing the servant Qian Niang, radiant with a smile, asked, "How's Father and Mother?"

Dumbfounded, the servant hurried home to report this to his master. In the meantime, the sick Qian Niang lying in bed sat up, dressed herself and without a word came out smiling to meet her other self. In a flash, the two Qian Niangs merged, dresses and all. Too bizzare a family tale to tell, the Zhangs kept it a secret, telling only a few relatives.

Forty years later the couple died. Both their sons passed the civil examination and became a vice county magistrate and county garrison commander respectively.

I have heard the story since my childhood although in widely different versions, and always regarded it as mere fiction. But in the last year of the Dali period (766-779), I met the Laiwu County Magistrate Zhang Zhonggui, who told me the story again in detail. Since he was Zhang Yi's own nephew and the details of the story he told were convincing, I have recorded it faithfully as it was told to me.

2. Ren the Fox Fairy

Shen Jiji

*Among the legends of the Wei, Jin and Southern
and Northern Dynasties (220-589), many fox-fairy
tales emerged. "Ren the Fox Fairy" marked a great
advance in the Tang Dynasty, not only in writing
teachnique but also in character depiction.*

*Except for not making her own clothes, Ren
appears to be a normal of flesh and blood, deeply
devoted to her lover until she is bitten to death by
hounds and reveals her true form. From the time
she and Zheng Liu first meet, she remains loyal to
him until she gives up her own life for him. The
author laments that she should "resist violation and
remain chaste and faithful to her lord till death,
while few women nowadays are equal to this!" And
this is perhaps his reason for writing the story.
Nevertheless, we cannot agree with the author in
having her arrange other girls to please the
playboy Wei Yin as an act of gratitude.*

*The story uses exaggeration and contrast to
describe Ren's beauty, while actions and details
reveal her nature and personality. This style can be*

7

found in many later fox-fairy tales, such as Strange Tales from Make-Do Studio.

Some say that Shen Jiji was a native of Wuxian County, Jiangsu Province, others, that he came from Wukang County, Zhejiang Province. During the Dezong reign of the Tang Dynasty, he worked first as Left Advisor and then as an editor and compiler of history and folklore, and in the second year (781 A.D.) of the Jianzhong period was demoted to the position of revenue manager in the army in Chuzhou, Zhejiang, where he worked his way up to become a vice bureau director in the Ministry of Rites. He is the author of the ten-volume Chronicles of Jianzhong.

Wei Yin, ninth son of the daughter of the Prince of Xinan, was a somewhat wild young lord and a heavy drinker. His cousin's husband, Zheng, whose personal name is not known but who was the sixth child of his family, had studied the military arts and was also fond of drinking and women. Since he was poor and had no home of his own, he lived with his wife's family. Zheng and Wei became inseparable. In the sixth month of the ninth year of the Tianbao period (750 A.D.), they were walking together through the capital on their way to a drinking party in the Xinchang quarter, when Zheng, who had some private business, left Wei south of the Xuanping quarter, saying he would join him later at the feast. Then Wei headed east on his white horse, while Zheng rode south on his donkey through the north gate of the Shengping quarter.

On the road Zheng came upon three girls, one of whom, dressed in a white gown, was exceedingly lovely. Pleasantly surprised, he whipped up his donkey to circle round them, but lacked the courage to accost them. Since the girl in white kept glancing at him in what seemed an encouraging way, he asked jokingly:

"Why should such beautiful girls as you travel on foot?"

The girl in white countered with a smile: "If men with mounts aren't polite enough to offer us a lift, what else can we do?"

"My poor donkey is not good enough for such lovely ladies as you," protested Zheng. "But it is at your disposal, and I shall be glad to follow you on foot."

He and the girl looked at each other and laughed, and with her two maids teasing them they were soon on familiar terms. He went east with these young women to Leyou Park, and dusk had fallen by the time they reached a magnificent mansion with massive walls and an imposing gate. The girl in white went in, calling back over her shoulder, "Wait a little!" One of her maids stayed at the gate and asked Zheng his name. Having told her, he enquired the name of the girl and learned that her surname was Ren and that she was the twentieth child in the family.

Presently Zheng was invited in. He had just tethered his donkey at the gate and placed his hat on the saddle, when the girl's sister—a woman of thirty or thereabouts—came out to greet him. Candles were set out, the table spread, and they had drunk several cups of wine when the girl, who had changed her dress, joined them. Then they drank a great deal and made merry, and late at night they went to bed together. Her coquetry and charm, the way she sang and laughed and moved—it was all exquisite and something out of this world. Just before dawn Ren said, "You had better go now. My brother is a member of the royal conservatory of music and serves in the royal guards. He'll be home at daybreak and he mustn't see you." Having arranged to come again, Zheng left.

When he reached the end of the street, the gate of that quartet was still bolted. But there was a foreign bread shop there where a light was burning and the stove had been lit. Sitting under the awning, waiting for the morning drum, Zheng began chatting with the shopkeeper. Pointing to where he had spent the night, asked, "When you turn east from here you come to a big gate—whose house is that?"

"Its all in ruins," said the shopkeeper. "There's no house left."

"But I was there," insisted Zheng. "How can you say there is no house?"

The shopkeeper understood in a flash what

had happened. "Ah, now I see it!" he exclaimed. "There's a fox fairy there, who often tempts men to spend the night with her. She has been seen three times. So you met her too, didn't you?"

Ashamed to admit the truth, Zheng denied this. When it was light he looked at the place again, and found the walls and the gate still there, but only waste land and a deserted garden behind.

After reaching home he was blamed by Wei for not joining him the previous day; but instead of telling the truth, Zheng made up an excuse. He was still bewitched by the fairy's beauty, however, and longed to see her again, unable to drive her image from his heart. About a fortnight later, in a clothes shop in the West Market, he once more came upon her accompanied by her maids. When he called out to her, she tried to slip into the crowd to avoid him; but he called her name repeatedly and pushed forward. Then, with her back to him and her fan behind her, she said: "You know who I am. Why do you follow me?"

"What if I do?" asked Zheng.

"I feel ashamed to face you," she replied.

"I love you so much, how could you leave me?" he protested.

"I don't want to leave you; I'm only afraid you must hate me."

When Zheng swore that he still loved her and became more insistent in his request, the girl turned round and let fall the fan, appearing as dazzlingly beautiful as ever.

"There are many fox fairies about," she told the young man. "It's just that you don't know them for what they are. You needn't think it strange."

Zheng begged her to come back to him and she said, "Fox fairies have a bad name because they often harm men; but that is not my way. If I have not lost your favour, I would like to serve you all my life." Asked where they could live, she suggested. "East of here you'll come to a house with a big tree towering above its roof. It's in a quiet part of town—why not rent it? The other day when I first met you south of the Xuanping quarter, another gentleman rode off on a white horse toward the east. Wasn't he your brother-in-law? There's a lot of furniture in his house you can borrow."

It so happened, indeed, that Wei's uncles, absent on official duty, had stored away their furniture with him. Acting on Ren's advice, Zheng went to Wei and asked to borrow it. Asked the reason, he said, "I have just got a beautiful mistress and rented a house for her. I want to borrow the furniture for her use."

"A beauty, indeed!" retorted Wei with a laugh. "Judging by your own looks, you must have found some monstrosity!"

None the less his friend lent him curtains, bed and bedding, dispatching an intelligent servant with him to have a look at the girl. Presently the servant ran back, our of breath and sweating. "Well?" asked Wei, stepping forward. "Have you seen her? What's she like?"

"Marvellous! I've never seen anyone so lovely!"

Wei, who had many relations and had seen many beauties in the course of his numerous adventures, asked whether Zheng's mistress was a match for one of these.

"No comparison!" exclaimed the servant. Wei mentioned four or five other names, but still received a negative reply. His sister-in-law, sixth daughter of the Prince of Wu, was a peerless beauty, as lovely as a fairy. "How does she compare with the sixth daughter of the Prince of Wu?" he asked.

But again his man declared that there was no comparison.

"Is that possible?" Wei exclaimed, clasping his hands in amazement. Then he hastily asked for water to wash his neck, put on a new cap, rouged his lips and went to call on Zheng.

It happened that Zheng was out and Wei, entering, found a young servant sweeping and a maid at the door, but no one else. He questioned the boy, who told him with a laugh that there was no one at home. But making a search of the rooms, Wei saw a red skirt behind a door and going closer discovered Ren hiding there. Dragged out from the dark corner, she was even more beautiful than he had been told. Mad with passion, he took her in his arms to assault her, only to meet with resistance. He pressed her hard, until she said, "You shall have your way, but first let me recover my breath." However, when Wei came on again she resisted as before. This happened three or four times. Finally Wei held her down with all his strength and the girl, exhausted and drenched with perspiration, knew she could hardly escape. Limp and inert, she gave him a heart-rending look.

"Why are you so sad?" he asked.

With a long sigh, she answered, "I pity Zheng with all my heart."

"What do you mean?" he demanded.

"He's over six feet tall but has failed to protect a woman—how can he call himself a man? You are young and rich, and have many beautiful mistresses. You have seen many like me. But Zheng is a poor man, and I am the only woman he loves. How can you rob him of his only love while you have so many? Because he is poor, he has to be dependent on others. He wears your clothes, eats your food, and so he is in your power. If he could support himself, we shouldn't have come to this."

At this, Wei, a gallant man with a sense of justice, desisted, composed himself and apologized. Then Zheng came back and they exchanged cordial greetings. And thenceforward Wei looked after all their needs.

Ren often met Wei and went out with him on foot or by carriage. He spent almost every day with her until they became the best of friends, taking great delight in each other's company. And because she was everything to him except his mistress, he loved and respected her and grudged her nothing. Even eating and drinking he could not forget her. Knowing Wei's love for her, Ren said to him one day: "I'm ashamed to accept such favours from you. I don't deserve such kindness. And I can't betray Zheng to do as you desire. I was born in Shaanxi and brought up in the capital. My family are theater people, and since all the women in it are the mistresses and concubines of rich men, they know every single courtesan in the capital. If you see some beautiful girl and cannot have her, I would like to get her for you to repay your kindness." Wei accepted her offer.

A dress-maker named Zhang in the market place took Wei's fancy with her clear complexion and fine figure. He asked Ren if she knew her, and she answered, "She is my cousin. I can get her easily." After about ten days, she brought this woman to him. A few months later, when Wei was tired of Zhang, Ren said, "Market girls are easy game. Try to think of someone most charming but hardly attainable, and I shall do my best for you."

"The other day at the Han Shi Festival,"[1] said Wei, "I went to Qianfu Temple with some friends

---

[1] On this day in early spring no stoves were lit and people ate cold food (*han shi*).

when General Diao had brought his musicians to play in the hall. One of them was a reed-organ player, a girl of about sixteen with two locks of hair over her ears. She was charming—quite lovely! Do you know her?"

"She's the general's favourite," answered Ren. "Her mother is my sister. I'll see what I can do."

Wei bowed to her, and Ren promised him her help. She became a frequent visitor at the general's house. After a whole month had passed, Wei urged her to make haste and enquired what her plan was. She asked him for two bolts of silk to use as a bribe, and these he gave to her. Two days later, he was having a meal with Ren when the general sent his steward with a black horse to beg her to go to his house. Hearing this summons, Ren smiled at Wei and said, "It is done!" It seemed that she had made the favourite fall ill with a disease which medicine was powerless to cure. At their wits' end, the girl's mother and the general had consulted a witch doctor; but Ren had shown this witch doctor her house and bribed her to say that the sick girl must be removed there.

Accordingly the witch doctor told the general, "The girl must not stay at home but should go and live in that house in the southeast, to imbibe the life-giving influences there." When they made enquiries and found it was Ren's house, the general asked her to let the girl lodge there. At first Ren declined, saying her house was too small, and only after repeated requests did she give her consent. Then the general sent the girl in a carriage with clothing and trinkets, accompanied by her mother, to Ren's house. As soon as she arrived, she was cured. Within a few days, Ren secretly introduced Wei to her, and a month later she was with child. But then her mother took fright, and carried her back hastily to the general; so this was the end of that affair.

One day Ren asked Zheng, "Can you lay your hands on five or six thousand coins? If so, I promise to make a profit for you."

When he had raised a loan of six thousand coins, she told him, "Go to the horse-dealers in the market. You will find a horse with a spot on its rump—buy it and take it home."

Zheng went to the market where he saw a man trying to sell a horse which, sure enough, had a black mark on its rump. Accordingly he bought it and led it home. His brothers-in-law scoffed, "Nobody wants a hack like that. What did you buy such a crock for?"

Soon after that, Ren told him: "The time has come to sell the horse. You should get thirty thousand for it." Then Zheng took the horse to the market, and was offered twenty thousand but refused to sell.

All the folk in the market marvelled: "Why does one offer such a price? Why does the other refuse to sell?"

When Zheng started to ride away, the would-be purchaser followed him to the gate and raised his offer to twenty-five thousand, but still Zheng would not sell. "Nothing doing under thirty thousand," he declared. Then, however, his brothers-in-law gathered round and pestered him into selling at just under thirty thousand.

Later he found out the reason for the buyer's insistence: This man was the groom of Zhaoying County, and one of his horses which had a black mark on its rump had died three years before. This fellow was to be discharged soon, and was due to be paid sixty thousand for keeping the horses. If he could buy a horse for half that sum and hand it over to the government, he would still be the gainer. He would be paid for three years' fodder which had never been consumed. That was why he had insisted on buying.

Once Ren asked Wei for some new dresses, as her old gowns were worn out. He wanted to buy silk for her, but she declined, saying she preferred ready-made clothes. Wei commissioned a shopkeeper named Zhang to get them, sending him to Ren to find out just what she wanted. When the shopkeeper saw her, he was so astonished that later he said to Wei, "That is no common woman, she must be from some noble house. It isn't right for you to keep her. I hope you will return her to her family soon, to avoid trouble." This shows how striking her appearance was.

However, they could not understand why she insisted on buying ready-made dresses instead of having them made to measure.

A year later Zheng was appointed a captain of Huaili Prefecture, with his headquarters at Jincheng. Now since Zheng had a wife, though he spent the day with his mistress he had to go home to sleep at night, and he missed Ren. So when he was going to his post he asked her to accompany him; but she refused.

"We should only be together for a month or two," she said. "It seems hardly worth it. It would be better to work out how much I shall need to spend while you're away, and let me wait at home till you come back." Although Zheng pleaded with her, she was adamant. Then Zheng asked Wei for a loan, and Wei came to persuade her too and to ask the reason. After some little hesitation she answered. "A witch told me it would be unlucky for me to go west this year. That's why I want to stay here."

But Zheng was so eager for her to go, he could think of nothing else. Both men laughed at her and demanded, "How can an intelligent girl like you be so superstitious?" They reasoned with her.

"If what the witch said was true," said Ren, "and I die because I go with you, won't you be sorry?"

"Nonsense!" declared the two men, and insisted again. Finally they persuaded her against her will.

Wei lent her his horse and saw them off at Lingao. The next day they reached Mawei. Ren was riding ahead on the horse with Zheng behind on his donkey, followed by her maid and other attendants. The gamekeepers outside the West Gate had been training their hounds at Luochuan for some ten days, and just as Ren was passing the hounds leaped out from the bushes. Then Zheng saw his mistress drop to the ground, turn into a fox and fly southward with the pack in hot pursuit. He ran forward and yelled at the hounds, but could not restrain them; and after running a few hundred yards she was caught. Shedding tears, Zheng took money from his pocket to buy back the carcass, which was then buried with a pointed stick stuck into the ground to mark the place. When he looked back, her horse was cropping grass by the roadside, her clothes were lying on the saddle, while her shoes and stockings were hanging on the stirrups like the skin shed by a cicada. Her trinkets had dropped to the ground, but everything else belonging to her had vanished, including her maid.

About ten days later Zheng returned to the capital. Wei was delighted to see him, and coming forward to greet him asked, "Is Ren well?"

With tears Zheng replied, "She is dead!"

Wei was stricken with grief at this news. They embraced each other and mourned bitterly, then Wei asked what sudden illness had carried her off.

"She was killed by hounds," answered Zheng.

"Even fierce hounds cannot kill men," protested Wei.

"But she was no human being."

When Wei cried out in amazement, his friend told him the whole story. He could only marvel and heave sigh after sigh. The next day they went together by carriage to Mawei, and after opening the grave to look at the carcass returned prostrated with grief. When they thought back over her behaviour, the only unusual habit they could recall was that she would never have her clothes made to measure.

Later Zheng became the inspector of the royal stable and a very wealthy man, keeping a stable of some dozen horses. He died at the age of sixty-five.

During the Dali period (766-779), I was staying at Zhongling and spent much time with Wei, who told me this story over and over again until I knew it inside out. Later Wei became a chancellor of the imperial court and concurrently Prefect of Longzhou, finally dying at his post in the northwest.

It is sad to think that a beast assuming human form should resist violation and remain chaste and faithful to her lord till death, while few women nowadays are equal to this! And what a pity that Zheng was not more intelligent. He simply appreciated her appearance without studying her nature. A really wise man would have probed the laws of change, investigated the nature of supernatural beings, and with his skilful pen recorded the gist of the mystery, instead of simply contenting himself with the enjoyment of her grace and charm. This is most unfortunate!

In the second year of the Jianzhong period (781), when I was Left Advisor, I left for Suzhou at the same time that General Bei Qi, Junior City Magistrate Sun Cheng, Bureau Director Cui Xu of the Ministry of Revenue, and Right Advisor Lu Chun were setting out to the Yangtze River Valley. We travelled together from the province of Shaanxi to Suzhou by land and along the waterways. With us too was ex-Advisor Zhu Fang, who was on a tour. As we floated down the Ying and Huai rivers in our boat, feasting by day and conversing at night, each of us told of some strange happenings. When these gentlemen heard the story of Ren, they were deeply moved and greatly astonished; and because they asked me to record this strange tale, I have written this narrative.

3. Madame Willow

Xu Yaozuo

This is a romance of chivalry and love through separation and reunion. Squire Li finds a good match of beauty with talent between Madame Liu (Madame Willow) and Han Yi; Xu Jun cannot bear to see such a perfect union torn apart by brute force and comes out to redeem it. For all her beauty and shrewdness, Liu, the heroine, relies completely on others, being passed from hand to hand like a piece of goods, and submitting herself to a brutal rough-neck. Filled with compassion for her, the author lashes out at the tumult of war and the wanton warlords but criticises the events with conventional ideas, revealing his rather pedantic mentality.

Xu Yaozuo, the author, was a successful candidate of the imperial examinations in the Tang Dynasty, Grand Proofreader and finally Grand Master of Remonstrance. According to The Chronicles of Tang Poetry, *Vol. 41, in the 16th year of the Zhenyuan period (800 A.D.), he was an advisor to the Western Expedition General. Six of his essays were collected in the* Literary Works of the Tang Dynasty, *Vol. 633, but not this story.*

23

A similar record was found in the Poetry of True Events, *by Meng Zhao, with a note on its source from which we can see that these events really did take place and were widely known at that time. As the story was sad and moving, it was later rewritten into several operas—*The Chained Purse, *by Wu Changru in the Ming Dynasty and* The Willow of Chang'an *by Zhang Guoshou in the Qing Dynasty (1644-1911).*

In the Tianbao period (742-756), there was a young poet in Changli named Han Yi. He was unconventional, lived with relatives on his mother's side of the family, and was very poor. Han had a good friend named Li who was an educated man of property, and who greatly admired men of letters and cared much about friendship. Li had a favorite concubine named Liu, meaning "Willow," who was a rare beauty, loved conversation, and excelled at singing and reciting poetry. Li had arranged a special house for her dwelling where he often dined and drank tea with Han Yi. He even rented a neighboring house to accommodate Han.

Being a social figure, Han had many important visitors. Liu would often peep through the door and murmur, "Could such a famed scholar as Master Han really be in want?" As Li himself was an ardent admirer of Han, he would never stint at anything to please his friend. On discovery of Liu's secret admiration for Han, he invited Han to dinner, at the height of which he rose to make a toast and declared, "Madame Liu's beauty finds no match and Scholar Han's literary talent is unrivalled. May I propose that the two of you unite?"

Thoroughly shaken, Han stood up to leave, protesting, "My dear friend, you've been kind enough to share your own clothes and food with me. How could I ever deprive you of your love?" Li insisted, however, and seeing this was his sincere wish, Liu presented herself, bowing deeply to both Li and Han, and took her seat at the table. Li seated his friend as the guest of honor and repeatedly toasted the couple till the end of the banquet. Li took out three hundred thousand coins to provide for Han's domestic needs. Since Han adored Liu's beauty and Liu his genius, the success and bliss of the union can well be imagined.

The next year Han Yi was chosen by the Vice-Minister of Rites, Yang Du, as a successful candidate in the imperial examinations. But he stayed in town for a year without accepting his honor and offcial appointment. Liu said to him, "You should visit your parents and bring honor to your family, as the ancient people did. How can you waste your time with a humble woman like me and delay your offcial appointment in the capital? You must go. I have enough to live on here until you return." So Han Yi went home to visit his parents. After a year, Liu ran out of food and had to pawn her jewelry to make ends meet.

In the last year of the Tianbao period, there was a rebellion in the country. The rebel army took both the east capital, Luoyang, and the west capital, Chang'an, and many people fled the cities. Fearing that her beauty would bring her trouble, Liu cut off her hair, damaged her looks and led the life of a hermit in the Faling Temple. At this time Hou Xiyi was transferred to Ziqing as Governor, appointing Han Yi to be his secretary on account of his literary merit. It was not until Emperor Suzong recovered the capital with his military might that Han was able to send a man by a small path to search for his sweetheart Liu. The man brought Liu some chips of gold in a white silk purse on which Han had written a short poem:

Willow by the terrace, my willow, is your beauty still with you?
Slim and green your branches, have they been plucked long ago?

Tears ran down her cheeks as Liu received the gold; even her maids wept with her. Taking a brush, she wrote down these lines:

Willow of virtue sprouts each year; her branches are made parting souvenirs.
A falling leaf ushers in autumn; can her beauty last till ever you come?

Soon, a general of ethnic minority origin in the Imperial Army named Shazhari, once decorated for

26

his valor, came to hear of Liu's rare beauty. He abducted her to his mansion and spent every night with her in a special chamber. Governor Hou was promoted vice-minister, and Han Yi went with him to the capital. There, he looked for Liu but failed to find her, and was filled with endless remorse.

One day at the Dragon Head Ridge, Han Yi saw an ox carriage screened on all sides, driven by a servant and followed by two maids. As he got nearer to the carriage he heard a soft whisper from inside, "Isn't that Squire Han Yi? I'm Willow." Then one of the maids was sent to tell him that Madame Liu was now being held by General Shazhari. Because there were others in the carriage, Liu asked him to wait by one of the city gates the next morning. Han did as requested, and found Liu in a carriage. She gave him a jade box filled with a scented ointment and wrapped in white silk. "I am afraid this is a parting gift for you and we will never meet again. Please remember me." With these words she turned the carriage around and drove away, waving her hand in a fluttering sleeve while Han Yi gazed in stupor until the carriage disappeared in the flying dust. He was overwhelmed with emotion.

Just then several generals from Ziqing were feasting in a restaurant, and invited Han to join them. Han consented, but his distraught manner and voice betrayed him among his friends. One gallant young police inspector, Xu Jun, said to him, with his hand on his sword, "Sir, you look so sad, something must be dreadfully wrong. Let me help you put it right." Han had no choice but to tell him his whole story.

"Please write down a few words for the lady and I'll bring her back to you right away," said Xu. He put on his uniform, slung his bow and arrows across his back and with a bodyguard behind him made straight for Shazhari's mansion. He waited outside until Shazhari left, gave him time to travel about half a kilometer, then tore open his jacket, baring his chest, and with the reins in hand, dashed through the front gate straight into the main hall, shouting, "The General has suddenly fallen ill and sent for Madame Liu!" Frightened out of their wits, the servants dared not look up to ask questions. The young officer rushed upstairs, showed the lady Han Yi's note, and took her downstairs and out of the house on horseback, leaving a cloud of dust behind. The horse raced along so fast that the reins snapped. In less than half an hour, they were in the restaurant. "Sir, I've honored my promise!" the young man proudly presented the lady to Han, to the amazement of all present. Liu and Han clasped each other's hands and wept in rapture while all others were deeply touched.

Nevertheless, Shazhari, the Emperor's favorite, was certainly no easy person to deal with. Worrying about the consequences, both Han and Xu begged the vice-minister Hou Xiyi for help. Hou was deeply shocked. He said, "All my life I've been prudent. How dare you do this, Xu Jun?" He hastily wrote a memorandum to the throne:

"Adjutant Inspector, Assistant Treasurer and Censor Han Yi, having passed the imperial examinations with honor, has served under me for some years with merit. He has a concubine who was separated from him during the years of tumult and lived with an honorable nun. Now that peace and prosperity have been restored in the country, people live in harmony throughout the land. However, General Shazhari has wantonly violated the Imperial Law. Considering himself excerpt from the law because of his past services, he went so far as to kidnap Madame Liu whom he had taken a fancy to, and seriously violated the social order. My subordinate, Police Inspector Xu Jun, whose family are from Youzhou and Jizhou, is a brave officer. He took Madame Liu by force and nobly returned her to Han Yi. However, he did this without my permission, and my own negligence is partly responsible."

Soon an edict was announced to the effect that Liu should be returned to Han Yi, and General Shazhari was granted two million coins in compensation. The matter was thus settled. Later, Han Yi, through a series of promotions, finally became the Secretariat Drafter.

We can say that Madame Liu was a devoted woman, but not resolute enough in character; Xu Jun a chivalrous man, but not prudent in character.

With her beauty and loyalty, Liu could compare with the two famous palace ladies-in-waiting, Feng and Ban, in the Han Dynasty[1]; with his talent, Xu had the courage of Cao Mo in the Spring and Autumn Period and Lin Xiangru in the Warring States Period[2]. The glory of historical events depends on action, and without their occurrence there can be no merit. It is a pity that Liu and Xu did not live in the right time or place, and their natural endowments were never fully exploited. Was this due to a lack of integrity and social responsibility or was it rather owing to lack of opportunity? I think it was a matter of opportunity.

---

[1] Emperor Yuandi of the Han Dynasty was watching a wild beast fight when a huge bear broke loose and rushed toward him. Lady of Handsome Fairness Feng stepped up and stood between the beast and the Emperor to protect him.

Once Emperor Chengdi wanted Lady of Handsome Fairness Ban to accompany him in a carriage on a tour. The lady dared to refuse on the grounds that in the past many monarchs had lost their empires because of lust for beautiful women.

[2] Cao Mo was a general in the State of Lu. Duke Huan of the State of Qi demanded a piece of land from the State of Lu as he had defeated the latter in battle. Dagger in hand, Cao argued with Duke Huan who was forced to relinquish his claim.

The powerful Prince of Qin attempted to humiliate the Prince of Zhao by making him play zither at a banquet. The quick-witted Minister Lin Xiangru of Zhao succeeded in removing the humiliation by getting the Prince of Qin to hit a clay wine cup in rhythm with his master.

4. The Dragon King's Daughter

Li Chaowei

The fairy tale, The Dragon King's Daughter, *is known to every household in China. The story is a fantasy with colorful characters, shining in romantic splendor. The hero Liu Yi encounters a number of mythical figures, such as the tearful and emotional Dragon King's daughter, the fiery and boisterous Prince of Qiantang and the cordial and honorable Lord of Dongting. Liu himself is righteous and compassionate. He will not bow under pressure or brute force, making him a man of integrity and capable of love. Although the events in the tale are far beyond the human world, they embody noble human qualities and are therefore very popular. What is important about the legend is its impact, which spread throughout the country in the centuries following the mid-Tang period. Shang Zhongxian's* Liu Yi of Dongting Lake *and Li Haogu's* Zhang Sheng Boils the Sea *of the Yuan Dynasty, Huang Shuozhong's* The Dragon Flute *of the Ming Dynasty and Li Yu's* The Mansion in the Mirage *of the Qing Dynasty are its progeny. Even*

now it is still very much alive in various forms of drama on the Chinese stage.

The author Li Chaowei's origins are unknown. Judging from the date near the end of the story, he must have lived during the periods of Dali and Zhenyuan (785—805) in the Tang Dynasty.

During the Yifeng period (676-679), a scholar named Liu Yi failed in the official examination and, as he was returning to the Xiang River Valley, decided to go and take his leave of a fellow provincial who was staying at Jingyang. He had ridden about three kilometers, when a bird flying up from the ground startled his horse and made it bolt and it had galloped three kilometers before he could stop it. Then he caught sight of a girl herding sheep by the roadside. She was amazingly beautiful but her finely arched eyebrows were knit, her clothes were soiled, and she was standing there listening intently as if awaiting someone's arrival.

"What has brought you to such a wretched state?" Liu asked.

The girl first expressed her gratitude with a smile; then, unable to restrain her tears, replied, "Unhappy creature that I am! Since you ask me the reason, how can I hide the deep resentment I feel? Listen then! I am the youngest daughter of the dragon king of Dongting Lake. My parents married me to the second son of the dragon king of the Jing River; but my husband, devoted to pleasure and led

33

astray by his attendants, treated me more unkindly every day. I complained to his parents, but they were too fond of their son to take my part. When I persisted in complaining, they grew angry and banished me here." Having said this, she broke down and sobbed.

"Dongting Lake is so far away," she went on. "It lies beyond the distant horizon, and I can get no word to my family. My heart is breaking and my eyes are worn out with watching, but there is no one to know my grief or pity me. Since you are going south and will pass near the lake, may I trouble you to take a letter?"

"I have a sense of justice," answered Liu, "and your story makes my blood boil. I only wish I had wings to fly there—why talk of trouble? But the lake is very deep, and I can only walk on land. How am I to convey your message? I fear I may be unable to get through, proving unworthy of your trust and failing in my own sincere wish to help you. Can you tell me how to make the journey?"

"I cannot say how I appreciate your kindness," said the girl, shedding tears. "If ever I receive a reply, I shall repay you even if it costs my life. Before you promised to help me, I dared not tell you how to reach my parents; but actually, to go to the lake is no harder than going to the capital."

Asked for directions, she told him, "South of the lake stands a big orange tree which is the sacred tree of the village. Take off this belt, put on another, and knock on the trunk three times. Someone will come to your call, and if you follow him you will have no difficulty. I have opened my heart to you besides trusting you with my letter. Please tell my parents what you have heard. On no account fail me!"

Liu promised to do as she said. Then the girl took a letter from her pocket and handed it to him with a bow, all the while looking eastward and weeping in a way that touched his heart.

When he had put the letter in his wallet, he enquired, "May I ask why you herd sheep? Do deities also eat cattle?"

"No," she answered. "These are not sheep, but rain-bringers."

"What are they?"

"Thunder, lightning, and the like."

Liu looked at the sheep closely, and saw that they moved proudly with heads held high. They cropped the grass differently too, although they were the same size as ordinary sheep and had the same wool and horns.

"Now that I am going to act as your messenger," he said, "I hope in future, when you get back to the lake, you won't refuse to see me."

"Certainly not!" she exclaimed. "I shall treat you as a dear relative."

Then they bid each other goodbye, and he started east. After a few dozen yards he looked back, but both girl and sheep had disappeared.

That evening he reached the county town and said goodbye to his friend. It took him over a month to get home, and he went without delay to Dongting Lake. He found the orange tree south of the lake, changed his belt, faced the tree and knocked three times. A warrior came out of the water, and bowed to him. "Why have you come here, honorable sir?" he asked.

Without telling him the story, Liu simply answered, "To see your king."

The warrior parted the waves and pointed the way, saying to Liu as he led him down, "Close your eyes. We will be there in no time."

Liu did as he was told, and soon they reached a great palace where he saw clustered towers and pavilions, millions of gates and arches, and all the rare plants and trees of the world. The warrior asked him to wait at the corner of a great hall.

"What place is this?" asked Liu.

"The Palace of the Divine Void."

Looking round, Liu saw that this palace was filled with every precious object known to man. The pillars were of white jade, the steps of jasper; the couches were of coral, the screens of crystal. The emerald lintels were set with cut glass, while the rainbow-colored beams were inlaid with amber. And the whole created an impression of strange beauty and unfathomable depth which defied description.

The dragon king was a long time in coming,

and Liu asked the warrior, "Where is the Lord of Dongting?"

"His Majesty is in the Dark Pearl Pavilion," was the reply. "He is discussing the Fire Canon with the Sun Priest, but will have finished soon."

"What is the Fire Canon?" Liu wanted to know.

"Our king is a dragon," was the reply, "so water is his element, and with one drop of water he can flood mountains and valleys. The priest is a man, so fire is his element, and with one torch he can burn down a whole palace. Since the properties of the elements differ, they have different effects. As the Sun Priest is expert in the laws of men, our king has asked him over for a talk."

He had barely finished speaking when the palace gate opened, a mist seemed to gather and there appeared a man in purple holding a jasper scepter. The warrior leaped to attention, crying, "This is our king!" Then he went forward to report Liu's arrival.

The dragon king looked at Liu and asked, "Are you not of the world of men?"

Liu replied that he was, and bowed. The king greeted him in return and asked him to be seated.

"Our watery kingdom is dark and deep, and I am ignorant," said the dragon king. "What has brought you, sir, from such a distance?"

"I am of the same district as Your Majesty," replied Liu. "I was born in the south, but have studied in the northwest. Not long ago, after failing in the examination, I was riding by the Jing River when I came upon your daughter herding sheep in the open country. Exposed to wind and rain, she was a pitiful sight. When questioned, she told me she had come to such a pass because of her husband's unkindness and his parents' neglect. I assure you, her tears as she spoke went to my heart. Then she entrusted this letter to me and I promised to deliver it. That is why I am here." He took out the letter and passed it to the king.

After reading the missive, the king covered up his face and wept. "Though I am her old father," he lamented, "I have been like a man blind and deaf, unaware that my child was suffering far away, while you, a stranger, came to her rescue. As long as I live, I shall never forget your kindness." He gave way to weeping, and all the attendants shed tears.

Presently a palace eunuch approached the king, who handed him the letter with orders to tell the women in the inner palace. Soon wailing was heard from within and in alarm the king bade his attendants, "Quickly tell the women not to make so much noise, or Qiantang may hear them!"

"Who is this man?" asked Liu.

"My younger brother," said the dragon king. "He used to be the Prince of the Qiantang River, but has now retired."

"Why must you keep it from him?"

"Because he is overbold," was the reply. "The

nine years of flood in the time of the ancient sage King Yao was due to one of his rages. Not long ago he quarrelled with the angels in heaven and flooded the Five Mountains. Thanks to a few good deeds I had to my credit, the heavenly emperor pardoned him; but he has to be kept here. The people of Qiantang are waiting still for his return."

He had scarcely finished when there came a great crash, as if both heaven and earth had been torn asunder. The palace shook and mist seethed as in burst a crimson dragon more than a thousand feet long, dragging after it a jade pillar to which its neck had been fastened by a gold chain. Its eyes were bright as lightning, its tongue red as blood, and it had scarlet scales and a fiery mane. Thunder crashed and lightning flashed around it, then snow and hail fell thick and fast, after which it soared up into the azure sky.

Panic-stricken, Liu had fallen to the ground. But now the king himself helped him up, urging, "Have no fear! All is well."

After a long time, Liu recovered a little. And when calm enough he asked leave to withdraw. "I had better go while I can," he explained. "I couldn't survive another experience like that."

"There's no need to leave," said the king. "That's the way my brother goes, but he won't come back that way. Do stay a little longer." He called for wine, and they drank to pledge their friendship.

Then a soft breeze sprang up, wafting over auspicious clouds. Amid flying pennons and flags and the sound of flutes and pipes, in came thousands of brightly dressed, laughing and chattering girls. Among them was one with beautiful, arched eyebrows who was wearing bright jewels and a gown of the finest gauze. When she drew near, Liu saw that she was the girl who had given him the message. Now she was shedding tears of joy, as she moved through a fragrant red and purple mist to the inner palace.

The king said with a laugh to Liu, "Here comes the prisoner from the Jing River!" He excused himself and went inside, and from the inner palace happy weeping was heard. Then the king came out again to feast with Liu.

Presently a man in purple strode up to stand by the king. He was holding a jasper scepter and looked vigorous and full of spirit. The king introduced him as the Prince of Qiantang.

Liu stood up to bow, and the prince bowed in return. "My unhappy niece was insulted by that young blackguard," he said. "It was good of you, sir, with your strong sense of justice, to carry the news of her wrongs so far. If not for you, she would have pined away by the Jing River. No words can express our gratitude."

Liu bowed and thanked him. Then the prince told his brother, "I reached the river in one hour, fought there for another hour, and took another hour to come back. On my return journey I flew to high heaven to report to the heavenly emperor; and when he knew the injustice done he pardoned me. In fact, he pardoned my past faults as well. But I am thoroughly ashamed that in my indignation I did not stop to say goodbye, upsetting the whole palace and alarming our honorable guest." He bowed again.

"How many did you kill?" asked the king.

"Six hundred thousand."

"Did you destroy any fields?"

"About four hundred kilometers."

"Where is that scoundrel, her husband?"

"I ate him."

The king looked pained.

"Of course that young blackguard was insufferable," he said. "Still, that was going rather far. It is lucky that the heavenly emperor is omniscient and pardoned you because such a great injustice had been done. Otherwise what could I have said in your defense? Don't ever do that again!" The prince bowed once more.

That evening Liu was lodged in the Hall of Frozen Light, and the next day another feast was given at the Emerald Palace. All the royal family gathered there, music was played, and wine and delicacies were served. Then bugles, horns and drums sounded as ten thousand warriors danced with flags, swords and halberds on the right-hand side, while one came forward to announce that this was the triumphal march of the Prince of Qiantang. This spectacular and awe-inspiring display impressed all who saw it.

Then to an accompaniment of gongs and cymbals, stringed and bamboo instruments, a thousand girls dressed in bright silks and decked with jewels danced on the left-hand side, while one came forward to announce that this music was to celebrate the return of the princess. The melodies were poignant and sweet, breathing such grief and longing that all who heard were moved to tears. When the two dances were over, the dragon king in high good humour made the dancers presents of silk. Then the guests sat down together to feast, and drank to their hearts' content.

When they had drunk their fill, the king rapped on the table and sang:

> *Wide the earth and grey the sky,*
> *Who can hear a distant cry?*
> *The fox lies snugly in his lair,*
> *But thunderbolts can reach him there.*
> *A true man, who upholds the right,*
> *Restored my daughter to my sight.*
> *Such service how can we requite?*

After the king's song ended, the prince made a bow and sang:

> *Life and death are fixed by fate,*
> *Our princess found a worthless mate.*

By River Jing she had to go,
In wind and frost, in rain and snow.
This gentleman her letter bore,
Then we restored her to this shore.
This we'll remember evermore!

After this song, the king and prince stood up and each presented a cup to Liu, who hesitated bashfully before accepting, then quaffed off the wine, returned the cups and sang:

Like a blossom in the rain,
The princess longed for home in vain,
I brought back tidings of her plight,
And all her wrongs were soon set right,
Now we feast, but soon must part,
For home again I needs must start.
Bitter longing fills my heart!

This song of his was greeted by loud applause.

The king brought out a jasper casket of rhinoceros horn which could part the waves, and the prince an amber dish bearing jade that shone at night. They presented these to Liu, who accepted the gifts with thanks. Then the inmates of the palace started piling silk and jewels beside him, until gorgeous materials were heaped up all around. Laughing and chatting with the company, he had not a moment's quiet. Sated at last with wine and pleasure, he excused himself and went back to sleep in the Hall of Frozen Light.

The next day he was feasting again in the Pavilion of Limpid Light when the Prince of Qiantang, heated with wine and lounging on the couch, said insolently, "A hard rock can be smashed but not made to yield, and a gallant man can be killed but not put to shame. I have a proposal to make. If you agree, all will be well between us. If not, we can perish together. How about it?"

"Let me hear your proposal," said Liu.

"As you know, the wife of the Lord of the Jing River is our sovereign's daughter," said the prince. "She is an excellent girl with a fine character, well thought of by all her kinsmen but unlucky enough to have suffered indignities at the hands of that scoundrel. However, that's a thing of the past. We would like to entrust her to you, and become your relatives for ever. Then she who owes you gratitude will belong to you, and we who love her will know she is in good hands. A generous man shouldn't do things by halves. Don't you agree?"

For a moment Liu looked grave. Then he rejoined with a laugh. "I never thought the Prince of Qiantang would have such unworthy ideas. I have heard that once when you crossed the Nine Continents, you shook the Five Mountains to give vent to your anger; and I have seen you break the golden chain and drag the jade pillar after you to rescue your niece. I thought there was no one as brave and just as you, who dared risk death to right a wrong, and would sacrifice your life for those you love. These are the true marks of greatness. Yet now, while music is being played and host and guest are in harmony, you try to force me to do your will in defiance of honor. I would never have expected this of you! If I met you on the angry sea or among dark mountains, with your fins and beard flying and mist and rain all around, though you threatened me with death I should consider you a mere beast and not count it against you. But now you are in human garb. You talk of manners and show a profound understanding of human relationships and the ways of men. You have a nicer sense of propriety than many gallants in the world of men, not to say monsters of the deep. Yet you try to use your strength and temper—while pretending to be drunk—to force me to agree to your proposal. This is hardly right. Although small enough to hide under one of your scales, I am not afraid of your anger. I hope you will reconsider your proposal."

Then the prince apologized. "Brought up in the palace, I was never taught etiquette," he said. "Just now I spoke wildly and offended you—your rebuke was well deserved. Don't let this spoil our friendship." That night they feasted together again as merrily as ever, and Liu and the prince became great friends.

The day after, Liu asked permission to leave. The queen gave another feast for him in the Hall of Hidden Light, which was attended by a great throng of men and women, maids and servants. Shedding tears, the queen said to him, "My daughter owes you so much, we can never repay you. And we are sorry to have to say goodbye." She told the princess to thank him.

"Shall we ever meet again?" asked the queen.

Liu regretted now that he had not agreed to the prince's request. His heart was very heavy. After the feast, when he bid them farewell, the whole palace was filled with sighing, and countless rare jewels were given him as parting gifts.

He left the lake by the way he had come, escorted by a dozen or more attendants who carried his bags to his home before leaving him. He went to a jeweller's at Yangzhou to sell some of the jewels, and though he parted with about one hundredth only he became a multi-millionaire, wealthier by far than all the rich men west of the Huai River.

He married a girl called Zhang, but soon she died. Then he married a girl called Han; but after several months she died as well, and Liu moved to Nanjing.

Loneliness tempted him to marry again, and a go-between told him, "There is a girl called Lu from Fanyang County, whose father, Lu Hao, used to be magistrate of Qingliu. In his later years he studied Taoist philosophy and lived by himself in the wilderness, so that now no one knows where he is. Her mother was named Zheng. The year before last the girl married into the Zhang family at

Qinghe, but unfortunately her husband died. Because she is young, intelligent and beautiful, her mother wants to find a good husband for her. Are you interested?"

So Liu married this girl on an auspicious day, and since both families were wealthy, the magnificence of their gifts and equipage impressed the whole city of Nanjing.

Coming home one evening about a month after their marriage, Liu was struck by his wife's resemblance to the dragon king's daughter, except that she was in better health and more lovely. Accordingly, he told her what had happened.

"I can't believe it," she replied. Then she told him that she was with child, and Liu became more devoted to her than ever.

A month after the child was born, Liu's wife dressed herself in fine clothes, put on her jewels, and invited all their relatives to the house. Before the assembled company she asked him with a smile, "Don't you remember meeting me before?"

"Once I carried a message for the dragon king's daughter," he replied. "That is something I have never forgotten."

"I am the dragon king's daughter," she said. "Wronged by my former husband, I was rescued by you, and I swore to repay your kindness. But when my uncle the prince suggested that we marry, you refused. After our separation we lived in two different spheres, and I had no way of sending word to you. Later my parents wanted to marry me to another river god—that stripling of the Zhuoqin River—but I remained true to you. Although you had forsaken me and there was no hope of seeing you again, I would rather have died than stop loving you. Soon after that, my parents took pity on me and decided to approach you again; but you married girls from the Zhang and Han families, and there was nothing we could do. After those girls had died and you came to live here, my family felt the match was possible. But I never dared hope that one day I might be your wife. I shall be grateful and happy all my life, and die without regret." So saying, she wept.

Presently she went on: "I did not disclose myself to you before, because I knew you did not care for my looks. But I can tell you now that I know you are attached to me. I am not good enough to keep your love, so I'm counting on your fondness for the child to hold you. Before I knew you loved me, I was so anxious and worried! When you took my letter, you smiled at me and said, 'When you go back to the lake, don't refuse to see me!' Did you want us to become husband and wife in future? Later when my uncle proposed the marriage and you refused him, did you really mean it or were you just offended? Do tell me!"

"It must have been fated," said Liu. "When first I met you by the river, you looked so wronged and pale, my heart bled for you. But I think all I wanted at the time was to pass on your message and right your wrong. When I said I hoped you wouldn't refuse to see me in future, that was just a casual remark with nothing behind it. The prince's attempt to force me into marriage annoyed me because I object to being bullied. Since a sense of justice had motivated my action, I could hardly marry the woman whose husband's death I had caused. As a man of honor I had to do what I thought right. So during our drinking I spoke from my heart, saying only what was just, with no fear of him. Once the time came to leave, however, and I saw the regret in your eyes, I was rather sorry. But after I left the lake, the affairs of this world kept me too occupied to convey my love and gratitude to you. Well, now that you belong to the Lu family and are a woman, I find my former feelings toward you were more than a fleeting passion after all! From now on, I shall love you always."

His wife was deeply moved and replied with tears, "Don't think human beings alone know gratitude. I shall repay your kindness. A dragon lives for ten thousand years, and I shall share my span of life with you. We shall travel freely by land and sea. You can trust me."

"I never thought you could tempt me with immortality!" laughed Liu.

They went to the lake again, where the royal entertainment once more given them beggars description.

Later they lived at Nanhai for forty years. Their mansions, equipage, feasts and clothes were as splendid as those of a prince, and Liu was able to help all his relatives. His perennial youth amazed everybody. During the Kaiyuan period (713-741), when the Emperor set his heart on discovering the secret of long life and searched far and wide for alchemists, Liu was given no peace and went back with his wife to the lake. Thus he disappeared from the world for more than ten years. At the end of that period, his younger cousin, Xue Gu, lost his post as magistrate of the capital and was sent to the southeast. On his journey Xue crossed Dongting Lake. It was a clear day and he was looking into the distance when he saw a green mountain emerging from the distant waves. The boatmen shrank back in fear, crying, "There was never any mountain here—it must be a sea monster!"

As they were watching the mountain approach, a painted barge came swiftly toward them and the men on it called Xue's name. One of them told him, "Master Liu sends his greetings." Then Xue understood. Invited to the foot of the mountain, he picked up the skirt of his gown and went quickly ashore. On the mountain were palaces like those on earth, and Liu was standing there with musicians before and bejewelled girls behind him, more splendid than in the world of men. Talking more brilliantly and looking even younger than formerly, he greeted Xue at the steps and took his hand.

"We have not been separated long," he said, "yet your hair is turning grey."

"You are fated to become an immortal and I to become dry bones," retorted Xue with a laugh.

Liu gave him fifty capsules, and said, "each of these will give you an extra year of life. When you have finished them, come again. Don't stay too long in the world of men, where you must undergo so many hardships." They feasted happily, and then Xue left. Liu was never seen again, but Xue often related this story. And fifty years later, he too vanished from the world.

This tale shows that the principal species of each category[1] of living creatures possesses supernatural powers—for how otherwise could reptiles assume the virtues of men? The dragon king of Dongting showed himself truly magnanimous, while the Prince of Qiantang was impetuous and straightforward. Surely their virtues did not appear from nowhere. Liu's cousin, Xue Gu, was the only other human being to penetrate to that watery kingdom, and it is a pity that none of his writings have been preserved. But since this account holds such interest, I have recorded it here.

---

[1] The ancient Chinese divided the animal kingdom into five categories: feathered, furred, hard-shelled, scaly and hairless. The chief species of these categories were phoenix, unicorn, tortoise, dragon and man. From man, the most intelligent of all, these others derived some of their virtues.

5. Prince Huo's Daughter

Jiang Fang

A devoted girl and a disloyal boy is an oft-told tale in Chinese classic novels and drama. Prince Huo's Daughter *is one of the earliest works of this kind, and it also contains attacks on the feudal class system. Although Li Yi, the boy, is from a declined family, the reputation of the Longxi Lis is still high. In contrast, Huo Xiaoyu, the girl, in spite of her fine upbringing, is doomed by her low class station. She is cruelly denied even a few years of happiness as an interlude in her life. The tragedy arouses immense sympathy among the people who admire her deep love and detest Li's treachery. However, the story runs beyond the relation of the boy and girl as Huo's revenge destroys the other innocent girls who later marry her husband. It seems the author has lost track of the cause of the tragedy but keeps punishing Li, the culprit, with endless paranoia. According to the chronicles, the mid-Tang poet Li Yi was "retarded in boyhood but sensitive to criticism and later very harsh with his wives and concubines." This became known as the*

Li Yi Malady. The end of the story seems to stick too closely to the facts to be considered a work of art.

The legend is well narrated and the dialogues reveal the speakers' characters. The story concentrates on only a few scenes so as to achieve great dramatic effect. Later Tang Xianzu, the great Ming Dynasty (1368-1644) classic dramatist, has turned it into two operas The Violet Flute *and* The Violet Hairpin, *the latter being one of his monumental "Four Linchuan Dreams."*

The author, Jiang Fang, a native of modern Yixing County, Jiangsu Province, was a Hanlin academician during the reign of Tang emperor Xianzong (806-820) and later demoted to magistrate of Lianzhou Prefecture. He has left a volume of poetry as well as this story which won him fame.

During the Dali period (766-779), there was a young man of Longxi whose name was Li Yi. At the age of twenty he passed one of the civil service examinations and the following year the best scholars of his rank were to be chosen for official posts through a further examination at the Ministry of Civil Affairs. In the sixth month he arrived at the capital and took lodgings in the Xinchang quarter. He came from a good family, showed brilliant promise, and was acknowledged by his contemporaries as unsurpassed in literary craftsmanship. Thus even senior scholars looked up to him. Having no mean opinion of his own gifts, he hoped for a beautiful and accomplished wife. But long and vainly did he search among the famous courtesans of the capital.

In Chang'an there was a match-maker named Bao, who was the eleventh child in her family. She had been a maidservant in the prince consort's family, but a dozen years before this had redeemed herself and married. Clever and with a ready tongue, she knew all the great families and was a past-master at arranging matches. Li gave her rich gifts and asked her to find him a wife, and she was very well disposed toward him.

One afternoon, some months later, Li was sitting in the south pavilion of his lodgings when he heard insistent knocking and Bao was announced. Gathering up the skirt of his gown, he hurried to meet her. "What brings you here so unexpectedly, madam?" he asked.

Bao laughed and responded, "Have you been having sweet dreams? A fairy has come down to earth who cares nothing for wealth but who admires wit and gallantry. She is made for you!"

When Li heard this he leaped for joy and felt as if he were walking on air. Taking Bao's hand he bowed and thanked her, saying: "I shall be your slave as long as I live!"

Asked where the girl lived and what her name was, Bao replied: "She is the youngest daughter of Prince Huo. Her name is Jade, and the prince doted on her. Her mother, Qingchi, was his favourite slave. When the prince died, his sons refused to keep the child because her mother was of humble birth, so they gave her a portion and made her leave. She has changed her name to Zheng, and people do not know that the prince was her father. But she is the most beautiful creature you ever saw, with a sensibility and grace beyond compare. She is well versed too in music and the classics. Yesterday she asked me to find a good match for her, and when I mentioned your name she was delighted, for she knows you by reputation. They live in Old Temple Lane in the Shengye quarter, in the house at the entrance to the carriage drive. I have already made an appointment for you. Go tomorrow at noon to the end of the lane, and look for a maid called Guizi. She will show you the house."

As soon as the match-maker left, Li started to prepare for the great occasion, sending his servant Qiuhong to borrow a black charger with a gilt bit from his cousin Shang who was adjutant general of the capital. That evening he washed his clothes, had a bath, and shaved. He could not sleep all night for joy. At dawn he put on his cap and examined himself in the mirror, fearing all might not go well. Having frittered away the time till noon, he called for the horse and galloped to the Shengye quarter. When he reached the place appointed, he saw a maid standing there waiting for him, who asked, "Are you Master Li?" He dismounted, told the maid to stable the horse, and went quickly in, bolting the gate behind him.

The match-maker came out from the house, smiling at him from a distance as she cried. "Who is this gate-crasher?" While they were joking with each other, he found himself led through the inner gate into a courtyard where there were four cherry trees and a parrot cage hanging on the northwest side.

At the sight of Li, the parrot squawked, "Here's a guest! Lower the curtain!"

Naturally bashful, Li had felt some scruples about going in, and now the parrot startled him and brought him to a standstill until Bao led the girl's mother down the steps to welcome him, and he was asked to go inside and take a seat opposite her. The mother, little more than forty, was a slender, attractive woman with charming manners.

"We have heard of your brilliance as a scholar," she said to Li, "and now that I see what a handsome young man you are too, I am sure your fame is well deserved. I have a daughter who, though lacking in education, is not ill-favoured. She should be a suitable match for you. Madame Bao has already proposed this, and today I would like to offer my daughter to you in marriage."

"I am a clumsy fellow," he replied, "and do not deserve such a distinction. If you accept me, I shall count it a great honor as long as I live."

Then a feast was laid, Jade was called by her

mother from the east chamber, and Li bowed to greet her. At her entrance, he felt as if the room had been transformed into a bower of roses, and when their eyes met he was dazzled by her glance. The girl sat down beside her mother, who said to her, "You like to repeat those lines:

When the wind in the bamboos rustles the curtain,
I fancy my old friend is near.

Here is the author of the poem. You have been reading his works so often—what do you think of him now you see him?"

Jade lowered her head and answered with a smile: "He doesn't live up to my expectations. Shouldn't a poet be more handsome?"

Then Li got up and made several bows. "You love talent and I admire beauty," he said. "Between us we have both!"

Jade and her mother looked at each other and smiled.

When they had drunk several cups of wine together, Li stood up and asked the girl to sing. At first she declined, but her mother insisted, and in a clear voice she sang an intricate melody. By the time they had drunk their fill it was evening, and the match-maker led the young man to the west wing to rest. The rooms were secluded in a quiet courtyard, and the hangings were magnificent. Bao told the maids Guizi and Wansha to take off Li's boots and belt. Then Jade herself appeared. With sweet archness and charming coyness she put off her clothes. Then they lowered the bed-curtains, lay down on the pillows and enjoyed each other to their hearts' content. The young man felt that he was in bed with a goddess.

During the night, however, the girl suddenly gazed at him through tears and said, "As a courtesan, I know I am no match for you. You love me now for my looks, but I fear that when I lose them your feelings will change, and then I shall be like a vine with nothing to cling to, or a fan discarded in the autumn. So at the height of my joy I cannot help grieving."

Li was touched, and putting his arm round her neck said gently, "Today I have attained the dream of my life. I swear I would sooner die than leave you. Why do you talk like that? Let me have some white silk to pledge you my faith in writing."

Drying her tears, Jade called her maid Yingtao to raise the curtain and hold the candle, while she gave Li a brush and ink. When not occupied with music, Jade was fond of reading, and her writing-case, brushes and ink all came from the palace. Now she brought out an embroidered case and from it took three feet of white silk lined with black for him to write on. The young man had a gift for contemporary composition, and taking up the brush wrote rapidly. He swore by the mountains and rivers, by the sun and the moon, that he would be true. He wrote passionately and movingly, and when he had finished he gave Jade his pledge to keep in her jewel box.

After that they lived happily for two years like a pair of kingfishers soaring on high, together day and night. But in the spring of the third year, Li came first in his examination and was appointed secretary-general of Zheng County. In the fourth month, before leaving to take up his post and to visit his parents in Luoyang, he gave a farewell party to all his relatives at the capital. It was the season between spring and summer. When the feast was over and the guests had gone, the young man and the girl were filled with grief at their coming separation.

"With your talents and fame," said Jade, "you have many admirers who would like to be related to you by marriage. And your old parents at home have no daughter-in-law to look after them. So when you go to take up this post, you are bound to find a good wife. The pledge you made me is not binding. But I have a small request to make, which I hope you will consider. May I tell you what it is?"

Li was startled and protested, "In what way have I offended you, that you speak like this? Tell me what is in your mind, and I promise to do whatever you ask."

"I am eighteen," said the girl, "and you are only twenty-two. There are still eight years before you reach thirty, the age at which a man should marry. I would like to crowd into these eight years all the love and happiness of my life. After that you can choose some girl of good family for wife—it will not be too late. Then I shall retire from the world, cutting my hair short and becoming a nun. This is the wish of my life and I ask no more."

Cut to the heart, Li could not hold back his tears. "I swear by the bright sun," he assured the girl, "as long as I live I shall be true to you. My only fear is that I may fail to please you—how can I think of anything else? I beg you not to doubt me, but rest assured. I shall reach Huazhou in the eighth month and send to fetch you. We shall be together again before very long." A few days later he said goodbye to her and went east.

Ten days after Li's arrival at his post, he asked leave to go to Luoyang to see his parents. Before he reached home, his mother had arranged a match for him with a cousin in the Lu family—a verbal agreement had already been reached. His mother was so strict that Li, though hesitating, dared not decline; accordingly he went through with the ceremonies and arranged a date for the wedding. Since the girl's family was a powerful one, they demanded over a million cash betrothal money and would call off the marriage if this were not forthcoming. Because Li's family was poor he had to borrow this sum; and he took advantage of his leave to look up distant friends, travelling up and down the Huai and Yangtze River valleys from the autumn till the next summer. Knowing that he had broken his promise to fetch Jade at the appointed time, he sent no message to her, hoping that she would give him up. He also asked his friends not to disclose the truth.

When Li failed to return at the appointed time, Jade tried to find out what had become of him, only to receive contradictory reports. She also consulted many fortune-tellers and oracles. This went on for more than a year, until at last she fell ill of sorrow; and, lying in her lonely room, went from bad to worse. Though no tidings had come from Li, her love for him did not falter, and she gave presents to friends and acquaintances to persuade them to find news of him. This she did so persistently that soon all her money had gone and she often had to send her maid out secretly to sell dresses and trinkets through an inn-keeper in the West Market.

One day Jade sent Wansha to sell an amethyst hair-pin, and on her way to the inn the maid met an old jade-smith who worked in the palace. When he saw what she was carrying, he recognized it. "This hair-pin is one I made," he said. "Many years ago, when Prince Huo's youngest daughter first put up her hair, he ordered me to make this pin and gave me ten thousand cash for the job. I have always remembered it. Who are you? And how did you come by this?"

"My mistress is the prince's daughter," replied the maid. "She has come down in the world, and the man she married went to Luoyang and deserted her. So she fell ill of grief, and has been in a decline for two years. Now she wants me to sell this, so that she can bribe someone to get news of her husband."

The jade-smith shed tears, exclaiming, "Can the children of nobles fall on such evil times? My days are nearly spent, but this ill-fated lady's story wrings my heart."

Then the old man led Wansha to the house of Princess Yanxian, and when the princess heard this story she too heaved sigh after sigh. Finally she gave the maid one hundred and twenty thousand cash for the hair-pin.

Now the girl to whom Li was engaged was in the capital. After raising the sum he needed for his marriage, he returned to his post in Zheng County; but at the end of the year he again asked for leave to go to Chang'an to get married. And he found quiet lodgings, so that his whereabouts would not be known. A young scholar, however, named Cui Yunming, who was Li's cousin and a kind-hearted man, had formerly drunk with Li in Jade's room and laughed and talked with her until they were on the best of terms. Whenever he received news of Li, he would tell Jade truthfully, and she had helped him so often with money and clothing that he felt deeply indebted to her.

When Li came to the capital, Cui told Jade, who sighed and exclaimed indignantly, "How can he be so faithless?" She begged all her friends to ask Li to come to her; but knowing that he had broken his promise and that the girl was dying, he felt too ashamed to see her. He took to going out early and coming back late in order to avoid callers. Though Jade wept day and night, unable to eat or sleep in her longing to see him, he never came. And indignation and grief made her illness worse. When the story became known in the capital, all the young scholars were moved by the girl's love while all the young gallants resented Li's heartlessness.

It was then spring, the season for pleasure trips, and Li went one day with five or six friends to Chongqing Temple to see the peonies in bloom. Strolling in the west corridor, they composed poems together. A close friend of Li's named Wei Xiaqing, a native of Chang'an, was one of the party. "Spring is beautiful and flowers are in bloom," he told Li. "But your old love nurses her grief in her lonely room. It is really cruel of you to abandon her. A true man would not do this. Think it over again!"

As Wei was sighing and reproaching Li, up came a young gallant wearing a yellow silk shirt and carrying a crossbow.

He was handsome and splendidly dressed, but attended only by a Central Asian boy with cropped hair. Walking behind them, he overheard their conversation; and presently he stepped forward and bowed to Li, saying, "Is your name not Li? My family comes from the east, and we are related to the royal house. Though I have no literary talent myself, I value it in others. I have long been an admirer of yours and hoped to make your acquaintance, and today I am lucky enough to meet you. My humble house is not far from here, and I have musicians to entertain you. I have eight or nine beautiful girls too, and a dozen good horses, all of them at your disposal. I only hope you will honor me with a visit."

When Li's friends heard this, they were delighted. They rode along after this young gallant, who swiftly turned corner after corner until they reached the Shengye quarter. Since they were approaching Jade's house, Li was reluctant to go any farther and made some excuse to turn back.

But the stranger said: "My humble home is only a stone's throw from here. Don't leave us now!" He took hold of Li's bridle and pulled his horse along.

In a moment they had reached the girl's house. Li was dismayed and tried to turn back, but the other quickly ordered attendants to help him dismount and lead him inside. They pushed him through the gate and bolted it, calling out, "Master Li is here!" Then exclamations of joy and surprise could be heard from the whole house.

The night before, Jade had dreamed that Li was brought to her bedside by a man in a yellow shirt and that she was told to take off her shoes. When she woke up she told her mother this dream, and said, "Shoes symbolize union. That means that husband and wife will meet again. But to take them off means separation. We shall be united then parted again—for ever. Judging by this dream, I shall see him once more and after that I shall die."

In the morning she asked her mother to dress her hair for her. Her mother thought she was raving and paid no attention, but when Jade insisted she consented. And no sooner was her hair done than Li arrived.

Jade had been ill so long that she could not even turn in bed without help. But on hearing that her lover had come she got up swiftly, changed her clothes and hurried out like one possessed. Confronting Li in silence, she fixed angry eyes on him. So frail she could hardly stand, she kept averting her face and then, against her will, looking back, till all present were moved to tears.

Soon several dozen dishes of food and wine were brought in. And when the company asked in astonishment where this feast had come from, they found it had been ordered by the young gallant. The table spread, they sat down. Jade, though she had turned away from Li, kept stealing long glances at him; and finally raising her cup of wine, she poured a libation on the ground and said, "I am the unhappiest of women, and you are the most heartless of men. Dying young of a broken heart, I shall not be able to look after my mother; and I must bid farewell for ever to my silk dresses and music, to suffer torments in hell. This is your doing, sir! Farewell! After death I shall become an avenging spirit and give your wives and concubines no peace."

Grasping Li's arm with her left hand, she threw her cup to the ground. Then, after crying out several times, she fell dead. Her mother placed her body on Li's knee and told him to call her, but he could not revive her.

Li put on mourning and wept bitterly during the wake. The night before the obsequies she appeared to him within the funeral curtain, as beautiful as in life. She was wearing a pomegranate-red skirt, purple tunic, and red and green cape. Leaning against the curtain and fingering the embroidered tassels, she looked at him and said, "You must still have some feeling for me, to see me off. That is a comfort to me here among the shades." With that she vanished. The next day she was buried at Yusuyuan near the capital. After mourning by her grave, Li went back; and a month later he married his cousin. But he was in low spirits after all that had happened.

In the fifth month, Li went with his wife to his post at Zheng County. About ten days after their arrival, he was sleeping with his wife when he heard soft hoots outside the curtain, and looking out he saw a very handsome young man hiding behind the hangings and beckoning repeatedly to his wife. Li leaped up in agitation and went round the curtain several times to look for the intruder, but no one was there. This made him so suspicious that he gave his wife no peace until some friends persuaded him to make it up and he began to feel a little better. About ten days later, however, he came home to find his wife playing her lute on the couch, when an engraved rhinoceros-horn case, little over an inch in diameter and tied with a flimsy silk love-knot, was thrown into the room. This case fell on his wife's lap. When Li opened it, he found two love-peas, one Spanish fly as well as other aphrodisiacs and love-charms. Howling like a wild beast in his anger, he seized the lute and beat his wife with it as he demanded the truth. But she could not clear herself. After that he often beat her savagely and treated her with great cruelty; and finally he denounced her in the court and divorced her.

After Li divorced his wife, he soon became suspicious of the maidservants and women slaves whom he had favoured, and some he even killed in his jealousy. Once he went to Yangzhou and bought a famous courtesan named Ying, who was the eleventh child of her family. She was so charming and beautiful that Li was very fond of her. But when they were together he liked to tell her about another girl he had purchased, and how he had punished her for various faults. He told her such things every day to make her fear him, so that she would not dare to take other lovers. Whenever he went out, he would leave her on the bed covered up with a bath-tub which was sealed all round; and upon his return he would examine the tub carefully before letting her out. He also kept a very sharp dagger and would say to his maids, "This is Gexi steel. It's good for cutting the throats of unfaithful women!"

Whatever women he had, he would soon grow suspicious of them, and he was a jealous husband to the two other wives he married later.

6. Governor of the Southern Tributary State

Li Gongzuo

In the middle of the Tang Dynasty, the empire was in turmoil. Provinces under military governors became independent regimes, and everywhere there were signs of decay. The bureaucracy split into parties and factions contending for ascendency which often ended in elimination of the losers together with their families. Owing to such bloody infighting and the influence of Buddhist ideology, people began to see life as a dream expressed in legends.

Setting his story in an anthill, the author Li Gongzuo vividly describes the spectacular dream journey of the hero Chenyu Fen. Though the story ends with a pessimistic view of life, like Gulliver's Travels *it contains strong criticism of the society of the time. The most fantastic feature of this legend is its setting in an anthill the excavation of which proves the authenticity of the fictitious subterranean world. The satire quickly gained popularity, and "A Dream of the Southern Tributary State" has become*

a popular proverb ever since. The legend was futher developed by Tang Xianzu into A Story of the Southern Tributary State *and by Che Renyuan into* A Dream of the Southern Tributary State *in the Ming Dynasty.*

The author Li Gongzuo, alias Zhanmeng, was a native of Longxi. He passed the highest imperial examination and became a magistrate's adjutant first in Zhonglin and later in Jianghuai during the reign of Emperor Xianzong. Four of his novels can be found in the Taiping Micellany.

Chunyu Fen, a native of Dongping and a well-known gallant of the Yangtze River region, was fond of drinking, hot-tempered and recklessly indifferent to conventions. He had amassed great wealth and acted as patron to many dashing young men. Because of his military prowess he had been made an adjutant of the Huainan Army, but in a fit of drunkenness he offended his general and was dismissed. Then in his disappointment he let himself go and gave his days to drinking.

Chunyu's home was some five kilometers east of Yangzhou. South of his house there was a huge old ash tree with great branches, thick with foliage, which shaded an acre of land; and under this tree Chunyu and his boon companions drank daily to their hearts' content. In the ninth month of the tenth year of the Zhenyuan period (794 A.D.), Chunyu got drunk, and two of his friends carried him home and laid him in the eastern chamber. "You had better have a sleep," they said, "while we give the horses some fodder and wash our feet. We shan't go until you feel better."

He took off his cap and rested his head on the pillow, laying there in a tipsy state, half dreaming and half awake. Presently he saw two messengers in purple, who entered to kneel before him and announce, "His Majesty the king of Ashendon has sent us, his humble subjects, to invite you to his kingdom."

Chunyu arose from his couch, dressed himself and followed the messengers to the gate, where he found a small green carriage drawn by four horses. Seven or eight attendants standing there helped him into this. Driving out of the gate, they made for the ash tree and—to Chunyu's amazement—headed down the hollow under the tree. However, he dared ask no questions. The scenery along the road—the mountains and rivers, trees and plants—looked different from the world of men. The climate too had changed. After they had travelled about 15 kilometers, city walls came into sight, and the highway began to be thronged with carriages and people. The footmen on the carriage kept calling out to clear the road and the pedestrians moved hurriedly out of their way. They entered a great city through a turreted red gate over which was inscribed in letters of gold "The Great Kingdom of Ashendon." The gate-keepers bestirred themselves and bowed low to them.

Then a rider cantered up, calling, "As His Highness the prince consort has travelled so far, His Majesty orders him to be taken to the East Hostel to rest." And he led the way.

Chunyu saw a gate in front swing open, and alighting from the carriage he passed through it. Here were brightly painted and finely carved balustrades and pilasters among terraces of blossoming trees and rare fruits, while tables and rugs, cushions and screens had been set ready in the hall where a rich feast was laid out. Chunyu was enchanted. Presently it was announced that the prime minister had arrived, and Chunyu went to the foot of the hall steps to await him respectfully. Dressed in purple and holding an ivory scepter, the minister approached, and they paid their respects to each other. This done, the minister said, "Though our land is far from yours, our king has invited you here because he hopes for an alliance with you by marriage."

"How can a humble person like myself aspire so high?" replied the young man.

The minister asked Chunyu to follow him to the palace. They walked a hundred yards and entered a red gate where spears, axes, and halberds were displayed and among several hundred officers who stood by the side of the road to make way for them was Chunyu's old drinking friend Zhou. Chunyu was secretly delighted, but dared not go forward to accost him.

Then the minister led Chunyu up to a court where guards were standing solemnly in formation, showing that they were in the royal presence. He saw a tall, imposing figure on the throne, wearing a white silk robe and a bright red cap. Overcome by awe, he did not look up, but bowed as he was directed by the attendants. "At your father's wish," said the king, "we have asked you to our unworthy kingdom to offer you our second daughter as your wife." When Chunyu kept his head lowered and dared not reply, the king told him, "You may go back to the guest house and prepare for the ceremony."

As the minister accompanied him back, Chunyu was thinking hard. Since his father was a frontier general who had been reported missing, it was possible that, having made peace with the border kingdoms, he was responsible for this invitation. Still the young man was bewildered and at a loss to account for it.

That evening, amid pomp and splendour, betrothal gifts of lambs, swans and silk were displayed. There was music of stringed and bamboo instruments, feasting by the light of lanterns and candles, and a concourse of carriages and horsemen. Some of the girls present were addressed as the nymphs of Huayang or Qingxi, others as the fairies of the upper or lower region. Attended by a large retinue, they wore green phoenix head-dresses, gold cloud-like garments and golden trinkets and precious stones that dazzled the eye. These girls frolicked and played charming tricks on Chunyu who found it hard to answer their clever repartee.

"On the last Spring Purification Festival,"[1] one girl said, "I went with Lady Lingzhi to Chanzhi Monastery to watch Youyan perform the Brahmana dance in the Indian Quadrangle. I was sitting with the girls on the stone bench on the north side when you and your young gallants arrived, and got off your horses to watch. you accosted us and teased us and made jokes—don't you remember how Qiongying and I tied a scarlet scarf on the bamboo? Then, on the sixteenth of the seventh month, I went with Shang Zhenzi to Xiaogan Monastery to listen to Monk Qisuan discoursing on the Avalokitesvara sutra. I donated two gold phoenix-shaped hair-pins and my friend one rhinoceros horn case. You were there too, and asked the monk to let you see them. After admiring them and praising the workmanship at some length, you turned to us and said, "These pretty things and their owners surely can't belong to the world of men!' Then you asked my name and wanted to know where I lived, but I wouldn't tell you. You kept staring at me as if you were quite lovelorn—don't you remember?"

---

[1] On this festival, which falls on the third day of the third month, people used to bathe in the rivers to "purify" themselves and so guard against evil during the coming year.

Chunyu replied by quoting the song:

Deep in my heart it is hidden,
How can I ever forget?

And the girls said, "Who could imagine that you would become our relative?"

Just then up came three men in magnificent clothes. Bowing to Chunyu, they declared, "By His Majesty's order we have come to be your groomsmen." One of them looked like an old friend.

"Aren't you Tian Zihua of Fengyi?" Chunyu asked him. When the other said that he was, Chunyu stepped forward to grasp his hand and they talked about the past.

Asked how he came to be there, Tian replied, "On my travels I met Lord Duan, the prime minister, and he became my patron." When Chunyu enquired if he knew of Zhou's presence there, he answered, "Zhou has done very well. He is now the city commandant and has great influence. On several occasions he has done me a favour."

They talked cheerfully until it was announced that the prince consort should go to the wedding. As the three groomsmen handed him his sword, pendants, robes and head-dress and helped him put them on, Tian said, "I never thought to attend such a grand ceremony for you today. You mustn't forget your old friends."

Several dozen fairy maids now began to play

rare music, piercingly tender and infinitely sad, the like of which Chunyu had never heard before. Dozens of other attendants held candles all the way down a kilometer-long path lined on both sides with gold and emerald-green screens vividly painted and intricately carved. He sat up straight in the carriage, rather nervous, while Tian joked to put him at his ease. The girls he had seen were arriving too in phoenix-winged carriages. When he reached the gate of Xiu Yi Palace, the girls were there too, and Chunyu was asked to alight. He went through a ceremony just like that in the world of men, at the end of which screens and fans were removed, enabling him to see his bride, the Princess of the Golden Bough. She was about fifteen, lovely as a goddess and well trained in the marriage ceremony.

After the wedding Chunyu and the princess came to love each other dearly, and his power and prestige increased daily. His equipage and entertainments were second only to the king's. One day the king took him and some other officials as his guards to hunt on the Divine Tortoise Mountain in the west, where there were high peaks, wide marshlands and luxuriant forests stocked with all kinds of birds and beasts. The hunters came back with a big bag of game that evening.

Another day Chunyu said to the king, "On my wedding day Your Majesty told me you had sent for me in compliance with my father's wishes. My father served formerly as a general at the frontier.

After a defeat he was reported missing, and I have had no news of him for eighteen years. Since Your Majesty knows where he is now, I would like to call on him."

"Your father is still serving at the northern frontier," replied the king quickly. "We are in constant touch. You had better just write to him. There is no need for you to go there." The king ordered the princess to prepare gifts to send to her father-in-law, and after a few days a reply came in his handwriting. He expressed his longing for his son and wrote just as in former letters, asking whether certain relatives were still alive and what news there was of their home-town. Since the distance between them was so great, he said, it was difficult to send news. His letter was sad and full of grief. He told Chunyu not to come, but promised that they would meet in three years' time. With this letter in his hands, Chunyu wept bitterly, unable to restrain himself.

One day the princess asked him, "Don't you ever want to take up an official post?"

"I am used to a carefree life," he answered. "I don't understand official work."

"Just take a post," she said, "and I will help you." Then she spoke to the king.

A few days later the king said, "All is not well in my southern tributary state, and the governor has been dismissed. I would like to use your talents to set their affairs in order. You might go there with my daughter." When Chunyu consented, the king ordered those in charge to get his baggage ready. Gold, jade and silk, cases and servants, carriages and horsemen formed a long baggage train when he and the princess were ready to leave. And since Chunyu had mixed with gallants as a young man and never dreamed of becoming an official, he found this most gratifying.

He sent a memorandum to the king, saying, "As the son of a military family, I have never studied the art of government. Now that I have been given this important post, I fear I shall not only disgrace myself but ruin the prestige of the court. I would therefore like to seek far and wide for wise and talented men to help me. I have noticed that City Commandant Zhou of Yingchuan is a loyal, honest officer, who firmly upholds the law and would make a good minister. Then there is Tian Zihua, a gentleman of Fengyi, who is prudent and full of stratagems and has probed deeply into the principles of government. I have known both these men for ten years. I understand their talents and consider them trustworthy, and therefore I ask to have Zhou appointed the chief councillor and Tian the minister of finance of my state. For then the government will be well administered and the laws well kept." The two men were then appointed to these posts by the king.

The evening of Chunyu's departure, the king

and queen gave a farewell feast for him south of the capital.

"The southern state is a great province," said the king. "The land is rich and the people prosperous, and you must adopt a benevolent policy there. With Zhou and Tian assisting you, I hope you will do well and come up to our expectations."

Meantime the queen told the princess, "Your husband is impetuous and fond of drinking, and he is still young. A wife should be gentle and obedient. I trust you to look after him well. Though you will not be too far from us, you will no longer be able to greet us every morning and evening, and I find it hard not to shed tears now that you are going away." Then Chunyu and the princess bowed, got into their carriage and started south. They talked cheerfully on the way, and several days later reached their destination.

The officials of the province, the monks and priests, elders, musicians, attendants and guards had all come out in welcome. The streets were thronged, while drums and bells could be heard for kilometers around. Chunyu saw a goodly array of turrets and pavilions as he entered the great city gate, above which was inscribed in letters of gold "The Southern Tributary State." In front there were red windows and a large gate with a fine view into the distance. After his arrival he studied the local conditions and helped all who were sick or distressed, entrusting his government to Zhou and

Tian, who administered the province well. He remained governor there for twenty years, and the people benefiting from his good rule sang his praises and set up tablets extolling his virtue or built temples to him. As a result, the king honored him even more: he was given fiefs and titles and exalted to the position of a grand councillor of state, while both Zhou and Tian also became well-known as good officials, and were promoted several times. Chunyu had five sons and two daughters. His sons were given official posts reserved for the nobility, while his daughters were married into the royal family. Thus his fame and renown were unrivalled.

One year the kingdom of Sandalvine attacked this province, and the king ordered Chunyu to raise an army to defend it. Chunyu made Zhou commander of thirty thousand troops to resist the invaders at Jade Tower City, but Zhou proved proud and reckless, underestimating the enemy. His troops were routed and, abandoning his armour, he fled back alone to the provincial capital at night. Meanwhile the invaders, after capturing their beggage train and arms, had withdrawn. Chunyu had Zhou arrested and asked to be punished, but the king pardoned them both.

That same month Zhou developed a boil on his back and died. Ten days later the princess died of illness too, and Chunyu's request to leave the province and accompany the hearse to the capital was granted. Tian, the minister of finance, was appointed deputy in his place. Bowed down with grief, Chunyu followed the hearse. On the way many people wept, officers and common citizens paid their last homage, while great crowds blocked the way and clung to the carriage. When he reached Ashendon, the king and queen were waiting outside the capital, wearing mourning and weeping. The princess was posthumously entitled Shun Yi (Obedient and Graceful). Guards, canopies and musicians were provided, and she was buried at Coiling Dragon Mount some five kilometers east of the city. During the same month, Zhou's son Rongxin also arrived with his father's hearse.

Now though Chunyu had been ruling over a tributary state outside the kingdom for many years, he had managed to keep on good terms with all the nobles and influential officers at court. After his return to the capital he behaved unconventionally and gathered around himself many associates and followers, his power growing so rapidly that the king began to suspect him. Then some citizens reported to the king that a mysterious portent had appeared and the state was doomed to suffer a great catastrophe: the capital would be removed and the ancestral temples destroyed. This would be caused by some man of foreign birth who was close to the royal family. After deliberation the ministers decided that there was danger in Chunyu's luxury and presumption; accordingly the king deprived him of his attendants and forbade him to have any further dealings with his associates, ordering him to live in retirement.

Conscious that he had not governed badly all these years in his province, but was being slandered, Chunyu was in low spirits. The king, sensing this, said to him, "You have been my son-in-law for more than twenty years. Unhappily my daughter died young and could not live with you till old age. This is a great misfortune." Then the queen took charge of his children herself, and the king said, "You have left your home for a long time. You had better go back now for a while to see your relatives. Leave your children here and do not worry about them. In three years we shall fetch you back."

"Isn't this my home?" asked Chunyu. "What other home have I to go back to?"

"You came from the world of men," replied the king with a laugh. "This is not your home." At first Chunyu felt as if he were dreaming, but then he remembered how he had come there and, shedding tears, asked for permission to return. The king ordered his attendants to see him off, and with a bow Chunyu took his leave.

The same two messengers dressed in purple accompanied him out of the gate. But there he was shocked to see a shabby carriage with no attendants or envoys to accompany him. He got into the carriage, however, and after driving some kilometers they left the city behind. They travelled the same way that he had first come by. The mountains, rivers

83

and plains were unchanged, but the two messengers with Chunyu looked so seedy that he felt let down. When he asked them when they would reach Yangzhou, they went on singing without paying any attention. Only when he insisted did they answer, "Soon."

Presently they emerged from the hollow and Chunyu saw his own village unchanged. Sadness seized him, and he could not help shedding tears. The two messengers helped him down from the carriage, through the door of his house and up the steps. Then he saw himself lying in the eastern chamber, and was so frightened that he dared not approach. At that the two messengers called his name aloud several times, and he woke up.

He saw his servants sweeping the courtyard. His two guests were still washing their feet by the couch, the slanting sun had not yet set behind the west wall and his unfinished wine was still by the east window—but he had lived through a whole generation in his dream! Deeply moved, he could not help sighing. And when he called his two friends and told them, they were equally amazed. They went out to look for the hollow under the ash tree, and Chunyu, pointing to it, said, "This is where I went in the dream."

His friends believed this must be the work of some fox fairy or tree spirit, so servants were ordered to fetch an axe and cut through the tree trunk and branches to find where the hollow ended.

It was some ten feet long, terminating in a cavity lit by the sun and large enough to hold a couch. In this were mounds of earth which resembled city walls, pavilions and courts, and swarms of ants were gathered there. In the ant-hill was a small, reddish tower occupied by two huge ants, three inches long, with white wings and red heads. They were surrounded by a few dozen big ants, and other ants dared not approach them. These huge ants were the king and queen, and this was the capital of Ashendon.

Then the men followed up another hole which lay under the southern branch of the tree and was at least forty feet long. In this tunnel there was another ant-hill with small towers, which swarmed with ants. This was the southern tributary state which Chunyu had governed. Another large, rambling tunnel of a fantastic shape ran westward for twenty feet, and in this they found a rotten tortoise shell as big as a peck measure, soaked by rain and covered by luxuriant grass. This was the Divine Tortoise Mountain, where Chunyu had hunted. They followed up yet another tunnel more than ten feet long in the east, where the gnarled roots of the tree had twisted into the shape of a dragon. Here there was a small earthen mound about a foot high, and this was the grave of the princess, Chunyu's wife.

As he thought back, Chunyu was very shaken, for all that they had discovered coincided with his dream. He would not let his friends destroy these ant-hills, and ordered that the tunnels be covered up as before. That night, however, there was a sudden storm, and the next morning when he examined the holes the ants had gone. Thus the prophecy that Ashendon would suffer a great catastrophe and that the capital would be removed was realized. Then he thought of the invasion by the kingdom of Sandalvine, and asked his two friends to trace it. They found that some six hundred yards east of his house was a river-bed long since dry, and next to it grew a big sandal tree so thickly covered with vines that the sun could not shine through it. A small hole beside it, where a swarm of ants had gathered, must be the kingdom of Sandalvine.

If even the mysteries of ants are so unfathomable, what then of the changes caused by big beasts in the hills and woods?

At that time Chunyu's friends Zhou and Tian were both in Liuhe County, and he had not seen them for ten days. He sent a servant posthaste to make enquiries, and found that Zhou had died of a sudden illness, while Tian was lying ill in bed. Then Chunyu realized how empty his dream had been, and that all was vanity too in the world of men. He therefore became a Taoist and abstained from wine and women. Three years later he died at home, in his forty-seventh year, just as predicted in the dream.

In the eighth month of the eleventh year of the

Zhenyuan period (795 A.D.), while on a journey from Suzhou to Luoyang I had stopped at Huaipu and met Chunyu by chance. I questioned him and looked at the ant-hills, going into his story very thoroughly. Believing it to be quite genuine, I have written this tale for those who may be interested. Although it deals with supernatural and unorthodox things, it may have a moral for the ambitious. Let future readers not think this narrative a mere series of coincidences, and let them beware of taking pride in worldly fame and position!

For, as Li Zhao, former adjutant general of Huazhou commented:

> *His reputation reaches to the skies,*
> *His influence can make a kingdom fall,*
> *And yet this pomp and power, after all,*
> *Are but an ant-heap in the wise man's eyes.*

7. Story of a Singsong Girl

Bai Xingjian

This story is similar to Prince Huo's Daughter *at the beginning, but ends very differently. As a rule, it was out of the question in feudal society for the son of a high official like Zheng of Yingyang to formally marry a courtesan. But singsong girl Li Wa was an exception. She takes so much pains to heal her disgraced, gravely ill lover Zheng that he not only fully recovers but eventually attains the position of a high official. The legend is based on a folk tale called* A Unique Flower. *Its conclusion perhaps reflects the aspiration of the people in those days.*

The legend bears upon different walks of life in the Tang Dynasty, with events naturally interwined, and defined by sharp contrasts, such as Li's drastically different attitude to Zheng before and after his misfortune, and the dramatic contest between the rival dirge singers. Each stage ends abruptly with a swift change of setting to deepen the effect upon the reader. Some descriptions, such as the heartlessness of the procuress, the plight of

the disgraced scholar begging for food and Li Wa's meticulous care for the recuperating Zheng are rendered in realistic detail. The vitality of the legend spawned many poems and songs in the Tang Dynasty. Later Shi Junbao's opera Courtesan Li *in the Yuan Dynasty and Xue Jinyan's legend* The Embroidered Tunic *in the Ming Dynasty were inspired by the legend.*

The author Bai Xingjian, alias Zhitui (776—826), was the great poet Bai Juyi's brother. Their ancestors lived in Taiyuan and moved to Xiagui (now Weinan in Shaanxi). He passed the highest imperial examination in the second year of the Yuanhe period (807) and was successively assigned Left Advisor, transit authorization official and protocal director. His works amounted to 20 volumes but are lost.

In the Tianbao period (742-756) the Lord of Yingyang, whose name and surname I will omit, was Governor of Changzhou. He was highly respected and extremely rich. When our story starts he was fifty and had a son of nearly twenty—an intelligent lad of outstanding literary ability, the admiration of all his contemporaries. His father loved him dearly and had high hopes of him. "This," he would say, "is the 'thousand-league colt' of our family." When the time came for the lad to take the provincial examination, his father gave him fine clothes and equipage for the journey, and money for his expenses in the capital. "With your gifts you should succeed at the first attempt," he said. "But I am giving you an allowance for two years, and a generous one at that, to enable you to work without worrying." The young man was quite confident too, and saw himself passing the examination as clearly as he saw the palm of his own hand.

Setting out from Changzhou he reached the capital in little more than a month and took a house in the Buzheng quarter. One day on his way back from the East Market, he entered the eastern gate of the Pingkang quarter to visit a friend who lived in the southwest part. When he reached Mingke Lane, he saw a house with a rather narrow gate and courtyard. The house itself, however, was a grand one, and from the gate you could see many buildings stretching back. One half of the double door was open and at it stood a girl, attended by her young maid. She was of an exquisite, bewitching beauty, such as the world had seldom seen.

When he saw her, the young man unconsciously reined in his horse and hesitated, unable to tear himself away. He deliberately dropped his whip and waited for his servant to pick it up, all the time staring at the girl. She, for her part, returned his gaze with a look of answering admiration. But in the end he went away without daring to speak to her.

After that he was like a man distracted, and

secretly begged a friend who knew the capital well to find out who she was.

"The house belongs to a courtesan named Li," his friend told him.

"Is it possible to get her?" he asked.

"She is very well off," said his friend, "because her previous dealings have been with rich and aristocratic families, who paid her lavishly. Unless you spend a million cash, she will have nothing to do with you."

"All I want is to win her," answered the young man. "I don't mind if she costs a million."

Some days later he put on his best clothes and set out, with a train of attendants behind him, for her house. When he knocked at the door, a young maid opened it.

"Can you tell me whose house this is?" the young man asked.

The maid did not answer, but ran back into the house calling out at the top of her voice: "Here's the gentleman who dropped his whip the other day!"

The girl replied with evident pleasure: "Ask him in. I'll come as soon as I've changed my clothes and tidied myself."

The young man hearing this was inwardly overjoyed as he followed the maid into the house. He saw the girl's mother—a grey-haired woman with a bent back—and bowing low said to her: "I hear that you have a vacant courtyard which you might be willing to let. Is that true?"

"I am afraid it is too shabby and small for a gentleman like you," she said. "You my take it if you like, but I wouldn't dare ask for any rent." She then took him into the reception room, which was a very splendid one, and asked him to be seated, saying: "I have a daughter who is very young and has a few accomplishments, but who enjoys the company of visitors. I should like you to meet her."

With that she called for her daughter. The girl had sparkling eyes and dazzling white arms, and moved with such consummate grace that the young man could only leap to his feet in confusion and did not dare raise his eyes. When they had greeted each other, he made a few remarks about the weather, conscious as he did so that her beauty was such as he had never seen before.

They sat down again. Tea was made and wine poured out. The vessels used were spotlessly clean. He stayed on until it was late and the curfew drum could be heard all around, when the old lady asked if he lived far away.

He answered untruthfully: "Several kilometers beyond Yanping Gate," hoping that they would ask him to stay.

"The drum has sounded," she said. "You will have to leave at once, if you don't want to break the law."

"I was enjoying myself so much," said the young man, "that I didn't notice how late it was.

My house is a long way off, and I have no relations in the city. What am I to do?"

"If you don't think our house too shabby," put in the girl, "what harm would there be in your spending the night here?"

He glanced several times at the old lady, who assented.

Calling his servants, he ordered them to bring two bolts of silk[1] which he offered for the expenses of a feast. But the girl stopped him and protested laughingly: "No, you are our guest. We would like to entertain you tonight with our humble household's rough and ready fare. You can treat us another time." He tried to refuse, but in the end she had her way, and they all moved to the western hall. The curtains, screens, blinds and couches were of dazzling splendour, the toilet-boxes, coverlets and pillows the height of luxury. Candles were lighted and an excellent meal was served.

After supper, when the old lady had retired, the young man and girl began to talk intimately, laughing and joking completely at their ease.

"I passed your house the other day," said the young man, "and you happened to be standing at the door. After that, I couldn't get you out of my head. Lying down to rest or sitting down to eat, I couldn't stop thinking of you."

"It was just the same with me," she answered.

---

[1] In the Tang Dynasty silk was often used as money.

"You know, I didn't come today simply to look for lodgings," he said. "I came hoping you would grant the wish of my life. But I wasn't sure what my fate would be...."

As he was speaking the old woman came back and asked what they were saying. Upon being told, she laughed and said: "'There is a natural attraction between the sexes,' When lovers are agreed, not even their parents can control them. But my daughter is of humble birth—are you sure she is fit to share your bed?"

The young man immediately came down from the dais and, bowing low, said: "Please accept me as your servant!" After that the old lady regarded him as her son-in-law; they drank heavily together and finally parted. Next morning he had all his baggage brought round to their house and made it his home.

Henceforward he shut himself up there, and his friends heard no more of him. He mixed only with actors, dancers and people of that kind, passing the time in wild sports and aimless feasting. When his money was spent he sold his horses and men-servants. In little over a year all his money, property, attendants and horses were gone.

The old lady had begun to treat him coldly, but the girl seemed more devoted to him than ever. One day she said to him: "We have been together a year, but I am still not with child. They say that the spirit of the Bamboo Grove answers prayers as surely as an echo. Shall we go to his temple and offer a libation?"

Not suspecting any plot, the young man was delighted. And having pawned his coat to buy wine and sacrificial meat, he went with her to the temple and prayed to the spirit. They spent two nights there and started back the third day, the young man riding a donkey behind the girl's carriage. When they reached the north gate of the Xuanyang quarter, she turned to him and said: "My aunt's house is in a lane to the east near here. Suppose we rest there for a little?"

He fell in with her wishes, and they had not gone more than a hundred paces when he saw a wide drive and their servant stopped the carriage, saying: "We have arrived," The young man got down and was met by a man-servant who came out to ask who they were. When told that it was Mistress Li, he went back and announced her. Presently a woman of about forty came out.

She greeted our hero and asked: "Has my niece arrived?" The girl alighted from the carriage and her aunt welcomed her, saying: "Why haven't you been here for so long?" They exchanged glances and laughed. Then the girl introduced him to her aunt, after which they all went into a side garden near the western gate. There was a pavilion set in a profusion of bamboos and trees amid quiet pools and summer-houses.

"Does this garden belong to your aunt?" the

young man asked.

The girl laughed, but instead of answering she spoke of something else.

Delicious tea and cakes were served. But almost at once a man galloped up on a Fergana horse which was all in a lather. "The old lady has been taken very ill," he gasped. "She is beginning to be delirious. You had better hurry back."

"I am so worried," said the girl to her aunt. "Let me take the horse and ride on ahead. Then I will send it back, and you and my husband can come along later." The young man was anxious to go with her, but the aunt whispered to her maid to stop him at the gate.

"My sister must be dead by now," she said. "You and I ought to discuss the funeral together. What good can you do by running after her in an emergency like this?" So he stayed, to discuss the funeral and mourning rites.

It grew late, but still the horse had not come back. "I wonder what can have happened," said the aunt. "You had better hurry over to see. I will come on later."

The young man set out. When he reached the house he found the gate firmly locked and sealed. Astounded, he questioned the neighbors. "Mistress Li only rented this house," they told him. "When her lease was up, the landlord took it back, and she moved away. She left two days ago." But when he asked her new address, they did not know it.

He thought of hurrying back to the Xuanyang quarter to question the aunt, but it was already too late. So he pawned some of his clothes to procure himself supper and a bed. He was too angry to sleep, however, and did not close his eyes from dusk till dawn. Early in the morning he rode on his donkey to the aunt's house, but although he knocked on the door for the time it takes for a meal, no one answered. At last his loud shouts brought a footman slowly to the door. The young man immediately asked for the aunt.

"She doesn't live here," answered the footman.

"But she was here yesterday evening," the young man protested. "Are you trying to fool me?" He enquired whose house it was.

"This is the residence of His Excellency Master Cui. Yesterday somebody hired his courtyard to entertain a cousin coming from a distance, but they were gone before nightfall."

Bewildered and nearly distracted, the young man did not know what to do. He went back to his old lodgings in the Buzheng quarter. The landlord was sorry for him and offered to feed him; but in his despair he could eat nothing, and after three days he fell seriously ill. In another fortnight he was so weak that the landlord feared he could not live, and carried him to the undertakers. As he lay there at the point of death, all the undertakers in the market pitied him and nursed him, until he was well enough to walk with a stick.

The undertakers then hired him by the day to hold up the mourning curtains, and in this way he earned just enough to support himself. In a few months he grew quite strong again, but the mourners' chants always made him regret that he could not change places with the dead, and he would burst out sobbing and weeping, unable to restrain his tears. When he went home he would imitate their chants. Being a man of intelligence, he very soon mastered the art and became the most expert mourner in the whole capital.

It happened that the undertakers in the East and West Markets at this time were rivals. The undertakers in the East Market turned out magnificent hearses and biers—in this respect they were unrivalled—but the mourners they provided were rather poor. Hearing of our hero's skill, the chief undertaker offered him twenty thousand cash for his services; and the experts of the East Market secretly taught the young man all the fresh tunes they knew, singing in harmony with him. This went on in secret for several weeks. Then the two chief undertakers agreed to give an exhibition in Tianmen Street to see which was the better. The loser would forfeit 50,000 cash to cover the cost of the refreshments provided. An agreement to this effect was drawn up and duly witnessed.

Tens of thousands of people gathered to watch the contest. The chief of the quarter got wind of the proceedings and told the chief of police. The chief of police told the city magistrate. Very soon all the citizens of the capital were hurrying to the spot and every house in the city was empty.

The exhibition started at dawn. Coaches, hearses, and all kinds of funeral trappings had been displayed for a whole morning, but still the undertakers from the West Market could establish no superiority, and their chief was filled with shame. He built a platform in the south corner of the square, and a man with a long beard came forward, holding a hand-bell and attended by several assistants. He wagged his beard, raised his eyebrows, folded his arms and bowed. Then, mounting the platform, he sang the *White Horse* dirge. Proud of his skill, he looked to right and to left as if he knew himself unrivalled. Shouts of approval were heard on every side, and he was convinced that he must be the best dirge singer of his time who could not possibly be surpassed.

Presently the chief undertaker of the East Market built a platform in the north corner of the square, and a young man in a black cap came forward, accompanied by five or six assistants and carrying a bunch of hearse-plumes in his hand. This was our hero.

He adjusted his clothes, looked slowly up and down, then cleared his throat and began to sing with an air of diffidence. He sang the dirge *Dew on the Garlic*, and his voice rose so shrill and clear that its echoes shook the forest trees. Before he had finished the first verse, all who heard were sobbing and hiding their tears. They started jeering at the chief undertaker of the West Market until, overcome by shame, he stealthily put down the money he had forfeited and fled, to the amazement of the crowd.

Now the Emperor had recently ordered the governors of outlying provinces to confer with him at the capital once a year. This was called the "Yearly Reckoning." Thus our hero's father happened to be at the capital too, and he and some of his colleagues, discarding their official robes and insignia, had slipped out to watch the contest. With them was an old servant, the husband of the young man's foster-nurse. Recognizing our hero's accent and gait, he wanted to accost him but dared not and wept. Surprised, the Lord of Yingyang asked him why he was crying.

"Sir," replied the servant, "the young man who is singing reminds me of your lost son."

"My son was murdered by robbers because I gave him too much money," said the Lord of Yingyang. "This cannot be he." So saying, he began to weep too and went back to his lodging.

The old servant then went again to ask some of the undertakers: "Who was that singer? Where did he learn such skill?" They told him it was the son of such a one, and when he asked the young man's own name, that too was unfamiliar. The old servant was so much puzzled that he determined to put the matter to the test for himself. But when the young man saw him he gave a start, and tried to hide in the crowd. The servant caught hold of his sleeve, and said: "Surely it is you!" Then they embraced and wept, and presently went back together.

But when the young man came to his father's lodging, the Lord of Yingyang was angry with him and said: "Your conduct has disgraced the family. How dare you show your face again?" So saying he took him out of the house and led him to the ground between Qujiang and Xingyuan. Here he stripped him naked and gave him several hundred strokes with his horsewhip, till the young man succumbed to the pain and collapsed. Then his father left, thinking he was dead.

However, the young man's singing-master had asked some of his friends to keep a secret watch on him, and now they came back and told the others what had happened. They were all greatly upset, and two men were dispatched with a reed mat to bury him. When they got there they found his heart still warm, and when they had held him up for some time he started breathing again. So they carried him home and gave him liquid food through a reed pipe. The next morning he recovered consciousness, but for a whole month he was unable to move his hands and feet. Moreover, the sores left by his father's thrashing festered and gave out such a stench that his friends could not stand it, and one night they abandoned him by the roadside.

The passers-by, however, took pity on him and threw him scraps of food, so that he did not starve. After three months he was well enough to hobble about with a stick. Clad in a linen coat—which was knotted together in a hundred places, so that it looked as tattered as a quail's tail—and carrying a broken saucer in his hand, he started to beg his way through the various quarters of the city. Autumn had now turned to winter. He spent his nights in lavatories and caves and his days haunting the markets and booths.

One day when it was snowing hard, hunger and cold had driven him into the streets. His bitter cry pierced all who heard it to the heart. But the snow was so heavy that hardly a house had its outer door open.

When he reached the eastern gate of the Anyi quarter, he went north along the wall until he came to the seventh or eighth house which he found had the left half of its double door open. This was the house where the girl Li was then living, although the young man did not know it.

He stood at the door wailing persistently. And hunger and cold had made his cry so pitiful that you could scarcely bear to hear it.

The girl heard it from her room, and said to her maid: "That is my lover. I know his voice." She flew to the door and found him there, so emaciated and covered with sores that he seemed scarcely human.

"Can it be you?" she exclaimed, deeply moved. The young man simply nodded, too overcome by anger and excitement to speak.

She threw her arms round his neck, then wrapped him in her own embroidered jacket, led him to the western chamber and said in a choked voice: "It is all my fault that this has happened to you." And with these words she swooned.

The old woman came hurrying over in great alarm, crying: "What is it?" When the girl told her who had come, she immediately raised objections. "Send him packing!" she cried. "What did you bring him in here for?"

But the girl looked grave and protested: "No! This is the son of a noble house. Once he rode in grand carriages and wore fine clothes. But within a year of coming to our house he lost all he had. And then we got rid of him by a contemptible trick. We have ruined his career and made him despised by his fellow men. The love of father and son is implanted by Heaven; yet because of us his father hardened his heart and tried to kill him, then abandoned him so that he was reduced to this state.

"Everyone in the land knows that it was I who brought him to this. The court is full of his relatives. Once the authorities come to investigate this business, we shall be ruined. And since we have deceived Heaven and injured men, no spirits will take our part. Do we want to offend the gods and bring such misfortune on ourselves?

"I have lived as your daughter for twenty years, and my earnings amount to nearly a thousand pieces of gold. You are over sixty now, and I would like to give you enough to cover your expenses for another twenty years to buy my freedom, so that I can live somewhere else with this young man. We will not go far away. I shall see to it that we are near enough to pay our respects to you both morning and evening."

The old woman saw that the girl's mind was made up, so she gave her consent. When she had paid her ransom, the girl had several hundred pieces of gold left, and with them she hired a few rooms, five doors to the north. Here she gave the young man a bath, changed his clothes, fed him first with hot gruel, which was easy to digest, and later on with cheese and milk.

In a few weeks she was giving him all the choicest delicacies of land and sea. She clothed him, too, in the finest caps, shoes and stockings she could buy. In a few months he began to put on weight, and by the end of the year his health was as good as ever.

One day the girl said to him: "Now you are strong again and have got back your nerve. Try to think how much you remember of your old literary studies."

After a moment's thought he answered: "About a quarter."

Then she ordered her carriage to be got ready,

and the young man followed her on horseback. When they reached the classical bookshop at the side-gate south of the Flag Tower, she made him choose all the books he wanted, to the tune of a hundred pieces of gold. With these packed in the carriage, she drove home. She now bade him set aside all other cares, to give his whole mind to his studies. Every evening he pored over his books, with the girl at his side, and would not sleep before midnight. If she saw that he was tired, she would advise him to write a poem or ode by way of relaxation.

In two years he had thoroughly mastered his subjects, having read all the books in the kingdom. "Now I can go in for the examinations," he said.

But she answered. "No, you had better revise thoroughly, to be ready for all contingencies."

After another year, she said, "Now you may go."

He passed the examination with high distinction at the first attempt, and his reputation spread through the Ministry of Rites. Even older men, when they read his compositions, felt the greatest respect for him and wanted to become his friends.

But the girl said: "Wait a little! Nowadays when a bachelor of arts has passed his examination, he thinks he deserves to become a high official and enjoy fame throughout the empire. But your shady past puts you at a disadvantage beside your fellow scholars. You must sharpen your weapons, to win a second victory. Then you can rival the best scholars."

Then the young man worked harder than ever, and his reputation grew. That year there was a special examination to select scholars of outstanding talent from all parts of the empire. The young man took the paper on criticism of the government and advice to the Emperor, and came out top. He was appointed Army Inspector at Chengdu. Many high government officials were now his friends.

When he was about to take up his post, the girl said to him: "Now that you have regained your proper status, I no longer feel I have injured you. Let me go back and look after the old lady till she dies. You must marry a girl from some great family, who is fit to sacrifice to your ancestors. Don't injure yourself by an imprudent match. Take care of yourself! I must leave you."

The young man burst into tears and said: "If you leave me, I shall cut my throat."

But still she insisted that they must part.

He pleaded with her even more passionately, until she said: "Very well. I will go with you across the river as far as Jianmen. Then you must send me back."

To that he consented.

In a few weeks they reached Jianmen. Before they left a proclamation had been issued announcing that the young man's father, who had been Governor of Changzhou, had been summoned to the capital and appointed Governor of Chengdu and Inspector of Jianmen. Twelve days later, the Governor of Chengdu reached Jianmen, and the young man sent in his card to the posting-station where he was staying. The Lord of Yingyang could not believe that this was his son, yet the card bore the names of the young man's father and grandfather, with their ranks and titles. He was astounded. He sent for his son and, when he arrived, fell on his neck and wept bitterly.

"Now you are my son again," he said, and asked him to tell his story. When he had heard it, the Lord of Yingyang was amazed and enquired where the girl was.

"She came this far with me," answered the young man. "But now she is going back again."

"That won't do," said his father.

The next day he took his son in his carriage to Chengdu but kept the girl at Jianmen, finding suitable lodgings for her. The following day he ordered a go-between to arrange the wedding and prepare the six ceremonies to welcome the bride. Thus they wee duly married. In the years that followed the girl proved herself a devoted wife and competent house-keeper, who was loved by all her relations.

Some years later both the young man's parents died, and he showed such filial piety in his mourning that a divine fungus appeared on the roof of his mourning-hut and the grain in that district grew three ears on each stalk. The local authorities reported this to the Emperor, and informed him too that several dozen white swallows had nested in the rafters of our hero's roof. The Emperor was so impressed that he immediately raised the young man's rank.

When the three years of mourning were over, he was successively promoted to various important posts. Within ten years he was governor of several provinces, while his wife was given the title Lady of Qiankuo. They had four sons, all of whom became high officials, the least successful of them becoming Governor of Taiyuan. All four sons married into great families, so that all their relations were powerful and prosperous and their good fortune was unequalled.

How amazing that a singsong girl should have shown a degree of constancy rarely surpassed by the heroines of old! It really takes one's breath away.

My great-uncle was Governor of Jinzhou, an official in the Ministry of Revenue, and later Inspector of Roads and Waterways. The hero of this story was his predecessor in these three posts, so that my great-uncle knew all the details of his adventures. One day during the Zhenyuan period (785-805), Li Gongzuo of Longxi and I happened to be talking of wives who had distinguished themselves by their integrity, and I told him the story of the Lady of Qiankuo. He listened with rapt attention, and asked me to write it down. So I took up my brush, dipped it into the ink, and jotted down this rough outline of the tale to preserve it. It was written in the eighth month of the year Yi Hai (795).

8. Grandpa of the East City

Chen Hongzu

This tale is probably based on real people and real events. Perhaps only the monologue of the hero, Jia Chang, at the end is fictitious, as it is quite common practice in historical biographies for the author to speak through the mouth of a character in the story. This is the life story of the Cockfight Boy Jia Chang which exposes the sybaritic life of Emperor Xuanzong of the Tang Dynasty that ushered in the fall of the great empire. Jia's reminiscence reveals the tragedy through a series of contrasts. The story itself is fascinating, with vivid details rendered by the author in a style appealing to the readers. It provides not only amusement but also a lot of historical information as well.

The author calls himself Chen Hongzu, of whom nothing is known.

In the Xuanyang quarter of Chang'an lived an old man called Jia Chang. Born in the first year of the Kaiyuan period (713), he was 98 in the Geng Yin year of the Yuanhe period (810). Neither dim in sight nor hard of hearing, he spoke with a clear mind and sound memory. His father, named Zhong, was said to be over seven feet tall and strong enough to pull an ox backward by the tail. He was a warrior in the Empress' Guards. In the fourth year of the Jinglong period (710), he followed Emperor Xuanzong into the Daming Palace and killed Empress Wei.[1] Then he stood guard for Emperor Ruizong when the Emperor ascended the throne, and became a decorated Imperial Guards officer. The Emperor ordered that his family be moved close to the Dongyun Gate of the Daming Palace.

When Jia Chang was seven, he impressed others with his agility in climbing and running, and was able to clamber up a pillar with bare hands to the beams in a house. He was not only eloquent in conversation but could even talk to birds. When Emperor Xuanzong was Prince of Linzi, he was fascinated by the popular cockfights there at the Qingming Festival each year. When he became Emperor, he had a huge chicken-house built between the East and West palaces and collected over a thousand fierce fighting fowls with names like Golden Feather, Iron Claw, Tall Cockscomb, and

---

[1] In the fourth year of the Jinglong period (710), Empress Wei poisoned Emperor Zhongzong and made Prince Wen Emperor and herself Regent. Li Longji, the late emperor's nephew, led the Royal Cavalry into the palace and killed the Empress Regent and her followers and installed his father as Emperor Ruizong. This is known in history as the Coup of Jingyun (the reign title of Emperor Ruizong).

Flaunting Tail. It took five hundred young soldiers chosen from the Imperial Guards to feed and rear these birds. Fanned by the Emperor's enthusiasm, cockfighting caught on and many illustrious families spent fortunes on fighting fowls and swaggered about them. Raising fowls became a fashion in every house, with the poorest playing with toy chickens.

One day on a tour of the city, the Emperor was amused to find Jia Chang toying with wooden chickens by the roadside near the Yunlong Gate, and summoned him to the palace to tend the royal fowls, granting him better food and clothing than those of the Imperial Guards. The little lad, merely three feet tall, could play with the fowls as if they were children. He could tell at a glance which one of them was strong or weak, brave or timid, thirsty, hungry or ill; indeed he knew them inside out. When he picked out a couple to fight, they obeyed his command like tamed slaves. Eunuch Wang Cheng'en, the chief butler of the chicken-house, reported this to the Emperor and the boy was summoned to the throne. His Majesty was very pleased with the boy and made him head of the 500 fowl-boys. As he was by nature honest and prudent, he soon won the Emperor's favor and received gold and silver and silk clothes as royal gifts almost every day.

In the thirteenth year of the Kaiyuan period (725), the Emperor went to Mount Tai to offer sacrifices and Jia Chang followed with three hundred fowls in cages. Unfortunately, at the foot of the great mountain, Jia chang's father died. The Emperor granted him leave to escort the remains of his father back to his birth place Yongzhou. The magistrate of the town provided all that he needed for the procession of the hearse to parade down the Luoyang highway. In the third lunar month of the fourteenth year, Jia Chang put on his cockfight uniform and paid respects to Emperor Xuanzong at Hot Springs. By this time he had become known as the Cockfight Prodigy, and there was a song about him:

Why should my son learn to write if cockfights and horse races pay more?

At thirteen, a brat named Jia has made a fortune the whole world envies.

Making cocks fight, he stands dressed in silk by His Majesty's side.

His father's hearse was escorted by guards a thousand li to Chang'an.

When Empress Zhaocheng was still only a princess consort, she gave birth to the future Emperor Xuanzong on the fifth day of the eighth lunar month. After the repression of Empress Wei's usurpation, the birthday became a national holiday, during which free beef and wine were issued to the people for three days. It became known as "The Feast." Meanwhile, there would be a jubilee at the

Xingqing Palace. Sometimes The Feast would also be held in Luoyang. On New Year's Day and the Qingming Festival, celebrations took place at Li Hill. On such occasions, music of all kinds was played and everyone from the palace attended, including the servants and maids. Wearing a golden helmet adorned with jade carvings, Jia Chang would appear in a short embroidered suit with brocade cuffs, holding a bell and a whisk, and parade his fighting fowls in a row on the square with his head held high. The fierce fowls would bristle up and flap their wings and sharpen their beaks and claws, preparing for a fight. They would step forward or backward, jump up or down to the command of his whip. After the duels were fought, the victors would strut back to the chicken-house, with the vanquished following behind in formation like the wild geese in the sky. On such occasions, not one of the multitude of now crestfallen wrestlers, sword players, acrobats, football players, tightrope walkers and pole-top performers would dare to enter the square. Wasn't Jia Chang like the heroic monkey or dragon trainer in the ancient lore? It was indeed his day.

In the twenty-third year of the period, His Majesty himself arranged Jia's marriage with the daughter of a well-known actor named Pan Datong. At the wedding, the jade he wore and the silk dress of his bride all came from the Inner Chamber of the Imperial Palace. His wife bore him two sons,

Zhixin and Zhide. In the Tianbao period, his wife, being a good dancer, quickly won the favor of Her Royal Highness Lady Yang. The Jia couple remained in court favor for forty years. Wasn't this due to their industry in art and prudence in life?

The Emperor was born in the year of the rooster. He had people dress up in court costumes and indulge in cockfights. There were already portents of the coming disaster which would destroy the years of peace, but the Emperor did not see them. In the fourteenth year of the Tianbao period, the military governor An Lushan and his rebel army took the eastern capital Luoyang and the strategic pass Tongguan, and the Emperor fled to Chengdu. Trying to follow the Emperor, Jia Chang rushed out on horseback at night from a side door of the palace, but fell into a ditch by the roadside. He was so badly injured that he could only limp along with a stick and take refuge in the Zhongnan Mountains. On days when cockfights would have been held, he would climb the hill and wail aloud, facing southwest, the direction in which the Emperor had fled.

In the past, when An Lushan came on mission to the Western Capital Chang'an he had seen Jia Chang outside the side gate of the city. After he had conquered both the eastern and western capitals, he offered a reward of a thousand taels of gold for the fabulous cockfight master. But Jia Chang changed his name and found sanctuary in a temple, sweeping the yards and ringing the bells in service of the Buddha. When Emperor Xuanzong returned to the Qingxing Palace, he abdicated in favor of his son Emperor Suzong. Jia Chang was now able to return to where he had lived before, but he found his house razed to the ground with nothing of value left. A poor commoner once again, he could get no admission to the palace. The next day, roving out of the South Gate of Chang'an, he ran into his wife in tatters and his two sons carrying firewood on their backs. All three looked desolate and hungry. With nothing to support them, Jia Chang embraced them and wept. Then he bade them farewell by the road, and settled himself permanently in a remote temple in Chang'an studying the scriptures of the Buddha.

In the first year of the Dali period (766), he followed the eminent monk Yunping of Zisheng Temple, where the Dharanipitaka was carved on stone tablets, near the Sea Pond in the eastern city. There, he recorded his name and interpreted the profound theories in the scriptures he read. With a sincere goodwill he converted the common people to Buddhism, built houses for the monks and planted beautiful flowers and fruit trees in the temple. In the day, he would work in the garden and water the bamboos; at night he meditated in a chamber. Yunping passed away in the third year of the Jianzhong period (782). After paying the last respect to the monk as his disciple, Jia Chang built a pagoda to house his ashes east of the Zhenguo

Temple outside the East Gate of Chang'an. There he planted a hundred pine trees around the pagoda and lived in a hut at its foot, burning incense day and night and keeping the place tidy in honor of his master.

When Emperor Shunzong was crown prince in the East Palace, he granted Jia three hundred thousand cash to build a memorial hall for Yunping with a chamber for fasting and a hostel for rent as a source of income for Jia Chang. Despite this, Jia gave himself only a cup of porridge and a liter of soup each day, a mat to sleep on and a suit of coarse cloth to wear. All the rest of the money went to Buddhist activities. He did not care where his wife had gone.

In the Zhenyuan period, his elder son Zhixin, now serving in the army in Binzhou, came to the capital with Grand Minister of Education Ma Sui and paid him a visit at the Changshou quarter. Jia Chang treated him as a stranger and told him to leave. Then the younger son Zhide came back to Chang'an as a silk merchant in both Luoyang and Chang'an. Each year he would send his father gold, silver and silk, which were all rejected. So they all left him, never to return again.

In the Yuanhe period, Chen Hongzu from Yingchuan went on an excursion with his friends out of the Chunming Gate. Following the scent of incense in a thick grove of bamboo and pine trees, they came to a pagoda and on dismounting met Jia

Chang. Listening to the pious old man talk, they failed to notice that it was already dark. Jia Chang asked them to stay the night and reminisced about his past in a steady voice. Then he went on to talk about the rule of the dynasty.

Chen Hongzu asked him to comment on the vicissitudes of the Kaiyuan period. Jia said, "When I was young, I used to entertain the Emperor with cockfights and was kept as one of the royal theatrical troupe living outside the palace. Therefore I didn't know much of what really went on in the court. Nevertheless, I can say this much: I have witnessed the Director of Eunuch Attendants Du Xian appointed military governor to the west of the desert and Censor, with the power of the State over a vast region. And also Ge Shuhan, Governor of Liangzhou who took the Rock Fort, held the City of Qinghai, invaded Mount White Dragon, crossed the Pamirs, pushed the frontier to the Iron Gate Pass and successfully ruled the eastern valley of the Ili River. However, his seven conquests earned him only the position of Censor. I have also learned that Zhang Shuo, when governing Youzhou, used to send long caravans laden with silks and clothes from Hejian and Jizhou, gauze from the Yangtze and Huai river valleys and brocades from Sichuan with the sole purpose of decorating the chambers and halls of the Inner Palace. Hezhou and Dunhuang depended on the crops grown by the Frontier Army for sustenance, and the surplus grain was transported to Linzhou and then via the Yellow River to the granaries in Taiyuan, as a reserve for famine in the Guanzhong area. The local grain was stored by the people themselves. When the Emperor offered sacrifices to the Five Mountains, thousands of officials followed him but they did not consume the grain of the local people. During the festivals in summer and winter each year, I would go home on holiday and take a walk in the town. I saw people selling white cloth and white clothes. And in the byroads and lanes, occasionally I would see someone looking for a bolt of black cloth as offerings to the gods for curing the sick. But black cloth could not be bought for any price, and had to be substituted with the black gauze used for headbands. Recently I went to the main streets with a stick. Looking all around, I could hardly find a hundred pedestrains in white. 'So where are the men?' I asked myself. 'Have they all been drafted?'

"In the twelfth year of the Kaiyuan period, the Emperor issued an edict announcing that vacancies of vice-ministers in the Three Central Departments (the Department of State Affairs, the Chancellery and the Secretariat) should be filled by prefectural executives, and that vacancies of central bureau directors should be filled by county magistrates. When I was forty, bureau directors in the Three Central Departments who were skilled in government and the penal law would be appointed prefectural executives, and those with less competence as county magistrates. Ever since I moved to the main avenue of the city, I have often seen officials demoted from the Three Central Departments, resting in low spirits on their way to be magistrates in prefectures. In these days, only those competent in governing with moral integrity are promoted, never the scholars who excelled in the imperial examinations. Such is the way things go."

At this point Jia broke into tears, and went on, "Formerly Emperor Xuanzong had the power and glory to receive tributes once every three years from the tribal chiefs in the north, east, south and west. In return, grand receptions would be held for their emissaries with feasts and silk costumes as presents, and they would leave on completion of their mission. None of them would remain in the capital. But now the tribesmen from the north live with residents in the capital, get married and raise families. And young people are influenced by them. Just look at the ornaments, clothes and shoes they wear—all different from those before. Hasn't everything gone crazy?"

Chen Hongzu dared not answer the question, and presently left the old man.

9. The Story of Yingying

Yuan Zhen

Of all the Tang legends, the story of Yingying is perhaps the most popular and widely known. It is a story of a scholar Zhang and a beautiful girl called Yingying. In gratitude to the scholar for saving her life and in admiration for his literary talent, Yingying begins a clandestine love affair with him despite her misgivings. This could not be tolerated by the Confucian ethical code nor could it last long. In the end Zhang abandons her.

The story delineates Yingying in detail—proud and poised, shy but yielding, following her own conflicting emotions with bold action—as a wellbred girl inextricably in love. The story is well knit with scenes of passionate love and icy parting that touch the reader's heart. However, the author makes a lengthy commentary at the end, reviling Yingying as a "femme fatale" and extoling Zhang's weak fickleness as "repentence." Lu Xun has rightly dismissed such preaching as "sheer hypocrisy and bad taste," an example of the inhumanity of the feudalistic morality.

The author Yuan Zhen (779-831), alias Weizhi,

was a native of Luoyang in the Tang Dynasty. In the ninth year of the Zhenyuan period (793), he passed the primary imperial examination, and ten years later the provincial exam, being appointed as an editor. In the first year of the Yuanhe period (806) he passed the national exam and was made Left Advisor, Commandant of Luoyang and Court Censor. Upright and outspoken, he offended the powerful eunuchs and conservative bureaucrats, and was demoted to sergeant in the army in Jiangling. His work there impressed the eunuchs, who finally made him Prime Minister. He died in the fifth year of the Dahe period (831) at his post of Military Governor.

Yuan's poems rank with Bai Juyi's, known as the Yuan-Bai School. The Changqing Collection of Yuan's Works *amounts to 60 volumes. This story is believed to be autobiographical. There were many later variations, the best known being* Strings of the West Chamber *by Dong Jieyuan of the Jin Dynasty and* The West Chamber *by Wang Shifu of the Yuan Dynasty.*

During the Zhenyuan period (785-805), there was a scholar named Zhang. Gentle and sentimental, handsome and erudite, he nevertheless appeared stoic and aloof, untouched by temptation for what was beneath him. He would keep company with boisterous friends at banquets only to please them, but would never abandon himself. And so, at the age of 23, he had still not been close to a woman. Asked why, he would answer: "Deng Tuzi[1] was driven by lust rather than beauty. I appreciate great beauty but have seen none so far. If I ever had, she would have remained in my heart. So I'm not a cold, indifferent man."

On a visit to Puzhou in Shanxi, Zhang stayed in a hostel for monks in Pujiu Temple. Just then a widow named Cui who was on her way back to Chang'an stopped at the temple. It turned out that both Madame Cui and Zhang were related to the same family of Zheng, and Madame Cui was Zhang's distant aunt. That year Military Governor Hun Jian died in Puzhou. A eunuch there named Ding Wenya did not know how to handle military affairs, and a mutiny broke out. The soldiers ransacked the city. The Cuis were a wealthy family with a lot of servants and slaves, and Madame Cui was in a panic, not knowing how to keep the family safe. Fortunately Zhang had some important friends in the army and was able to seek their protection. A fortnight later, the Emperor sent Inspector Du Que to restore order there, and the upheaval and pillage were over.

To show her gratitude to Zhang for his help, Madame Cui gave a banquet there in his honor. She

---

[1] Deng Tuzi was a man in the last years of the Warring States Period. Although his wife was ugly, he still had five children with her and was regarded as a lustful man.

said to Zhang, "I am a widow, devoted to my children. It was dreadful that we ran into such a horrible riot that threatened our lives. My son and daughter indeed owe their lives to you, a debt far beyond any ordinary kindness. Today I've told them to come and pay their respects to you as their elder and express their thanks to you." First she summoned her teenage son Huanlang, who was gentle and handsome. Then she called for her daughter, urging, "Come and bow to your elder cousin who saved your life." However, the girl didn't appear, saying that she was too sick to see Zhang. Madame Cui became angry, insisting, "You owe your life to Cousin Zhang. Without him, you wouldn't be here today. How can you refuse to see him?"

After a while, the girl appeared. Although plainly dressed and without make-up, she had full blossoming cheeks and a fringe of hair that veiled her brow. It was a face that took Zhang's breath away. He immediately bowed to her. The girl casually sat by her mother, her eyes mildly reproaching her mother for making her come out to meet this cousin. Her delicate frame seemed hardly able to carry her. Zhang asked about her age, to which Madame Cui responded, "She was born in the seventh month of the Jia Zi year and is now 17." Throughout the dinner, Zhang tried to bring her into conversation but to no avail. In spite of this, he fell completely for her beauty but found no opportunity to express his feelings for her.

Yingying had a maid called Hongniang. Zhang secretly gave her many gifts, and tried to tell her of his feelings for Yingying, but Hongniang was startled and ran away, her face flushed. Zhang was mortified. However, she returned the next day. Zhang, greatly embarrassed, apologized to her and did not mention the matter again. The maid said, "Sir, I dare not pass on your words to my mistress or anyone else. But you know relatives of the family well. Why don't you make your proposal through them?"

"Ever since I was a child I have never liked company. Even when I was among pretty girls I did not look at them. So I never imagined that I would lose possession of myself as I have now. At dinner last night, I could hardly contain myself. Since then, I forget where to stop on the road and can't even remember whether I have eaten or not. I'm afraid I won't be able to last long like this. If I asked a match-maker to make the proposal, it would take at least three months. By then I would be dead. Tell me please, what should I do?" Zhang pleaded.

"Miss Cui is a chaste, self-possessed lady. She will not stand any impudence even from her family elders, much less her servants. But she is very fond of poetry and writing, and often indulges herself in them. Why don't you write her a love poem? That's all I can suggest," the maid said. Hearing this, Zhang was overjoyed. He instantly wrote two poems and gave them to her.

That night Hongniang returned with a sheet of colored writing paper, saying, "Miss Cui told me to deliver this to you." It was a poem entitled "On the Night of the Full Moon."

In the west chamber I wait for the moon to rise, leaving the door ajar,
The shadow of flowers rustling by the wall suggests a coming visitor.

Zhang was quick to see what was implied. It was the fourteenth day of the second lunar month, the eve of the full moon. In Yingying's garden there was an apricot tree near the east wall which could easily be scaled.

The next evening was the fifteenth; the moon was full. Zhang climbed over the wall and got to the west chamber. Indeed, the door was half open, and Hongniang was asleep in a bed. Zhang woke her up, and the girl exclaimed, "How did you get in here?"

"Miss Cui sent for me in the letter you gave me. Please tell her I'm here now," Zhang explained. In a minute the maid returned, saying, "She's coming!" Zhang grew tense with excitement, thinking he would soon achieve his desire. Then Yingying appeared formally dressed. Sternly, she said, "It was because my whole family owed our lives to you that Mother presented me to you. Why now do you send me lewd poems through my spoiled maid?

You began with gallantry saving others from disaster but have ended up attempting to prey upon one of them. This is seduction in place of ravage; how much different is one from the other? I first intended to keep this a secret, but that would be covering up someone's misconduct, which is immoral. If I had told Mother about you, it would have been a betrayal to your past kindness which would not be right either. And I didn't think I could make myself clear enough to you through my maid. So I wrote that short poem to seek an opportunity to do so myself. To make it work, I chose my words with care so that you would not fail to come. Knowing that this is against the ethical code, I can't help feeling ashamed of myself. I only wish that you will abide by convention and avoid unseemly conduct." With these words, she left. Zhang was dumbfounded, not knowing what to do. He climbed back over the wall, his dream utterly shattered.

A few nights later, Zhang was sleeping alone beneath a window when suddenly he was shaken awake. He sat up with a start and found Hongniang carrying pillows and bedding into the room. She patted him on the shoulder, whispering, "Come on, she's coming! Why are you still sleeping?" Laying down the pillows side by side, she made the bed and left. Zhang rubbed his eyes, thinking he was still in a dream, but waited with trepidation. In a minute, Yingying emerged, helped along by Hongniang. Shy and delicate, she seemed scarcely able to move her limbs, in sharp contrast to her proud former self.

It was the eighteenth. A crystal clear moon was hanging aslant in the sky, flooding half the bed with a silver light. Zhang grew buoyant with life, feeling he was with an angel come down to earth. After a spell, the bell of the temple began to chime, ushering in the dawn. Hongnian came and urged Yingying to leave. Sobbing, Yingying was led away. Throughout that night she had not uttered a word.

Zhang watched the approach of dawn dubiously. "Was it but a dream after all?" he asked himself. When it was light enough to see, he found powder on his arms, fragrance on his clothes and tears still glimmering on the mat of the bed. Then, for a fortnight, there was no sign of Yingying. Zhang was writing a 30-line couplet, "A True Rendezvous." It was hardly finished when Hongniang showed up again. Zhang asked her to take it to Yingying. She resumed her visits again, leaving in the morning, returning at night. This went on for about a month in the west chamber. Zhang inquired about her mother's intentions. Yingying sighed, " I have no way to sway her mind," and expressed her wish to be formally married.

Soon Zhang was to leave for Chang'an and told Yingying so. Yingying made no objections, but was evidently melancholy. She did not show up for two nights before his departure, and Zhang had to leave westward for the capital. But he returned to Puzhou again a few months later. Yingying was very good at writing prose and poetry. Zhang had asked more than once for her work but never saw a word by her. He sent her his own articles, but she did not even care much to read them. In fact, Yingying's writing technique was superb, but she never showed off. She was swift and eloquent in conversation but rarely talked to others. Her feelings for Zhang were deep but never expressed in words. Even in her sadness, she still looked placid, and nobody could tell whether she was angry or glad. When she played the *qin* zither, the music would be plaintive and repining. When Zhang overheard it and begged her to play more, she would decline, making her all the more desirable to him.

As the date of the imperial examination was drawing near, Zhang had to go to Chang'an again. On the eve of departure, he was beside himself, signing with grief. Yingying knew in her heart that they might never meet again. She made herself up and said slowly to Zhang in a gentle voice, "Our love began with lust and may end with your desertion which only serves me right, and I will not complain. But if you were to remain faithful despite the way we began, then that would be a kindness to me. Then our sacred vows would eventually be fulfilled. So why are you so sad at this parting? There is little I can do to soothe you. You have often said that I play music well, but I have never agreed to play for you because I was shy. Now that you're leaving, let me satisfy your wish." She had the *qin* laid out and cleaned, and started playing "Prelude to the Dance in a Rosy Gauze Costume." She had scarcely played a few notes when the tune ran into confusion, no longer intelligible to the ear. Everyone listening wept. Yingying stopped abruptly and left in tears, running into her room, refusing to come out again. The next morning Zhang left.

Zhang failed the examination the following year but chose to stay on in the capital. He wrote to Yingying, trying to console her. Her answer is recorded as follows:

"As I hold your letter between my hands, I feel deeply your loving caresses. It is sadness and happiness combined. You generously gave me a box of flower ornaments and a lipstick. But for whom shall I make myself up with these presents of yours? They will only increase my longing and sighing. From the letter I know you are now reviewing your lessons in peace; I regret that I have been abandoned. Since that is fate, what more is there to say? Since last fall, I have sensed that something is lost to me for ever. Sometimes, in a lively crowd, I force myself to laugh but alone, in the deep of the night, tears flow down my cheeks in streams. Even in dreams, I grieve for the breaking of our union. Love still lingers on in my heart as though the rendezvous would never end, but my awakened soul has already left with the dream. Although half of the bed is still warm, yet you are far, far away. It has been almost a year now since our parting. Chang'an is a place of pleasure where delights are beckoning at every corner. I'm grateful that you haven't forgotten my poor self and still long for me, although my gratitude cannot compensate your kindness. But our sacred vow shall never change.

"I first met you at occasional dinners as cousins. Tempted through my maid, I secretly gave myself to you. Indeed it was hard to contain a maiden's heart. You enticed me as Sima Xiangru with a *qin*,[1] but I didn't reject you as Maiden Gao with a spindle.[2] When we lay in the same bed, the bliss was eternal. Blinded by love, I thought I had found my destiny. But who could have thought it would turn out to be a fantasy; there was no real engagement at all. I was filled with shame for giving myself up so readily, and could never serve you openly. Now this cannot be altered, what else can I do except sighing? If you are gentle and will deign to embrace me, I will live again even though I am dead. But, if you are shrewd and care little about feelings, preferring your own career to our

---

[1] Sima Xiangru in the Han Dynasty played the *qin* to woo Zhuo Wenjun. She eloped with him and they lived happily ever after.

[2] In the Jin Dynasty a Maiden Gao was accosted by her neighbor; she responded by throwing a spindle of her loom at the rascal, costing him two of his front teeth.

secret love, which you may regard as a scandal, and break your own vow owing to circumstances, then I will, without changing my heart, wither away like fallen petals and leaves trodden upon under your feet. I have spoken in candor. My tears prevent me from saying more. Please take care, take good care of yourself.

"I am sending a jade bracelet for you, which was my favorite piece of jewelry when I was a little girl. Jade symbolizes hardness in character, and the shape of the bracelet is a ring, an endless cycle. Together with it, there is a strand of raw silk and a spotty bamboo tea grinder. These things are not valuable. But the jade stands for your firmness and its circular shape my heart that never changes. My tears mark the bamboo and the silk represents my thoughts of you. I use them to express my feelings and as witness to our everlasting love. Although our hearts are close, our bodies are far apart beyond hope of reunion. While my grievous remorse congeals, my spirit is flying across a thousand kilometers to rejoin you. Please take good care of yourself. The spring winds often bring illness, so pay attention to your diet. Take care and stop longing for me."

Zhang passed the letter among his friends and the story spread about the town. His friend Yang Juyuan, also a poet, wrote a short poem "Ode to Maiden Cui":

A young man more handsome than Pan Lang[1],
Fresh like the sweet herb after spring thaw,
The playboy scholar's heart was broken
On receiving a letter from Xiao Niang[2].

Yuan Zhen from Henan also wrote a poem in rhyme with Zhang's "A True Rendezvous":

A faint moonlight shone through the curtain,
While fireflies flit across the night sky.
Dark horizon loomed dimly in the gloaming,
With bush trees ranked in low silhouette.
A wind whistled through the bamboos in the
*   yard,*
Like phoenixes singing in the parasol trees.
The bed curtains hung dreamily like a mist,
Their hooks were jingling in the breeze.
The goddess arrived in state,
Followed by angels in the clouds.
Silently she entered late at night,
Leaving before dawn in a haze.
Her silk shoes sparkled with shiny pearls,
Her trousers were lavishly embroidered.
Her jade hairpin was gorgeous like a phoenix,
Her shawl a rainbow across her shoulders.

---

[1] Pan Lang here refers to Pan Yue, a noted scholar in the Jin Dynasty, known to be very handsome and later often so referred to.

[2] Xiao Niang, the name of a lady in a well-known family in east China, which became a substitute for ladies in the Tang Dynasty.

He said he hailed from the abode of immortals,
And came to pay tribute to the Azure Jade
Palace.
He said he hailed from the Luo River valley,
And came to visit with the beautiful maiden.
Although she mildly resisted the enticement,
Yet a glowing warmth had been kindled.
Her head bowed, her hair drooping in tremors,
She stepped back to reveal her beauty.
Shyly turning her rosy cheek aside,
She was carried onto the curtained bed.
The Mandarin ducks crossed their necks,
The halcyons were cooing together.
Although she knitted her brows,
Her lips were burning red.
Her breath smelt of orchid,
Her skin smooth, her muscles lithe.
Barely with strength to turn a wrist,
She coiled herself so tender and sweet.
Pearls of sweat dripping down in strings,
Her hair dishevelled like wild bushes.
Indeed the union was eternal,
But the bell of dawn began to chime.
It was indeed hard to part,
And love refused to leave.
Her face full of misery,
They both made a sacred vow.
A bracelet she left to embody union,
And a knot to bind the hearts together.

Tears streaming down in the mirror,
Insects flew round the flickering light.
The dawn was breaking, faintly glowing,
Before the candle light burned out.
Her sweet scent lingered on his clothes,
The pillows stained with her lipstick.
He returned to the Luo River valley riding on a
*   wild goose,*
And flew to Mount Song blowing a bamboo
*   flute.*
As her heart grieved by the pond,
His thoughts were roaming over the lotus.
She played the zither to vent her grief,
And looked up in anticipation for the return of
*   the wild goose.*
It was hard to cross the sea,
Nor easy to soar beyond the sky.
Floating clouds had no anchorage,
Only the flute player remained in the tower.

When friends heard the story they could not understand how it had ended like this. But Zhang said he cherished no rosy dreams about it. Yuan Zhen, his closest friend, asked him why. Zhang said, "Most great beauties created by god bring disaster either to herself or to others. With her exquisite charm, if Yingying had married into a wealthy family, she could have played havoc with wind and rain or caused calamities I couldn't name. History tells us that King Zhou of the Yin Dynasty and

King You of the Zhou Dynasty [1] were both mighty enough to rule a nation of a million strong, but perished despicably just because of a woman who dispersed their crowds, had the monarchs butchered and made a laughingstock of them. I don't have the moral strength to defeat such femme fatale, so I must control my own feelings." His audience nodded with deep sighs.

Over a year later, Yingying married another man, and Zhang had also taken a wife. He happened to pass Cui's house and asked through her husband to see her as his cousin. But Yingying did not show up. Zhang was clearly filled with grief. When Yingying heard of it, she wrote him a poem without showing herself.

> I'm afraid I've lost weight and also my looks.
> Tossing in my bed a thousand times, I can't leave it.
> Not for others that I wouldn't get up,
> It is because of you I've waned and feel ashamed.

A few days later, Zhang was about to leave, when she sent him another poem.

> You it was that deserted me,
> Why today should you see me?
> With sentiments of bygone days,

---

[1] These two were respectively the last kings of the two very early dynasties at the dawn of Chinese civilization.

You should express your pity for the one right before your eyes.

He never heard of her again. Most people praised Zhang for making amends for his sins. To my friends, I would often point out the moral of this story as a warning not to repeat Zhang's mistake, or, if they had already done so, to control themselves in future.

One day during the Zhenyuan period, my friend Li Gongchui stayed with me in my house. I told him this story which fascinated him. So he wrote a poem, titled "Ode to Yingying."

10. Wushuang the Peerless

Xue Tiao

This is a tortuous love story, a typical legend in which the hero and heroine meet and separate through drastic ups and downs in life. Wang Xianke, the hero, is well depicted. His love for Wushuang is so fervent and sincere that although he is plunged into despair many times, he persists to the end, and finally, miraculously, succeeds. His friend Bailiff Gu is an outstandingly chivalrous man of a few words who plays an important part in the events. Through the story the reader can gain a glimpse of life in the late Tang Dynasty. In those days bribery was often the lubricant to get things done, and the palace maids were simply wretched slaves. Although the story covers quite a long period, the events are closely knit, and the descriptions true to life in the psychology, language and history of that time. Only the drug supposedly able to make a person return to life after death given by the Taoist priest is a little far-fetched and unbelievable "and the bailiff's willingness to take his own life, with a number of other innocent lives in return for Wang's sumptuous gifts goes beyond chivalry" and is hard to accept. In the Song and Yuan dynasties which followed, the theme of the tale was often repeated in ballads and drama. Later, in the Ming Dynasty, the brothers Lu Can and Lu Cai turned it into Story of a Pearl.

The author Xue Tiao (830-872) was a native of Yongji, Shanxi. Having passed the civil service examination, he was appointed Imperial Adjutant and Secretary in the 11th year of the Xiantong period (870) by Emperor Yizong, and the following year was writing edicts for the Emperor at the post of bureau director respectively in the Ministry of Revenue and the Ministry of War. However, he was found dead at his post, probably poisoned, and was postumously promoted to Vice-Minister of Revenue.

Liu Zhen, a courtier during the Jianzhong period (780-783), had a nephew called Wang Xianke whom he brought up in his own family because Wang's father had died. Liu's daughter Wushuang (The Peerless) was a few years younger than Wang and the two children played together; while Liu's wife was so fond of her nephew that she gave him pet names. Several years passed, during which Liu was as kind as could be to his widowed sister and her son.

One day Wang's mother fell ill, and as she lay dying she said to Liu: "I have only this one child, and you know how I love him. I am sorry that I shan't live to see him marry. Wushuang is a beautiful, intelligent girl, and I love her dearly too. Don't marry her into any other family. I entrust my son to you. If you consent to their marriage, I shall die content."

"Set your mind at rest—you will recover," said Liu. "Don't worry about anything else." But the lad's mother died, and Wang took her coffin back to his house at Xiangyang for burial.

After the three years' mourning, he thought: "I am all alone in the world. I had better take a wife and have children. Wushuang is old enough to marry, and my uncle surely won't go back on his word even though he is now a high official." So he got his luggage ready and went to the capital.

By this time Liu was land tax commissioner and had a magnificent mansion, crowded with high-ranking visitors. When Wang called on him, Liu lodged him in the family school with his own children. But although acknowledged as his nephew, for a long time the young man heard nothing about the marriage. He had caught one glimpse of Wushuang from a window and she was as radiantly beautiful as a goddess come down to earth. He fell madly in love with her; but, afraid his uncle would not consent to their marriage, sold all that he had to raise several million cash. With this money he tipped his uncle's and aunt's attendants and servants lavishly, and gave feasts and drinking parties until he had gained free access to the inner court of the house. He also treated with the greatest respect the cousins among whom he lived. On his aunt's birthday, he pleased her by buying novel and rare presents—trinkets of carved rhinoceros horn and jade. And about ten days later, he sent an old woman to her to ask for Wushuang's hand.

"This is what I want too," said his aunt. "We must have a talk about it."

A few days later a servant informed him, "The mistress has been talking to the master about the marriage. But, judging by the way the master behaved, there seems to be some hitch." When Wang heard this he fell into despair and could not sleep all night, for fear his uncle would refuse him. However, he went on doing his best to please him.

One day Liu went to the court but came galloping home at dawn, perspiring and out of breath, able only to gasp: "Bolt the gate! Bolt the gate!" The whole household was thrown into confusion, and no one could guess what had happened. Presently Liu told them. "The troops at Jingyuan have revolted, and Military Governor Yao Lingyan has entered the Hanyuan Hall in the Imperial Palace with an armed force! The Emperor has left the palace by the North Gate, and all his ministers have fled with him. Concern for my wife and children made me come back to put my affairs in order. Call Xianke at once to look after my family, and I shall marry Wushuang to him."

At this Wang was surprised and overjoyed. He thanked his uncle who, having loaded twenty baggage animals with gold, silver and silk, said to him, "Change your clothes and take these things out by Kaiyuan Gate, then hire rooms in some quiet inn. I shall bring your aunt and Wushuang after you by a roundabout route from Qixia Gate."

Wang did as he was told, waiting in an inn outside the city; but by sunset they had still not arrived, and since noonday the city gates had been closed. Tired of looking south for the arrival of his uncle's family, Wang mounted his horse and rode with a torch in his hand around the city until he came to Qixia Gate. This gate was bolted too and there were guards there holding staffs, some standing and some sitting.

"What has happened in the city?" he ventured to ask, dismounting from his horse. "Has anyone passed this way?"

"Marshal Zhu Ce has made himself Emperor," said one guard. "In the afternoon a richly dressed man who had four or five women with him tried to leave through this gate. Everybody in the street knew him. They said he was Liu, the land tax commissioner, so the officer in charge dared not let him pass. Later in the evening horsemen came to arrest him, and took all his family to the north part of they city."

Wang burst out sobbing, and returned to his inn. Toward midnight the city gates burst open and torches shone bright as day as shouting soldiers armed with swords and other weapons poured out to hunt down and kill any runaway courtiers. Abandoning the baggage, Wang fled in fright.

After three years spent in his country house at Xiangyang, when news came that the rebellion had been suppressed, order restored in the capital and the whole empire pacified, he returned to Chang'an to find out what had become of his uncle. He had reached the south of the Xinchang quarter and was reining in his horse, wondering where to go, when someone accosted him; and looking carefully he saw that it was his former servant Saihong. This Saihong had served Wang's father, and Liu finding him useful had kept him on. Wang grasped his hand and they shed tears.

"Are my uncle and aunt well?" asked the young man.

"They are living in the Xinghua quarter," Saihong told him.

Wang was overjoyed and cried, "I shall go there then."

"I am a freeman now," said Saihong. "I am staying with a man who has a small house of his own and make a living by selling silk. It is late. You had better spend the night with me, and we can go together tomorrow." Then Saihong took him to his house where they had a good meal with plenty to drink. Later in the evening word came that, because Liu had worked for the rebels, he and his wife had been executed while Wushuang had been taken to the palace as a maid.

In his grief Wang cried aloud till all the neighbors were moved to pity.

"Wide though the world is," he told Saihong, "I have no folk of my own. Where can I go?" Then he asked, "Are there any of the old family servants left?"

"Only Wushuang's maid Caiping," replied Saihong. "She is working now in the house of General Wang, captain of the imperial guards."

"If I cannot see Wushuang again," sighed Wang, "I shall die content if only I can see her maid."

He paid a visit to the general, who had been his uncle's friend, told him the whole story from beginning to end and asked to redeem the maid with a good sum of money. The general was touched by his story, and agreed. Wang then rented a house, where he lived with Saihong and Caiping.

One day Saihong said: "Young master, you are a grown man now, you should find some official post instead of moping at home all the time." Wang let himself be persuaded, and asked the general's help. The general recommended him to City Magistrate Li, and the latter was able to have him appointed magistrate of Fuping and concurrently master of the Changle posting-station.

Several months later, a report came that a certain palace official was taking thirty handmaids to the imperial mausoleum to set the place in good order. They would travel in ten curtained carriages and put up at the Changle posting-station.

"I hear the palace maids selected are all girls from good families," Wang told Saihong. "I wonder if Wushuang is among them. Could you find out for me?"

"There are thousands of palace maids," retorted Saihong. "Why should Wushuang be one of these?"

"Go anyway," urged Wang. "You never know."

Saihong accordingly pretended to be a station officer and went to boil tea outside the curtain of the girls' room. Wang had given him three thousand cash and told him: "Stay by the stove. Don't leave the spot. And if you see her, report to me at once." But the palace maids kept out of sight on the other side of the curtain, and could only be heard talking together at night. When it grew late and all was still, Saihong washed his bowls and stoked his fire but dared not sleep. Suddenly someone called from the other side of the curtain: "Saihong! Saihong! How did you know I was here? Is my betrothed well?" Then there was the sound of sobbing.

"Our young master is now in charge of this posting-station," said Saihong. "He thought you might be here today, so he sent me with his greetings."

"I cannot say any more now," the girl replied. "Tomorrow after we leave, you will find a letter to my betrothed under the purple quilt in the northeast pavilion." After saying this she moved away. Presently he heard a great commotion inside and cries of "She has fainted!" The officer in charge shouted for a cordial. It was Wushuang who had fainted.

Saihong hurried to report this to Wang, who in desperation demanded, "How can I see her?"

"Wei Bridge is under repair," suggested Saihong. "You might pretend to be the officer in charge and stand near where the carriages pass. When Wushuang recognizes you, she will draw the curtain and you will see her."

Wang did as Saihong proposed. When the third carriage passed, the curtain was drawn and the sight of Wushuang filled him with grief and longing. Meantime Saihong had found the letter under the quilt in the pavilion. There were five sheets of paper with a printed design covered with the girl's writing and telling all that had befallen her and her utter misery. Wang shed bitter tears as he read it, certain in his heart that they would never meet again. But in a postscript to the letter she wrote, "I have heard that a bailiff named Gu in Fuping is a man you can turn to in trouble. Could you ask him to help?"

Wang requested his superior officer to relieve him of his duty at the posting-station, and went back to serve as magistrate of Fuping. He called on Bailiff Gu in his country house, then for a whole year paid him frequent visits and tried in every way to please him, making him innumerable presents of embroidered silk and precious jewels. But not a word did he breathe all that time of his request. And when his term of office expired, he stayed on in the county.

One day Gu came to see him and said, "I'm a rough soldier, getting on in years. There's not much I can do for anyone. But you have treated me well, and I feel you must want something of me. I have a sense of chivalry, and I appreciate your friendship so much I mean to repay you even if it costs me my life."

Wang shed tears and bowed, then told him the whole story. When he had heard it, Gu looked up at the sky and clapped his head with his hand several times. "This is very difficult!" he exclaimed. "I shall try to help, but don't expect quick results."

Wang bowed again and responded, "If I can only see her again alive, I don't mind how long I have to wait."

Half a year passed without any news. Then one day there came a knock at Wang's door and a letter was delivered from Gu, which said, "My envoy to Mao Mountain has returned. Come over." Wang galloped there at once, but Gu said nothing. When asked about his envoy, he replied, "I have kille him. Drink some tea." Later that night he asked, "Do you have a maid in your house who knows Wushuang?" Wang told him that Caiping did and at once had her brought there. After looking her over carefully, Gu smiled approvingly and said, "I shall borrow her for a few days. You may go back now."

A few days later it was rumoured that some high official had passed through the county, and one of the palace maids had been put to death. Filled with misgivings, Wang asked Saihong to make enquiries, and found that the girl executed was Wushuang. He wept and sobbed. "I had hoped that Gu could help," he sighed, "but now she is dead! What shall I do?" He shed tears and groaned, unable to restrain himself.

That same night, after midnight, Wang heard violent knocking at the door and when he opened it found Gu there with a stretcher.

"This is Wushuang," Gu told him. "To all appearances she is dead, but her heart is still warm. She will revive tomorrow, and you can give her some medicine. But you keep this quiet!" Wang carried the girl inside and kept watch. At dawn her limbs grew warm and she opened her eyes, but the sight of Wang made her cry out and faint away. He tended her and gave her cordials till night, when she recovered.

Gu told Wang, "Today I am repaying your kindness in full. I heard that a priest in Mao Mountain had a strange drug. Anyone who takes it appears to die suddenly but actually revives within three days. So I sent someone to ask for it, and managed to get one pill. Yesterday I asked Caiping to disguise herself as an imperial envoy and give

Wushuang this pill, ordering her to commit suicide because she was connected with the rebel party. At the mausoleum I pretended to be a relative, and redeemed her body with a hundred bolts of silk. I had to give big bribes to all the people on the way, to avoid being discovered. You must not stay here any longer. Outside the door you will find ten porters, five horses and two hundred bolts of silk. Take Wushuang away with you before dawn, changing your names and covering up your tracks to avoid trouble."

Before daybreak, Wang and Wushuang left. They travelled through the gorges until they reached Jiangling, where they stayed for some time. When they heard nothing from the capital to alarm them, Wang took his wife back to his country house at Xiangyang, where they remained all their life and where they had many children.

There are many vicissitudes, strange encounters and separations in human life, but I have heard of nothing comparable to this story, which I often say is unique in history. Wushuang lost her freedom during troubled times, but Wang remained loyal to his love and finally won her, thanks to the strange measures taken by Gu. After overcoming so many difficulties, the young couple were eventually able to escape and return to their home, where they lived happily as husband and wife for fifty years. A remarkable story!

11. The Man With the Curly Beard

Anonymous

The three characters in the story, the Red Whisk Maid, Li Jing and the Man with the Curly Beard were called "The Gallant Trio" by their contemporaries, and they deserved the title. The Red Whisk Maid is shrewd and pretty, Li Jing steadfast and handsome and the Man with the Curly Beard magnanimous. The interplay of the three leaves a deep impression on the reader's mind. Although not much description is given to Li Shimin, who was later to become Emperor Taizong of the Tang Dynasty, his image as a brilliant young man with regal grace is very much evident. All this contributes to the success of the legend in characterization and development as well.

The legend is an annecdote about the early days of the Tang Dynasty to testify that a real sovereign must be mandated by Heaven. Although the Man with the Curly Beard appears "Magnificent and kingly," he knows his place before the Son of Heaven and dares not go against the will of God. The moral of the story is: "Any subject who vainly

153

attempts to rebel is like a praying mantis dashing itself against the wheel of a chariot," a warning to *those with such intentions against the Dynasty.*

Judging from the sophistication in narration, the legend must have been written in the late Tang Dynasty. However, its author's name cannot be ascertained. According to Hong Mai's Random Thoughts from a Private Study *(Vol. 12), the author of "The Man with the Curly Beard" is Du Guangting.* The History of the Song Dynasty, "Chapter on Literature," *also records it as Du's work. Du Guangting, alias Binzhi, was a native of Jinyun County, Zhejiang, who called himself Dong Yingzi, and is known to have been a prolific writer. But recent research only affirms his contribution as rewriting the legend and not creating it. Later in the Ming Dynasty, Zhang Fengyi and Zhang Taihe co-produced the legend,* The Red Whisk, *and Ling Chucheng,* The Curly-bearded Man.

When Emperor Yangdi of the Sui Dynasty (605-618) visited Yangzhou, Councillor Yang Su was ordered to guard the West Capital. Now Yang Su, that proud noble, plumed himself on the fact that in those unsettled times no one in the empire had greater power or prestige than he. Giving free rein to his love of luxury and pride, he ceased to behave like a subject. He received both officials and guests seated on a couch, and went about supported by beautiful maids, in his behaviour usurping the Emperor's prerogatives. He became worse, too, in his old age when, forgetting his duty to his sovereign, he made no attempt to save the realm from utter ruin.

One day Li Jing, later to become the Duke of Wei but then a private citizen, asked for an interview in order to offer advice on government policy. Yang Su, as usual, received him sitting. Li approached and said with a bow, "The empire is in a turmoil and the bold are contending for power. As chief councillor to the imperial house, Your Highness should be thinking of how to rally good men, and should not receive visitors sitting."

Yang Su was impressed and stood up to apologize. After talking with Li he was very pleased with him and accepted his memorandum.

Now while Li had been discoursing brilliantly, one of Yang's maids—a very beautiful girl who was standing in front of them holding a red whisk—had watched him intently. When he was leaving, she said to the officer at the door, "Ask him his name and where he lives." Li told the officer. The girl nodded and withdrew, and Li went back to his hostel.

That night, just before dawn, there was a soft knocking at Li's door, and when he got up he found a stranger there in a cap and a purple gown, who was carrying a stick and a bag. Asked who he was, the stranger said, "I am the maid with the red whisk in Councillor Yang's house." Then Li quickly let her in. When she took off her outer gown and cap, he saw she was a beautiful girl of about nineteen with a fair complexion, dressed in bright clothes. She bowed to him, and he returned the bow.

"I have served Yang Su for a long time," said the girl, "and seen many visitors. But there has never been any one like you. The vine cannot grow by itself, but needs a tree to cling to. So I have come to you."

"But Councillor Yang has great power in the capital; how can it be done?" said Li.

"Never mind him—he's an old imbecile," she replied. "Many maids have left, knowing that he will fall; and he makes very little effort to get them back. I have thought it over carefully. Don't you worry." Asked her name, she told Li it was Zhang, and that she was the eldest in her family. He found her an angel in complexion, manner, speech and character. Both happy and alarmed at this unexpected conquest, he had not a moment's peace of mind. Inquisitive people kept peeping through his door, and for a few days a half-hearted search was made for her. Then Li and the girl dressed in fine clothes and fled on horseback from the capital to Taiyuan.

On the way they stopped at a hostel in Lingshi. The bed was made, meat was boiling in the pot, Zhang was combing her long hair in front of the bed and Li was currying the horses at the door, when suddenly a man of medium height with a curly red beard rode up on a sorry-looking donkey. He threw down his leather bag before the fire, took a pillow and lay down on the bed to watch the girl comb her hair. Furious but uncertain what course to take, Li went on grooming the horses. The girl looked intently at the stranger's face, holding her hair in one hand while with the other she signed to Li behind her back to prevent his flaring up. Then, quickly pinning up her hair, she curtseyed to the stranger and asked his name. Still lying on the bed, he answered that it was Zhang.

"My name is Zhang too," she said. "We may be cousins." With a bow she asked his position in the family, and he told her he was the third child. When she informed him that she was the eldest in her family, the stranger laughed and replied, "Then you are the eldest of my younger cousins."

"Come and meet my cousin," she called to Li, who bowed to him and sat down with them by the fire.

"What are you boiling?" asked the stranger.

"Mutton. It should be cooked by now."

"I am famished," said the man with the curly beard. While Li went out to buy bread, he took a dagger from his waist and cut up the mutton. They ate together, and after they had finished, the stranger sliced up what was left and gave it to the donkey. He was very quick in all his movements.

"You seem a poor fellow," the stranger remarked to Li. "How did you get hold of such a marvellous girl?"

"I may be poor but I am no fool,"said Li. "I wouldn't tell anyone else, but I won't hide anything from you." And he described how it had come about.

"Where are you going now?" asked the other.

"To Taiyuan," said Li.

"By the way, I have come uninvited: have you any wine?"

Li told him that west of the hostel was a wineshop, and fetched him a pint of wine. As they ate together, he said to Li: "Judging by your looks and behaviour, you are a stout fellow. Do you know anybody remarkable in Taiyuan?"

"I used to know a man whom I thought truly great," replied Li. "My other friends are only fit to be generals and captains."

"What is his name?"

"His name is Li too."

"How old is he?"

"Only twenty."

"What is he now?"

"He is the son of a provincial general."

"He sounds like the man I am looking for," said the stranger. "But I will have to see him to make sure. Can you arrange a meeting?"

"I have a friend named Liu Wenjing who knows him well," said Li. "We can arrange an interview through Liu. But why do you want to see him?"

"An astrologer told me there had been a strange

portent at Taiyuan, and I should look into it. You are leaving tomorrow—when will you arrive?"

Li calculated how long it would take, and the stranger said, "Meet me at daybreak the day after you arrive at Fenyang Bridge." Then he got on his donkey and made off so swiftly that he was at once lost to sight.

Li and the girl were both amazed and delighted. "Such a brave fellow will not deceive us." They said. "We need not worry." After some time they whipped up their horses and left.

On the appointed day they entered the city of Taiyuan, and were very pleased to meet the stranger again. They went to find Liu, and told him, "A good fortune-teller wants to meet Li Shimin.[1] Will you send for him?" Liu thought highly of Li, so he immediately sent a messenger to him asking him to come. Presently Li Shimin arrived, wearing neither coat nor shoes, but with a fur coat thrown over him. He was overflowing with good spirits, and his appearance was very striking.

The curly-bearded man, sitting silently at the end of the table, was struck from the moment of his entry. After drinking a few cups with him he called Li aside and said, "This is undoubtedly the future

---

[1] Later to become the second emperor, historically known as Emperor Taizong, of the Tang empire, reigning from 626-649.

emperor." When Li told Liu this, the latter was overjoyed and highly pleased with himself too.

After Li Shimin had left, the man with the curly beard declared, "I am eighty per cent certain, but my friend the Taoist priest must see him too. You two go back to the capital, but meet me one afternoon at the wineshop east of Mahang. If you see this donkey and another lean one, that means my priestly friend and I are there, and you can go straight up." Then he left, and again they did as they were told.

On the appointed day they went to the wineshop and saw the two donkeys. Lifting up the skirts of their robes they went upstairs, and found the curly-bearded man and a priest drinking there. They were pleased to see Li, asked him to sit down and drank about a dozen cups together.

"Downstairs in the cupboard," said the man with the curly beard, "you will find a hundred thousand cash. Get a quiet place to lodge your wife, and meet me again another day at Fenyang Bridge."

When Li went to the bridge, he found the priest and the curly-bearded man already there, and they went together to see Liu. They discovered him playing chess, and after greeting him they started chatting. Liu sent a note to invite Li Shimin to watch the game. The priest played with Liu, while the curly-bearded man and Liu watched.

When Li Shimin arrived, his appearance struck awe into them all. He bowed and sat down, looking so serene and talking so well that the atmosphere seemed to freshen and splendour to be shed all around. At the sight of him the priest turned pale, and as he made his next move he said, "It's all up with me. I have lost the game, and there's no help for it. What more is there to say?" He stopped playing and took his leave. Once outside he said to the curly-bearded man, "There is no place for you in this country. You had better try your luck elsewhere. Don't give up or lose hope." They decided to leave for the capital.

To Li the curly-bearded man said, "The day after you arrive, come with your wife to my humble lodgings. I know you have no property. I want to introduce my wife to you and talk things over. Be sure not to fail me." Then he sighed and left.

Li rode back to his lodgings. Later he went with his wife to the capital to call on the curly-bearded man. The latter's house had a small, plain wooden door. When they knocked, a man opened the door, bowed to them and said, "The master has been looking forward to your arrival for a long time." They· were led through inner doors, each more magnificent than the last. Forty girl attendants stood in the court, and twenty slaves led the way to the east hall where they found a great display of rare and precious objects. There were so many fine caskets, cupboards, head-dresses, mirrors and trinkets that they felt they had left the world of men. After they had washed they changed into rich and strange garments, and then their host was announced. He came in wearing a gauze cap, with a fur coat thrown over him, his whole appearance magnificent and kingly. When they had greeted each other cordially, he called his wife to come out, and they discovered that she was a beauty too. They were invited into the central hall, where there was a fine feast spread—richer than the banquets given by princes—and while they feasted twenty women musicians played music which sounded as if made in paradise. When they had eaten their fill, wine was served. Then servants carried out from the east hall twenty couches covered with embroidered silk. They removed the covers, and Li saw that the couches were laden with account books and keys.

"This is all the treasure I possess," said the man with the curly beard. "I turn it all over to you. I meant to make my mark in the world, and fight with brave men for ten years or more to carve out a kingdom. But now that the true sovereign has been found, why should I stay here? Your friend Li Shimin of Taiyuan will be a truly great ruler, who will restore peace to the empire after three or four years. With your outstanding gifts, if you do your best under his serene guidance, you will certainly reach the top rank of councillors. And your wife with her great beauty and discernment will win fame and honor through her illustrious husband. Only a woman like her could recognize your talent, and only a man like you could bring her glory. An able minister is bound to find a wise monarch. It is no accident that when the tiger roars the wind blows, and when the dragon bellows the clouds gather. You can use my gifts to help the true monarch and achieve great deeds. Go to it! Ten years from now, several hundred kilometers southeast of China, strange happenings will take place—that will be when I realize my ambition. When that time comes, will you both drink toward the southeast to congratulate me?" He bid his servants pay their respects to Li and his wife, saying, "From now on they are your master and mistress." Then the curly-bearded man and his wife put on military uniform and rode off, attended by one slave only. Soon they were out of sight.

Taking over the curly-bearded man's house, Li became wealthy and used his fortune to help Li Shimin to conquer the whole empire.

During the Zhenguan period, while Li was left minister and acting prime minister, the southern tribesmen reported that a thousand big ships and one hundred thousand armed troops had entered the kingdom of Fuyu, killed the king and occupied the land. By now all was peaceful there again. Li realized that the curly-bearded man had succeeded. On his return from court he told his wife, and they put on ceremonial dress and drank to the southeast to congratulate their old friend.

From this we see that imperial power is not won by any great man who aspires to it, let alone any man who is not great. Any subject who vainly attempts to rebel is like a praying mantis dashing itself against the wheel of a chariot, for Heaven has willed that our empire should prosper for a myriad generations.

It has been suggested that much of Li's military strategy was taught him by the man with the curly beard.

12. Guo Yuanzhen

Niu Sengru

"A gallant slaying the demon" is another strand of popular tales in the Tang legends. The Chinese have always revered strong and selfless heroes who stand up against evil, no matter what the cost to themselves. Guo Yuanzhen is typical of this kind of story. Daring and upright, Guo defeats the demon and mobilizes the villagers to vanquish their foe. The story is exciting, humorous and absorbing with events closely knit together. It is a clear, simple piece of work with considerable success.

The author Niu Sengru (780-848), alias Si'an, was a native of Lingtai, Gansu. He passed the advanced imperial examination in the 21st year of the Zhenyuan period (805), and serving under Emperor Muzong, was gradually promoted to be Vice-Minister of Revenue, and later under Emperor Wenzong to be Minister of War. His opposition to Li Deyu became known historically as the "Dispute Between the Niu and Li Parties." Under Emperor Wuzong, he was demoted to be a minor official in

Huizhou, Guangdong, and died on his way back to court under Emperor Xuanzong. His works A Collection of Strange Tales *amount to 10 volumes.* Guo Yuanzhen *is taken from the current 4-volume edition which is not the original.*

Having failed the advanced imperial examination during the Kaiyuan period, Guo Yuanzhen was on his way from Jinzhou to Fenzhou. He lost his way in the dark for some time before he dimly saw a light far away. Thinking it must be a human dwelling, he made straight for it. After eight or nine li (4.5 kilometers), he came to a mansion with an imposing gate, inside which the hall and corridors were all brightly lit and laden with food and sacrifices as if for a wedding, except that not a soul could be seen. Guo tied his horse to a post in the corridor and walked up a few steps into the hall, wondering where he had found himself. Then, from the bed-chamber east of the hall, he heard the endless sobs of a woman crying.

"Who is that crying, a human or a ghost?" shouted Guo. "Why is this place so lavishly laid out with no one here but you crying alone?"

"In our ancestral temple there's a General Black who can bring disaster or blessings upon us. But every year he wants a new bride whom our people must choose from the village. Although I'm not pretty, this year my father has traded me in for five hundred strings of coppers without telling me. Tonight, all the village girls pretended to have a feast with me here and made me drunk, then they locked me in and left," the female voice answered. "This means they have betrothed me to General Black. Even my parents have left me to die. I'm overcome with grief and fear. Are you a decent man? If you can save me, I will be your loyal servant all my life."

"When will the general come?" asked Guo indignantly.

"At the second watch."

"I feel ashamed to be a man. I'll do all I can to save you, even at the cost of my life. I can't bear to see you die at the bloody hands of a devil," said Guo.

The girl's sobbing gradually ceased. Guo sat on the steps leading to the west chamber, and had his horse taken to the north of the hall with his servant standing in front as a wedding attendant.

Soon a carriage arrived escorted with torches and lanterns. Two soldiers in violet uniforms entered but left immediately, muttering, "There's a minister in here."

The next moment, two other soldiers in yellow repeated the process with the same words. "Perhaps I do look like a prime minister. I'll lick that devil," Guo said to himself.

Slowly General Black alighted from his carriage.

His attendant reported to him what the guards had found. The general said, "Proceed."

With spears, swords and bows and arrows in hands, the soldiers escorted the general into the temple, before the steps to the east of the hall. Guo sent up his servant to announce to the general, "Scholar Guo asks your honor for an interview," and Guo rose to his feet with his palms together to show his respect.

"How do you come to be here?" asked the general.

"I'm told the General is to be married tonight. May I be your best man at the ceremony?" answered Guo.

Delighted, the general invited him to sit down and have a drink with him. Guo had a sharp knife in his bag with which he could kill the general. Tactfully he asked, "Has the General ever tried dried deer meat?"

"That is rather hard to find here," the general remarked.

"I have some fine dried deer meat here which I procured from the Royal Chef. Would you like a taste of it?" asked Guo.

The general was evidently pleased. Guo left the table and took out the dried meat with the knife. He sliced the meat, put it on a plate and extended the plate to the general who put out his hand to take it without any suspicion. Guo dropped the plate, grabbed the general's hand and boldly severed it.

With a shriek, the general bolted out, followed by his guards in panic. Guo took off his jacket and wrapped up the dripping hand. He sent his soldiers to look around and found it was dead quiet outside. So he opened the door of the east chamber and said to the crying girl, "Here's General Black's hand. From the trail of his blood, we can see his end is not far away. Now you're saved and can come out to dine."

The girl turned out to be very pretty, barely in her late teens. She dropped on her knees before him and said, "I swear to be your loyal slave and servant." Guo consoled her. When it was light enough, he opened the wrapping and found only the trotter of a pig in it.

Then distant wailing could be heard, growing louder as the people came near. They were the girl's parents, brothers and old village folks who were carrying a coffin to bury her body. They were astonished to find her alive and well with Guo Yuanzhen. When Guo told them what had happened the senior villagers became angry with him for having hurt their guardian god. They said, "General Black is our guardian god whom we have worshipped for many years. Each year we offer a girl to marry him so that he will see that there will be no natural disasters in this area;

otherwise we will soon be assailed with thunder storms and hail, sure as hell. How dare you, a wayfarer from elsewhere, to hurt our sacred god and bring a curse upon us? You should be slaughtered as a sacrifice for General Black or tied up and sent to the town court for punishment." And they ordered the young men to arrest him.

Guo shouted above their voices, "Listen. You have lived long lives and yet gained little wisdom. I've seen much of the world and have a better understanding of it than you. Any god must be appointed by Heaven to be a guardian down here on Earth, just as a prince is ordered by the Son of Heaven to govern a state. Am I right?"

"Yes. You're right," echoed the men.

"If the prince ravaged women in his state, wouldn't the Son of Heaven be angry? If he oppressed and tortured his subjects wouldn't the Son of Heaven vanquish him with his armed forces?" Guo went on. "If what you called 'General' were a god, how could his hand turn out to be a pig's trotter? Would Heaven appoint a promiscuous monster as a general? After all, he is nothing but a dirty beast. Why shouldn't I kill him in the name of Providence? It was because none of you ever had the guts to protect your young innocent girls from the beast that Heaven was angered. How do you know that I was not sent by Heaven to get rid of this monster? Now follow me, and we'll do away with this devil for good. All right?"

"All right!" shouted the crowd, now fully awakened. "We're at your service."

Guo ordered them to arm themselves with bows and arrows, swords and spears, rakes and hoes, and follow him to track down the wounded beast. After going ten kilometers, they traced the trail to a cavity in a large tomb. They began digging until the opening was wide enough for them to see what was inside. They found a cave the size of a house with a huge pig bereft of its left trotter, lying bleeding on the ground. It tried to dash through the fire and smoke but was beaten to death by the crowd. The country folks rejoiced and wanted to give a banquet in Guo's honor for celebration. Guo refused, saying, "I've done what is right for the people. I'm not a hired hunter."

Now the redeemed girl announced to her parents and the villagers that she was leaving, "I had the fortune to be a member of this clan, your own flesh and blood. I've never left my family or committed any crime punishable by death. But for five hundred thousand coppers, you have betrothed me to a monster, and left me locked up in an empty house at his mercy. Is this how people should behave? If not for the brave and righteous Squire Guo, where would I be at this moment? I was sent to death by my own parents, but saved by Squire Guo. I beg to go with him never to return to this village again." She kept kowtowing to Guo and nothing he could say could dissuade her from leaving with him. In the end, Guo took her home as his concubine, and she bore him several sons. Guo rose to distinction when his sons eventually became prominent ministers in the court.

Such is Fate. One might be born in a remote land, and thrown to a monster, yet still not perish in misery. Isn't that clear?

13. The Kunlun Slave[1]

Pei Xing

The two main characters in this legend—the Girl in Red and the Kunlun Slave are quite unusual. The former is born of a rich family but taken as a concubine by a powerful official. Yearning for freedom and true love, she cleverly offers herself to a man she loves through mime, which was outrageous in those days. The author brings in an underdog, the Kunlun Slave, who helps to bring the young couple together with his superhuman skills and wit. The story criticizes the privileges of officialdom in exploiting the poor and glorifies those who dare to fight against oppression. It had a strong influence on later generations in the country, which is exemplified in Liang Bolong's drama The Girl in Red *and Mei Yujin's* The Kunlun Slave *in the Ming Dynasty.*

The author Pei Xing served under Emperors Yizong and Xizong. Between 860 and 874 he served as Secretary for Gao Bing, Military Governor of

---

[1] During the Tang Dynasty, slaves brought to China from the South Seas were commonly known as Kunlun slaves.

Jinghai and later Vice-Military Governor of Chengdu. His three-volume collection Legends *has been lost, and only a few separate editions, such as this story, have been preserved in the* Taiping Miscellany. *They are not the original versions.*

During the Dali period (766-779) there was a young man called Cui, a palace guard of the Thousand Bulls Order, whose father was a high official and a close friend of a minister. One day his father told him to call on the minister to ask after his health. Now Cui was a handsome young man, rather bashful and quiet but with a very good manner. The minister ordered his maidservants to raise the curtains and ask him in. And as Cui bowed and delivered his father's message, the minister took a fancy to him; accordingly he made him sit down and talk.

There were three ravishingly beautiful maids there, who peeled red peaches into golden bowls, then poured sweetened cream over the peaches and presented them. The minister ordered one maid who was dressed in red to take a bowl to Cui; but the young man was too shy in the presence of girls to eat. Then the minister ordered the girl in red to feed him with a spoon, and Cui was forced to eat a peach while the girl smiled teasingly.

When the youth rose to go, the minister said, "Come again when you have time. Don't stand on ceremony." He told the girl in red to see him out.

Cui looked back at her as he left the courtyard, and she raised three fingers, turned up the palm of one hand three times, then pointed to the little mirror she wore on her breast and said, "Remember!"

When Cui had given his father an account of his visit, he went back to his study lost in thought. He became silent and low-spirited, and rapt in sad thoughts would eat nothing. All he did was to chant a poem:

Led by chance to a fairy mountain,
I gazed into star-bright eyes.
Through a red door the moon is shining,
There forlorn a white beauty lies.

None of his servants knew what was on his mind. But there was a Kunlun slave in his family called Melek who watched him for a time, then asked:

"What is troubling you that you look so sad all the time? Why not tell your old slave?"

"What do fellows like you understand?" retorted Cui. "Why pry into my private affairs?"

"Just tell me," urged Melek, "and I promise to get you what you want, be it far or near."

Impressed by his confident tone, Cui told him the whole story. "That's simple," said Melek. "Why didn't you tell me earlier, instead of moping like that?"

When Cui told him what signs the girl had made, Melek said, "That's easy to understand. When she raised three fingers, she meant that there are ten rooms in the minister's house where the maids live, and she lives in the third room. When she turned up one palm three times, she was showing fifteen fingers, for the fifteenth of the month. And the little mirror on her breast stood for the full moon on the night of the fifteenth. That is when she wants you to go to her."

Cui was overjoyed. "Is there any way for me to satisfy my longing?" he asked.

Melek smiled and said, "Tomorrow night is the fifteenth. Give me two lengths of dark blue silk to make two tightly fitting suits. The minister keeps a fierce dog to guard the girls' quarters and kill any stranger who attempts to break in. It is one of the famous Haizhou breed, swift as lightning and fierce as a tiger. I am the only man in the world who can kill this hound. Tonight I shall beat it to death for you."

Cui gave him meat and wine and next evening he left, carrying an iron hammer with chains attached to it. After the time it takes for a meal he came back, saying, "The dog is dead. Now there is nothing to stop us."

Just before midnight, the slave helped Cui to put on his dark blue suit, and with the young man on his back vaulted over about a dozen walls until they came to the girls' quarters. They stopped at the third room. The carved door was not locked, and the bronze lamp inside shed a faint light. They heard the girl sigh as she sat there expectantly. She was putting on emerald ear-rings and her face was newly rouged, but there was sadness in her face as she chanted:

> *Oh, the oriole cries as she longs for her love,*
> *Who beneath the bright buds stole her jewel*
> *   away;*
> *Now the blue sky is cold and no message has*
> *   come,*
> *So she plays her jade flute every sorrowful day.*

The guards were asleep and all was quiet. Cui lifted the curtain and entered. For a moment the girl was speechless; then she jumped off the couch and grasping Cui's hand said, "I knew a clever man like you would understand the signs I made with my fingers. But by what magic art did you come here?"

Cui told her all the planning had been done by Melek, and that the Kunlun slave had carried him there.

"Where is Melek?" asked the girl.

"Outside the curtain," he answered.

Then she asked Melek in, and offered him wine in a golden bowl.

"I come from the northern borderland and my family used to be rich," the girl told Cui. "But my present master was commander of the army there and forced me to be his concubine. I am ashamed that I could not kill myself and had to live on in disgrace. Though I powder and rouge my face, my heart is always sad. We have fine food in jade utensils and incense in golden censers; we wear the softest silk and sleep under embroidered coverlets, and we have mother-of-pearl screens and jewels. Yet these things cannot make me happy, when all the time I feel I am a prisoner. Since your servant has this strange skill, why not rescue me from my jail? If I were free again, I could die content. But I would like to be your slave, and have the honour of serving you. What do you say, sir?"

Cui changed colour and said nothing, but Melek answered, "If your mind is made up, it is quite simple."

The girl was overjoyed.

Melek asked first to be allowed to take out her baggage. After he had made three trips, he said, "I fear it will soon be dawn." Then with Cui and the girl on his back he vaulted over about a dozen high walls, just as when they had come in. And all the time the minister's guards heard nothing. Finally they returned to Cui's quarters, and hid the girl there.

The next morning, when the minister's household discovered that the girl was gone and the dog was dead, the minister was appalled. "My house is always well guarded and locked," he said, "yet now someone seems to have flown in and out leaving no trace. This must be the work of no common adventurer. Don't let word of this get out, for fear harm should come of it."

The girl remained hidden in Cui's house for

two years. Then, one spring day when she rode in a small carriage to Qujiang to see the flowers, she was recognized by one of the minister's household. When the minister learned of her whereabouts, he was amazed and summoned Cui to question him. In fear and trembling, the young man dared not conceal the truth, but told the minister the whole story and how he had been carried there by his slave.

"It was very wrong of the girl," said the minister. "But since she has served you so long, it is too late to demand justice. However I feel in duty bound to get rid of your Kunlun slave: that man is a public menace."

Then he ordered fifty guards, armed to the teeth, to surround Cui's house and capture the Kunlun slave. But Melek, a dagger in his hand, vaulted over the wall as swiftly as if he had wings, like some huge bird of prey. Though arrows rained down, they all fell short, and in a flash he made good his escape.

Cui's family was thrown into a panic. The minister too regretted what he had done, and was afraid. Every night for a whole year he had himself guarded by servants armed with swords and halberds.

Over ten years later, one of Cui's household saw Melek selling medicine in the market at Luoyang. He looked as vigorous as ever.

14. Scarlet Thread

by Yuan Jiao

In the latter half of its rule, the Tang Dynasty began to deteriorate. Its military governors continually fought one another, wreaking havoc upon the people. In despair, the people could do nothing to stop this and instead sought refuge in religion or in tales of some great swordsman who would save them from their misery. The heroes in such legends are often obscure figures like servants or slaves at the bottom of the society, who show their hidden power or skill only at critical moments. These legends reflect the people's hope for a normal life, and this is why the swordsmen are made so brilliant in the stories.

In this story, Scarlet Thread succeeds in restraining two belligerent warlords from going to war with one daring stroke, and so rescues the people from senseless slaughter. She is a woman at once charming and brave, ordinary but peerless. The story is full of adventures with lyrical scenes that add to its success. Hence "the theft of the gold box by Scarlet Thread" became a familiar topic *among the people ever after. In tradition, most of the swordsmen are ready to fight and die for their closest friends, but this story emphasizes the idea of paying a debt of gratitude, with a touch of the Buddhist Samsara.*

The author Yuan Jiao, alias Zhiqian or Zhiyi, was a son of Prime Minister Yuan Zi and born in Runan, Henan. He was Prefectural Governor of Guozhou and a bureau director in the Ministry of Rites. His works are collected in the Ganze Folk Songs, *including "Scarlet Thread." In the Ming Dynasty, it was rewritten by Liang Chenyu into a drama called* Dame Scarlet Thread.

Scarlet Thread was a maid in the house of Xue Song, the Military Governor of Luzhou[1]. As she could play the Ruan (a stringed instrument) and was well read in history and classics, Xue entrusted his personal letters and files to her. Once during a grand army banquet, Scarlet Thread whispered to the governor, "The Jie-drum[2] in the band sounds sad tonight. There must be something wrong with the drummer." Well versed in music himself, Xue

---

[1] Xue Song was the grandson of the renowned Marshal Xue Rengui who had served both Emperors Taizong and Gaozong at the beginning of the Tang Dynasty. He was first Military Governor successively of four prefectures and later the Zhaoyi Army in five prefectures—Luzhou, Zezhou, Xingzhou, Luozhou and Cizhou.

[2] A percussion instrument popular in ancient Central Asia.

agreed. He summoned the drummer who told him, "My wife died yesterday, but I did not dare to ask for leave." Xue granted him leave immediately.

After the Zhide period (756—757), there was still disorder in the areas of Hebei and Hezhong. The Emperor stationed the Zhaoyi Army commanded by Xue Song in Fuyang to bring the region east of the Taihang Mountains under control. He then made Xue marry his daughter to the son of Tian Chengsi, Military Governor of Weibo, and arranged for Xue's son to marry the daughter of Ling Huzhang, Military Governor of Huazhou, binding the three governors together through marriage. However, Tian was suffering from eczema which got worse in summer. He often grumbled, "If only I could be stationed east of the Taihang Mountains, merely breathing the cool dry air there would give me a few more years of life." So he picked out a task force of 3,000 tough brave warriors, who he called the Outer House Boys, and paid them well. He would often deploy 300 of them to guard the Weizhou city at night. Then he selected an auspicious date to take Luzhou by force and then make his headquarters there.

Xue Song was deeply upset on hearing of this. Day and night, he sighed and muttered to himself, not knowing how to deal with the impending clash. Late one night, after the door of his house was closed, Xue was pacing back and forth with a stick in the courtyard, attended only by his maid Scarlet

Thread. "My Lord has not eaten or slept well for a month. Is this due to something going on in the neighboring prefecture?" asked Scarlet Thread.

"It's a matter of life and death for many people, something beyond your comprehension."

"Although my position is humble, maybe I can help."

Xue Song told her the critical situation between his and Tian's prefectures and said, "I have inherited my peerage and territory from my grandfather, which are the honorable rights endowed upon me by the state. If I lose my territory, I will lose what took generations to build."

"This is simple enough. Don't worry, my Lord. Please allow me to pay Weizhou a visit and have a look at the situation there, and see what I can do about it. I'll set out at the first watch tonight and return at the third watch. Please give me a fast horse and a letter of introduction for the governor there. The rest you will hear when I'm back," the girl said confidently.

"How foolish of me! I never knew you were such an extraordinary girl. But what if you should fail and precipitate the disaster instead?" Xue exclaimed.

"I never fail in my tasks," said Scarlet Thread, and she went to her room, to get ready packing. Soon she appeared with her hair tied in a Wuman [1]

---

[1] An ancient tribe inhabiting present-day Southwest China.

knot, adorned with a gold phoenix hairpin, wearing a short violet jacket and a pair of black silk shoes. A dagger engraved with the figure of a dragon was slung across her chest, and on her forehead was written the name of the god Taiyi. She parted with a bow and disappeared in the twinkle of an eye.

Xue Song closed the door and sat in the hall, with his back to the candle. Though not a heavy drinker, that night he downed over a dozen goblets and still remained sober. When the bugle for dawn sounded in the breeze, he imagined he heard something like the drip from a leaf in the yard. With a start he asked who was there. It was Scarlet Thread.

"How did your trip go?" asked Xue anxiously.

"I've accomplished my task," she replied.

"Were there any casualties?"

"Nothing as serious as that. I have simply brought back a small gold box from his bed as a souvenir," Scarlet Thread went on, "I arrived at Weizhou before midnight. Passing through several doors, I got into his bed-chamber. I could hear the Outer House Boys snoring full blast in the corridor and see the governor's guards patrolling the courtyard, passing watch words around. I opened the door to the left of the chamber and approached his bedside. Your kinsman Tian was curled up, fast asleep. His pillow was made of engraved rhino leather, his hair tied with a yellow ribbon and a seven-star sword lay half under the pillow. Beside the sword, there was an open gold box engraved with the owner's date of birth and the name of the god of Polaris, and filled with precious perfume and jewels. Although by day this man was an ambitious commander, having everything his way, yet did it occur to him now in his dream that his life was hanging by a thread in my hands? If I captured and then released him, it would only cause a lot of hard feelings. At that moment the candle flame was flickering and the incense already in ashes; guards were posted all around with arms ready, some leaning their drooping heads on the screen, some snoring erect with towels and dusters in their hands. I took down their hairpins and earrings, and tied up their uniforms in bundles, and still they slept on. Then I brought this gold box home. Once I had left the west gate of the city, I continued for about two hundred li (one hundred kilometers), enjoying the beautiful scenery along the way—the Bronze Bird Pavilion towering above the Zhang River flowing toward the east, a gentle breeze caressing the wilderness at dawn and the moon lingering above the tree tops. I set out on my mission with misgivings but returned with a light heart and forgot the long hard journey altogether. I had performed my task in order to repay my debt of gratitude for your kindness to me. Although it took me a good half of the night to cover the seven hundred li both ways and to enter hostile territory across five or six towns, this was done in the hope of relieving my Lord's anxiety, and so there was no hardship to speak of."

The next day Xue Song sent a courier to Tian Chengsi with a letter, saying, "I received a visitor from Weizhou last night who showed me a gold box which he said he had taken from beside your pillow. I dare not keep it, but rather would seal it up and return it to you." The courier set out forthwith and arrived at midnight. There he found Tian's warriors searching throughout the entire house for the gold box, leaving no stone unturned. He knocked on the door with his whip and asked for an urgent interview. Tian came out immediately. When the courier presented Tian with the gold box, the governor fell aghast in a heap on the floor. He arranged for the courier to sleep in his house and treated him to food and gifts. The next day he sent his own courier to Xue Song with thirty thousand bolts of silk, two hundred thoroughbred horses and other valuables, along with a message which said, "It is only by your generosity that my head still remains on my shoulders. I will correct my mistake and make no more trouble for myself. From now on I will humbly obey you and never dare to claim parity with you due to the marriage between our children. Whenever you go out on a mission, I will closely follow your carriage and push your wheels forward. If you come to my place I will clear the way for you myself, whip in hand. I kept the Outer House Boys merely as servants and guards against thieves, and with no other intention at all. Now they have been discharged to till the land where they belong."

Since then, friendly contacts grew busy between Hebei and Henan. However, Scarlet Thread begged to leave Xue's house. The governor said, "Why, you were brought up in my house. Where do you want to go? Now I need you more than ever. How can you say you want to leave me?"

Scarlet Thread expained: "In a former life I was a man, traveling across the country trying to cure the sick with my knowledge of medicine that I had learned from medical classics. I came upon a pregnant woman with worms in her belly. I managed to kill the worms, but also killed the mother and the twins inside her. Thus I took away three lives at once. The King of Hell punished me, turning me into a woman and housemaid in this life, with the nature of a thief. Fortunately I was born in your house and am now nineteen years of age. All these years I've been given silk dresses to wear and delicious food to eat. My Lord's kindness to me was beyond praise. Today the country is undergoing reform that will bring lasting peace and prosperity for hundreds of generations to come. But there are a handful of those who want to disrupt this course. They must be wiped out. The day before yesterday I carried out the mission to Weizhou in order to clear my debt of my gratitude to you. I struck fear into the rebel's heart so that life and peace could be maintained between the two regions and the officers and soldiers would content themselves with holding their own territory. This is all I can do as a woman to atone for the sins of my former life and restore my former status as a man. Now I shall forsake and transcend this mortal world, purify my soul and seek for immortality in my own way."

"Since you will not stay, let me present to you a thousand taels of gold to cover the costs of your life of seclusion," Xue offered.

"I'm talking about my next life. Nothing can be arranged for me now," said Scarlet Thread.

Xue realized there was no holding her, and launchred a grand farewell party in her honor. Among the numerous distinguished guests, he chose Leng Chaoyang to recite a poem dedicated to her:

> *The caltrop song is sung on Mulan's boat,*
> *To bid farewell to one in a high tower.*
> *She leaves us now like Princess Luo in a mist,*
> *Only the river flows on for ever.*

Xue Song burst into tears at these words, and Scarlet Thread fell on her knees sobbing. Pretending to have had too much to drink, she left the table. Nobody can ever tell where she has gone.

15. The Story of Lady Yang (Part I)

Yue Shi

Ever since the time of Emperor Xuanzong and his favorite concubine Yang Yuhuan in the Tang Dynasty, the story of their love has been told far and wide, and is still as alive as ever. This is a saga based on historical records and legends threaded together with descriptions to give it integrity. In his early days, the Emperor was a mighty sovereign who put an end to the continuous power struggles in the court and turned a new page in the history of the Tang Dynasty known as the Prosperous Kaiyuan Period. Later on however, he grew idle and fatuous, trusting all his power to the Machiavellian Li Linpu and Yang Guozhong, and indulged himself in wine, women and song. This brought about the An-Shi Rebellions [1] and the eventual fall of the great empire. His decline in power also led to the tragedy of his romance with his dearest Lady Yang. As the initiator of the great tragedy, he is despicable; as the protagonist, pitiable.

---

[1] *An-Shi refers to An Lushan, a rebel governor, and Shi Siming, his general, both killed by their sons.*

Part One of the story is devoted to his sybaritic life with the Yang family, and Part Two describes his heart-rending memories of his lost love. It is through this contrast that the author expresses his own disgust and compassion for this historical romance and provides a lesson for future generations. For Lady Yang, the author shows much sympathy. Though it is because of her fatal charms that the Emperor has fallen, she remains purely an innocent political sacrifice.

This tale is chosen from Vol. 38 of a Ming-Dynasty hand-written script compiled by Zhang Zongxiang.

The author Yue Shi (930—1007), alias Zizheng, was a native of Yihuang County, Jiangxi. Living through the end of the Southern Tang Dynasty and into the early Song Dynasty, he passed the civil service examination and was appointed Editor and Writer of Historical Works, and Director of the Bureau of Waterways and Irrigation. A renowned scholar, in particular as a geographer, he was the author of The World in Peace. *He compiled novels such as* Immortals of the Caves *and* The Guangzhuo Legends. *As a folklore writer, his works include* The Green Pearl *and* The Story of Yang Yuhuan. *He was an important novelist of the early Song Dynasty.*

Lady Yang's real name was Yang Yuhuan. She was a native of Huayin County, Hongnong

Prefecture, but later moved to Dutou Village, Yongle County, Puzhou. Her great grandfather was Yang Lingben, Magistrate of Jinzhou Prefecture. Her father Yang Xuanyan was a revenue manager in the government of Shuzhou Prefecture where Yuhuan was born. There she once fell into a pond in front of the county seat; it later became known as "Lady Yang's Descent." She became an orphan very young and lived with her uncle who was a clerk in the government of Henan. In the eleventh lunar month of the 22nd year of the Kaiyuan period (A.D. 734), she became the concubine of Prince Shou, the son of Emperor Xuanzong. Six years later, the Emperor visited the Hot Springs Palace and instructed Gao Lishi (his favorite eunuch) to take her out of Prince Shou's residence to become a nun in the Taoist Taizhen Temple inside the Imperial Palace. There, she was given the Taoist name "Taizhen" (Exalted Originality). In the seventh month of the 4th year of the Tianbao period (A.D. 745); the Emperor made the daughter of the General of the Left Guard, Wei Zhaoxun, the consort of Prince Shou. In the same month, in the Phoenix Garden, Yang Yuhuan, now Yang Taizhen, was made "Guifei" (Honored Consort) by the Emperor ("Guifei" was the highest ranking imperial concubine). Her endowment was equal to half that of the Empress. On the day of the title-confering, the song "Costume of Rainbow and Feather" was played throughout the entire palace. In the evening the Honored Consort, or Lady Yang for short, was given a gold hairpin and an ornate jewelry box. That evening His Majesty came to her dressing room and placed in her hair a sparkling gold hairpin from which hung a violet pearl pendant, which he had personally chosen from the Imperial Jewelry Room. The Emperor was so pleased with her that he declared to all his attendants in the Inner Palace (harem): "Of all my treasures, Lady Yang is the most precious I've ever acquired." To celebrate his conquest, he composed a song "Possesion of the Jewel."

Sometime earlier, at the beginning of the Kaiyuan period, Emperor Xuanzong had doted on Lady Wu who bore him a son. Being also very beautiful, Lady Wu had no equal among her peers. However, she died in the eleventh month of the 21st year in the Kaiyuan period. In the entire Inner Palace there was no one to replace her. The Emperor sunk into an abyss of despair. Now that Lady Yang had come, like a candle in the night, to dispel the shadow of Lady Wu, the Emperor loved her more than ever.

Lady Yang had three sisters. All three were very beautiful, and their sparkling repartee greatly entertained the Emperor. Their visits to the palace were therefore much longer than the usual. In the palace, Lady Yang was called "Niangzi" (Madame) but treated as if she were the empress. The day she was entitled Honored Consort, her father Yang

Xuanyan was postumously granted the title of Governor of Jiyin, and her mother Lady Li of Longxi Prefecture. Later on, Yang Xuanyan was further entitled Minister of War and his wife Lady of the Liang Princedom. Her uncle, Yang Xuangui, was appointed Grand Master of Imperial Entertainments, and her distant cousin Yang Zhao became a vice-minister with several other court titles. Her elder brother Yang Xian also had a high position in court. Her younger cousin Yang Qi married Princess Taihua, who was Lady Wu's daughter. Because of this, of all the Emperor's daughters, Princess Taihua was his favorite, and was endowed with a mansion attached to the palace. Thus the Yang family could sway virtually the entire country. A word from them was as good as the Emperor's own and was immediately carried out to the letter by governments at all levels. Everyday rare goods from all parts of the country were delivered by footmen and caravan to their houses.

In those days An Lushan was still Military Governor of Fanyang. The emperor trusted him so much that he called him "my son." He was feasted several times in the palace, but each time he would kowtow only to Lady Yang and never to His Majesty. The Emperor asked him why; and he answered, "We northern tribesmen don't know our father but only our mother." With a laugh, the Emperor pardoned him and ordered the whole Yang family from Yang Xian down to call An Lushan "brother" and feast together as one family. They got on well together at first but later fell out while contending for power.

In the seventh month of the fifth year of the Tianbao period, Lady Yang lost control of herself owing to jealousy and offended the Emperor, who had her sent away to her brother forthwith in a cart. By noon the Emperor found he had lost his appetitite because of her absence and became irascible. His attendant Gao Lishi knew the cause and begged permission to bring Lady Yang back. Meanwhile, he sent over a hundred cartloads of garments, rice, flour and wine to her. At first, Yang's sisters and brother Xian were crying together for fear of impending punishment, but seeing the increasing flow of food supplies, including even food from the Emperor's table, they felt reassured. Without Lady Yang's presence, the Emperor felt desolate and restless. He would have the eunuchs flogged when they appeared before his eyes, and some of them were scared to death because of this. Gao finally got permission to bring her back. By nightfall, he opened the Anxingfang gate and led her in. The next morning, Emperor Xuanzong was beside himself with joy to see his favorite back. On her knees, Yang tearfully repented her faults before him. The Emperor called in the acrobats from both ends of the capital to entertain her, and her sisters brought in sumptuous food to celebrate the reunion. From then on Lady Yang was given ever more attention by the Emperor and the rest of the Inner Palace never saw His Majesty again.

In the seventh year of the Tianbao period, Emperor Xuanzong promoted Yang Zhao to Censor-in-chief and Acting Mayor of the capital, and renamed him Guozhong (loyal to the country). The Emperor made Lady Yang's eldest sister Lady of the Han Princedom, her third sister Lady of the Guo Princedom and her eighth sister Lady of the Qin Princedom, all on the same day. And each of them was granted one hundred thousand coppers to buy cosmetics. Nevertheless, Lady of the Guo Princedom was so proud of her natural beauty that she preferred to present herself before the Emperor without any make-up. On that Du Fu the poet wrote:

> By permission of His Majesty,
> Lady of Guo often rides into the palace.
> Lest the rouge smear her cheeks,
> She has merely brushed her eyebrows.

Emperor Xuanzong presented her with a luminous pearl, Lady of the Qin Princedom a special headgear and Yang Guozhong a unique bed-curtain—all priceless treasures. Such was the Emperor's magnanimity to the Yang family. Moreover, he issued three edicts in one day to appoint Yang Xian Chief Minister for Dependencies with the honorific title "Supreme Pillar of State," and his gate guarded with the ceremony due to officers of the third rank. The five residences of the Yang brothers and sisters were all clustered in Xuanyang Quarters, with magnificent gates equal to those of the Imperial Palace, far beyond the normal convention; even their servants and carriages were conspicuous in the capital. The five houses vied with one another in ostentation and luxury. Their construction all cost fabulous money. When one of them outshone the rest, the other four would quickly pull down their own buildings and have them rebuilt and refurbished through night and day in order to catch up. Food from the Emperor's table and tributes from all parts of the land were shared by all five of them. From the time that Emperor Xuanzong ascended the throne, no one could compare with them in wealth and luxury.

Wherever the Emperor went, he would take his favorite concubine along. When she preferred to ride a horse, Gao Lishi would hold the reins, with a whip in hand ready for her use. In the palace seven hundred embroiderers and weavers and several hundred sculptors and carpenters were kept working for the birthdays and festivals to be held there all year round. Xuanzong sent a special envoy Yang Yi to Guangdong to collect novel and rare tributes. Military Governor of Lingnan (Guangdong), Zhang Jiuzhang, and Chief Executive of Guangling, Wang Yi, were both promoted because of the rare, exquisite jewels and costumes they sent to Lady Yang on the occasion of the Dragon Boat Festival. Zhang became Grand Master of Imperial Entertainments, and Wang Vice-Minister of Revenue.

Xuanzong had a special bed-curtain made together with a long pillow and an extra large quilt to accommodate himself and his brothers together in bed. Not long after, in the second month of the ninth year of the Tianbao period, Lady Yang stole the eldest Prince Ning's purple jade flute and played it without permission. Thereby she offended the Emperor again and was driven out of the palace. Her brother Yang Guozhong was deeply worried and asked Ji Wen, a friend who had strong influence among the eunuchs, for help. Ji Wen spoke at court: " Lady Yang was merely a woman led astray by her fantasy. She deserves capital punishment for offending Your Majesty. As she was Your Majesty's favorite, she ought to be punished only within the palace. Why not grant her a place for burial here instead of leaving her disgraced out in the cold?" When Xuangzong ordered Eunuch Zhang Taoguang to take Lady Yang to her brother's house, she begged Zhang in tears: "Please tell His Majesty I deserve to die for my conduct. Everything on me came from His Majesty except my hair and skin which were given by my parents. Now I have nothing to give His Majesty but this." At this she cut off a lock of hair and asked Zhang to take it to Xuanzong. Meanwhile, having expelled his favorite, Xuanzong felt lost without her. Eunuch Zhang recounted Lady Yang's parting words to the Emperor who was deeply shaken and filled with pity for her. Xuanzong quickly sent Gao Lishi to bring her back. He loved her more than ever, and granted Yang Guozhong the title of Military Governor of Jiannan for recompense, with special permission for him to stay in the capital instead of at his post at Jiannan.

On the night of the Lantern Festival in the first month of the tenth year in the Tianbao period, all five Yang families turned out on the street to enjoy the spectacle but were caught in a jam with Princess Guangning's horse guards before the West City Gate. Clearing the way vigorously, a Yang servant accidentally caught his whip on the princess' dress, causing her to fall off her horse. Hurrying to the rescue, her husband Cheng Changyi also received several blows. The princess protested to the Emperor in tears, and the case ended up with one Yang servant executed and Cheng Changyi suspended from court sessions. This only inflated the Yang family's arrogance more than ever. They entered and left the Forbidden Palace as they pleased; no officer, high or low, dared look them in the eye. A popular saying arose: "Don't cry when you have a daughter, and don't laugh when you have a son," while another went: "Men are no longer made officers in court whereas girls become the Emperor's concubines. It is your darling daughter that brings honor to your gate." It could be seen how much people envied the Yang families.

One day Xuanzong held a party in the Qinzheng (Diligent Administration) Hall. In the courtyard there was a woman acrobat, Aunt Wang, who could balance a very tall pole on her head with a wooden platform in the shape of twin hills at the top; a little boy would somersault between the two "hills" in mid-air while Aunt Wang was dancing below. This boy was a prodigy named Liu Yan. At only ten, he was appointed proofreader in the Palace Library. Xuanzong summoned him to his box and Lady Yang put him on her lap. Combing his hair, she asked him to compose a poem on Aunt Wang's performance. He immediately chimed: "In the yard a hundred shows are on, but only the tall pole captures the eyes of all. Who says the somersaults are not thrilling? Have a look at the little boy at the top." It brought down the house, and the Emperor ordered an ivory scepter and a yellow embroidered gown be given to him.

On another occasion, the Emperor gave a banquet for his brothers. The magnolias were in full bloom, but he himself was not in the right mood. As Lady Yang rose to dance, half drunk, to the music of "Costume of Rainbow and Feather," he was fascinated and forgot his troubles. Inspired by the power of the music and the dance, he composed two melodies, one titled "Return of the Crimson

Clouds," to describe ten fairies he had dreamed of, and the other, titled "Riding the Waves," to recall the Dragon King's Daughter he had met in another dream. He gave both to the Palace Chamber of Music and Drama and also to his own brothers.

Then a woman dancer Xie Ahman from Xinfeng County was presented to Xuanzong. The royal couple were very pleased with her performance. A special music and dance party was arranged in the palace with the most illustrious band: Prince Ning played the flute, Xuanzong the drum, Lady Yang the *pipa* guitar, and so on and so forth. They played from morning till noon indulging in their own performance with Lady of the Qin Princedom sitting primly as their only audience. At the finale, the Emperor playfully begged her for a tip. The lady answered, "Who dare say His Majesty's sister-in-law has no money to spend?" leaving a tip of three million coppers at once.

Indeed the instruments of this band could not have been found elsewhere. Lady Yang's *pipa* was made of a hard sandalwood brought to the palace as a tribute by Eunuch Bai Jizhen from a mission to Sichuan. It gleamed like jade, ingrained on the surface with a pattern of twin-phoenixes formed by gold and scarlet lines. The strings were imported from the Middle East in 498. They were made of silk, washed with water, to become glossy like strings of pearls. The purple jade flute was believed to have once been owned by the Moon Goddess Chang'e. An Lushan presented three hundred wind instruments to the Emperor, all made of fine quality jade. Lady Yang played her *pipa* so well that all the princes, princesses and Yang's sisters studied the instrument under her. Each time they learned a melody, they would offer her presents. One day Lady Yang said to Xie Ahman, "You're poor and have nothing to offer me. Let me give you something instead." She told her maid Hong Taoniang to give Xie a piece of jade marked with red spots.

Lady Yang was also good at playing the *qing*, a percussion instrument of carved hollow jade that produces crisp sharp sounds when struck. Often she could produce new tunes with it and get better results than the professionals in the Court of Imperial Sacrifices and the Imperial Orchestra. Therefore Xuanzong ordered for her a special *qing* made of green jade from Lantian with a wooden frame elaborately decorated and set upon a pedestal of two cast gold lions.

Early in the Kaiyuan period, the palace gardens were planted with flaming peonies. Xuanzong had them moved in front of the Eaglewood Pavilion east of the Xingqing Pond. Now the peonies bloomed in a roaring blaze. Xuanzong would ride his priceless horse Dazzling White, followed by Lady Yang, on a litter carried by footmen, enjoying the spectacle. The Emperor wanted the theater orchestra to play 16 tunes in the procession. At the head stood Li Guinian, the greatest singer of the day, clapper in hand ready to sing. But Xuanzong said, "How can you sing old songs in the presence of Lady Yang while we are enjoying such fabulous flowers?" He told Li to get some royal golden stationery and ask Secretary Li Bai to compose three verses to the tune of Qingpingle (verse with 46 characters in rhyme each) on it. His mind still clouded from the drinks, Li completed his task at one stroke.

Verse One:

Clouds are her clothes and flowers her complexion,
The spring breeze caresses the blossoms with dew.
If she fails to appear atop the Jade Mountains,
We'll rendezvous on the moonlit Jasper Stage.

Verse Two:

A peony laden with fragrant dew,
A fairy on the drizzling Mount Wu low in mood.
You may ask who is over there—
My lovely Feiyan decked out in the latest fashion.

Verse Three:

Blooming flowers laugh with the radiant Beauty,

And the monarch watches them beaming.
All the sadness and sorrows are blown away,
From the royal couple in the Eaglewood
Pavilion.

Li Guinian ran back to the Emperor with the newly written verses, and Xuanzong ordered the Imperial Theater Troupe to set them to music and start rehearsing. Lady Yang filled the crystal glasses with grape wine from West Liangzhou (modern western Gansu) and recited the poems with deep emotion while Xuanzong accompanied her on a jade flute, dragging the ending note of each verse to please her. When she finished her wine, Lady Yang tidied her hair and bowed with her palms together repeatedly to the Emperor in gratitude. After that Xuanzong placed Li Bai far above his peers in his estimation. However, Gao Lishi was still nursing a deep hatred for the poet who had once made him take off his boots. One day when Lady Yang was reciting Li Bai's verses, Gao cut in with a jibe: "I thought Your Highness would hate Li Bai, but you seem only to admire him." Lady Yang was astonished and asked, "Why? Did he insult me?" Gao replied, "He compares you to Zhao Feiyan[1] which actually deprecates you." Lady Yang was convinced, and on each of three occasions when the

---

[1] Zhao Feiyan was a queen in the Han Dynasty famous for her talent in dancing. But she was later disgraced and committed suicide.

Emperor wished to promote the genius poet, she dissuaded him.

One day Xuanzong was reading the *Biography of Emperor Chengdi of the Han Dynasty* in a chamber in the Hundred Flowers Courtyard. A little later, Lady Yang entered. She smoothed his collar and asked, "What are you reading?"

Xuanzong replied, "You'd better not ask or there'll be no end of it."

Lady Yang took over the book and found the following:

When Emperor Chengdi of Han discovered Zhao Feiyan, she was very slim and light of figure. Lest she might be blown away by the wind, the Emperor had a crystal tray made and carried by maids for her to sing and dance upon. Moreover, a seven-gem pedestal was built for her, sprayed with perfumes to protect her delicate limbs." And so it went on.

"No strong wind can carry you away," Xuanzong bantered, for Lady Yang was a little plump.

"My performance of the 'Costume of Rainbow and Feathers' has surpassed all our ancestors!" said Lady Yang.

"Can't you take a joke? Well then, I have a very fine screen put away somewhere. I'll give it to you as recompense. All right?" coaxed the Emperor.

The screen was named Rainbow, carved with figurines of great beauties of the past. Each about three inches tall, they were surrounded by sparkling gems in the form of clothes, furniture and artware: crystals intricately edged with tortoise shell and rhino horn strung together with pearls. It was indeed a priceless work of art given by Emperor Wendi of the former Sui Dynasty to his daughter Princess Yicheng as her dowry that followed her to a northern state. Later in the first year of the Kaiyuan period, the northern state was vanquished by Emperor Taizong of Tang, and the screen was returned with Empress Xiao to the court of the Tang Dynasty. Now it became Emperor Xuanzong's present for his cherished concubine.

16. The Story of Lady Yang (Part II)

Yue Shi

In the last year of the Kaiyuan period, a kind of "milky tangerine" was brought to the court as a tribute from Jianglin Prefecture. Emperor Xuanzong had ten saplings planted in Penglai Palace, and in the ninth month of the tenth year of the Tianbao period, the grown trees began to bear fruit. The Emperor gave some tangerines to the prime minister and said, "Not long ago I had the saplings planted in the palace. Now I have reaped a harvest of over a hundred and fifty delicious tangerines which are as good as the orginal ones. It's a small miracle, isn't it?"

In return, the prime minister presented a memorial to him full of eulogy: "I believe that what Nature has cultivated cannot be altered, but here is something unprecedented brought forth by exceptional incidence. From this we can see that only sages are able to rule the world; their own vitality combining with the power of nature to achieve universal harmony. Growing tangerines and pomelos is no exception; the fruit are called by different names in the north and the south as arranged by Nature, but their Yin and Yang remain unchanged. Your Majesty follows the mandate of Heaven and the natural customs and habits of the people, and so achieves national concord; Your Majesty's munificence, like the rain and dew, nurtures everything in the country. The plants and grass have their own natural gifts endowed by Mother Earth. And so this rare fruit from the south delivers delicious progeny in the royal garden. Its base is covered with white frost, its fragrance permeates the beautiful palaces; its golden color sets the royal garden aglow in the sun…." Deeply flattered, the Emperor shared out all the fruit among the officials, keeping a twin tangerine for himself and Lady Yang. "This fruit seems to understand me. It symbolizes our union," he said, sitting closer to Lady Yang, and shared the tangerine with her. He had the event painted in a picture to hand down to posterity.

Lady Yang, being born in Sichuan, was very fond of lichees. As the same fruit from southern Guangdong was even better in taste, every year it was carried by express relay horse non-stop from Guangdong to the capital, and none of its delicious taste was lost overnight.

Once, Xuanzong was playing dice with Lady Yang and was about to lose the game unless he threw a four. He kept shouting at the top of his voice for a four until the spinning dice actually settled on the four. The Emperor ordered Gao Lishi to give out crimson silk to celebrate his truimph and so it became a ritual of the game.

In those days there was a white parrot in the palace named Snowy Lady, which could talk like a human being. One morning she flew to Lady Yang's dressing table, squawking, "Snowy was attacked by a bird of prey in her dream last night." Xuanzong told Lady Yang to make Snowy Lady repeat the Buddhist classic Prajnaparamitahrdaya sutra until she learned it by heart so as to avert the misfortune. One day the royal couple went on an excursion to another palace, taking Snowy along on a pole attached to their sedan. Suddenly a hawk swooped down on the parrot and killed her. Deeply grieved, the Emperor and Lady Yang buried her in a grave, calling it "The Parrot Tomb."

Vietnam presented as a tribute fifty Kapur balls shaped like cicada chrysalis to the Emperor. According to Persian merchants, such balls grew only on ancient borneo camphor trees. They were called "Ruilongnao" (auspicious camphor) in the palace. Xuanzong gave ten of them to Lady Yang, who secretly sent three of the ten to An Lushan through a caravan courier. She also sent him jade boxes and porcelain bowls all encased in wrought gold.

In the eleventh year of the Tianbao period (752), Prime Minister Li Linpu died. Xuanzong gave this vital position to Yang Guozhong along with over forty other titles. Moreover, in the following year

Yang was placed directly in charge of construction, a lucrative job. His eldest son Yang Xuan married Lady Yanhe, daughter of the Crown Prince, and was appointed Grand Master of Imperial Entertainments, Chamberlain for Ceremonials and Vice-Minister of Revanue. His younger son Yang Pei married Princess Wanchun. Lady Yang's first cousin, Vice-Director of the Palace Library Yang Jian, married Lady Chengrong. Thus in the Yang family, there was one imperial consort, two princesses, three princedom ladies and three ladies. Also in the twelfth year of the same period, Lady Yang's father was given the posthumous title of Defender-in-chief and Duke of the Qi Princedom and her mother, Lady of the Liang Princedom. An ancestral temple was built by the government with an inscription on stone written by the Emperor himself. Lady Yang's uncle, Yang Xuangui, was appointed Minister of Works. The sons and daughters of the princedom ladies were all related to the ruling house in one way or another.

Each year in the tenth lunar month, the Emperor would come to Huaqing Palace to spend the winter there until the following spring. As always, he would be accompanied by Lady Yang in his carriage. In the Palace was a Dressing Chamber where Lady Yang did her make-up and a Lotus Pond where she took her bath. Yang Guozhong's residence was on the south of the East Gate of the Palace opposite to Lady of the Guo Princedom's whereas Lady of the Han Princedom's house was connected with that of Lady of the Qin Princedom. When Xuanzong visited one of them he would call on the rest as well, accompanied by the royal band. When he went out on an excursion, each house would send out a guard of honor dressed in one color, bearing arms to form a colorful procession marching in front of and to the rear of the Emperor. Each time, after they had passed, glistening golden flowers, boots, pearls, jewels and precious stones could be collected by the handfuls. Some onlookers who bent down to have a closer look at the gorgeous carriages found themselves caught with perfumes lasting several days. Hundreds of camels and horses paraded with the Guard of Honor of the Governor of Jiannan carrying the colors at the head. The guards were given drinks before setting out and feasts on return. The streets in this area were constantly overflowing with tributes and presents from far and near, including pets and horses, singers and slaves.

After the death of Lady of the Qin Princedom, the power and influence of Lady of the Guo Princedom, Lady of the Han Princedom and Yang Guozhong grew more than ever. Lady of the Guo Princedom and Yang Guozhong made no effort to cover their intimate relationship even in public. When they went to court, they would ride in a trio, whipping their horses and laughing all the way with a retinue of over a hundred carrying torches in full blaze. In gorgeous costumes, they paraded, wearing no mask or veil, before the admiring throngs that lined the streets. Indeed, all marriages in the ten Yang families had to be arranged by Ladies of the Han and Guo Princedoms, at the cost of 1,000 strings of coppers each before Emperor Xuanzong gave his permission.

On the first day of the sixth month in the fourteenth year of the Tianbao period, Xuanzong came to Huaqing Palace to celebrate Lady Yang's birthday. He ordered the children's orchestra to play a new song in Longevity Hall. The song did not have a title as yet. Just then a tribute of lichees arrived from the south, and so the song was named "Sweet Smell of Lichee" to a mighty cheer that reverberated through the valley nearby.

In the eleventh lunar month that year, An Lushan started a rebellion in Fanyang, accusing Yang Guozhong, Lady of the Guo Princedom and Lady Yang of their crimes and sins in the capital. But no one dared mention the bad tidings to the Emperor. At first Xuanzong wanted to delegate his power in the court to Crown Prince Li Heng as successor to the throne while he himself would take the army to quell the rebellion. When Xuanzong asked Yang Guozhong's opinion, Yang was frightened out of his wits. He hurried home and broke the tidings to his cousins, saying, "That would be the end of us. The day the Crown Prince comes into power, we're all dead!" In tears the

Yang sisters told Lady Yang of the situation. She kowtowed to the Emperor, begging for his mercy and pity on her family. Xuanzong put off his expedition.

In the sixth lunar month the following year, the strategic Tongguan Pass fell; the Emperor fled to Sichuan with Lady Yang. At Mahui, in apprehension of a mutiny, General Chen Xuanli of the Dragon Army of the Right cried out to his troops, "Look, the empire is crumbling down. Isn't this brought about by Yang Guozhong's ruthless exploitation of the people? How can we allow him to escape punishment?"

"He must be punished!" the soldiers roared.

Just then a peace mission from Tubo (Tibet) had arrived and were consulting Yang Guozhong in front of the post station. A sergeant shouted, "Yang is now conspiring with the Tubo people for a rebellion!" Immediately, the troops closed in from all sides and killed Yang Guozhong and his son Yang Xuan. The Emperor was obliged to come to the entrance of the post station and reward the troops with food and drinks. The troops refused to fall out. Xuanzong asked why. Gao Lishi answered, "They have punished Yang Guozhong for his crimes, but his sister Lady Yang still remains at Your Majesty's side. How can they leave without fear for what they have done? Your Majesty, please take this into account." The Emperor turned back into the station. There was a side lane leading to his house, but he could not move a step further. For a long while, he stood alone in the lane, leaning on a stick, his head bent on his chest. "Please, Your Majesty, make the decision in the name of peace for the country," begged the Metropolitan Record Keeper Wei E. Then Xuanzong went into the house and took Lady Yang out by the hand until they came to the horse track before the north wall. Then he dropped her hand and ordered Gao to end her life.

Choking with tears in her throat, Lady Yang was distraught with grief. "Please Your Majesty take good care of yourself. I have indeed failed to live up to the expectation of the nation and have no regrets leaving this world. Please allow me to pay my last respects to the Buddha," she begged.

"May Honored Consort be given a good birth in your next life," the Emperor responded.

Then Gao Lishi strangled her with a long gauze cloth under a pear tree in front of the Buddhist temple. Just then a tribute of fresh lichees arrived from Guangdong. Wailing aloud, the Emperor ordered Gao to lay the fruit beside her body as a sacrifice. However, the troops still remained where they were. So Lady Yang's body was laid in a bed covered with an embroidered quilt and moved into the courtyard. General Chen Xuanli and a few others were called in. The general uncovered her head and confirmed she was dead. He announced, "Lady Yang is dead," and the troops left. She was

215

buried in a pit, north of the road about half a kilometer away from the west wall of the town. She was then thirty-eight. Holding a bunch of lichees in his hand, Xuanzong said to Zhang Yehu, "All the way from here to Sword Gate are twittering birds and fallen flowers, clear streams and green hills, only to recall my grief for Honored Consort."

Once Emperor Xuanzong wanted to pay a visit to Lady of the Guo Princedom, but he was stopped at the palace gate by Chen Xuanli, on the ground that a monarch could not call on a subject without giving prior notice. Another time, when Xuanzong living in Huaqing Palace wanted to go on a night excursion around the time of the Lantern Festival, Chen Xuanli protested, saying, "Outside the palace is wilderness, so Your Majesty has to be well prepared before going on a night excursion." On both occasions, as well as on other similar ones, the Emperor could not all but heed well-grounded remonstrations. This created favorable conditions for honest officials to speak out their minds, as evidenced in the Mawei Incident.

Earlier on, a Taoist named Li Xiazhou wrote a metaphorical poem:

The man from the Swallow City left,
The horses didn't return from the fort.
If you ever see a ghost under the hill,
A gauze dress will hang on a bracelet.

"The man" refers to An Lushan who was born

in Jimen, a city in the north. "The fort" refers to the strategic pass Tongguan which fell to the rebel army. "A ghost under the hill" refers to the character "wei" which forms the name of the town Mawei where Lady Yang was strangled. "A gauze dress" refers to the cloth Gao used to strangle her to death, and "a bracelet" refers to Lady Yang's pet name, Yuhuan, meaning "Jade Bracelet."

In the later years of the Tianbao period there was a children's song: "The wig is thrown into the river while a yellow dress flows with the stream." Now the prophesy of both riddles had come true, for in her life Lady Yang often wore a false bun as hairdress with a yellow skirt to match.

Before the rebellion, An Lushan was a frequent visitor to the court, and was swayed by Lady Yang's charms. When he heard of her tragic death at Mawei, he sighed with grief for days. It seemed there was also some other reason that led to his rebellion against Yang Guozhong.

Lady of the Guo Princedom left the capital before her sister. The news of Yang Guozhong's death overtook her when she arrived at Chencang. In a panic on learning that the county magistrate Xue Jingxian was going to arrest her, she rushed into a bamboo grove and first killed her son Pei Hui and then her daughter. Yang Guozhong's wife Pei Rou begged her, "Please madame, won't you do me the same favor?" So the Lady killed her and her daughter. Then she slit her own throat but did not die, and was thrown into prison. "Are you the regular army or rebels?" she gasped. "A bit of both," answered the warden. The blood clogged her throat and she too died. All the bodies were moved to a pit under a willow tree east of the town wall.

The Emperor set off from Mawei and came to the Fufeng Road, which was lined with flowers. There beside a temple stood a stalwart Chinese photinia tree which Xuanzong stopped to admire and named "The Upright Tree"; his mind was still dwelling on his lost love. When he entered a valley, he was caught by a long drizzling rain lasting a fortnight. The distant ringing of bells across the hills inspired him to compose the song "Ringing Bells in the Rain" to express his endless remorse and sorrow.

In the second year of the Zhide period (757), Chang'an, the capital, was recovered. The Emperor returned to Chang'an from Chengdu in the eleventh lunar month and sent some officials to hold a memorial service to his late Honored Consort. He even intended to move her tomb to the capital but was dissuaded by powerful eunuchs like Li Fuguo. After Suzong was enthroned Vice-Minister of Rites Li Kui said, "The troops killed Yang Guozhong for treason. If the late Honored Consort was moved back, they might take it badly." The new Emperor took the counsel.

As Xuanzong had already abdicated the throne and become the Emperor Emeritus, he could only secretly send some eunuchs to move Lady Yang's remains to another spot. The body had been wrapped with a violet quilt when buried, but its flesh had decomposed and only the silk perfume bag still remained on her chest. After she was reburied, the eunuch in charge brought back the perfume bag and presented it to Xuanzong, who kept it in his sleeve. He then had a portrait of Lady Yang drawn and hung in the chamber in the palace so that he could gaze at it night and day, sighing in tears.

After his abdication, Xuanzong moved to the Xingqing House in the south of the palace. One night he went up the Qinzheng Pavilion, scanning the southern skies alone. Seeing nothing but the moon in a haze, he sang in verse, "The trees in the yard have grown up, yet my expeditionary troops have not returned." No sooner had he finished than he felt there was a distant refrain from a by-lane beyond the palace wall. He asked Gao Lishi, "Wasn't that a voice of the former royal troupe? Go find him in the morning." The next morning Gao spotted the singer in one of the by-lanes and took him to the palace. The man admitted he had been a member of the troupe before. Later, Xuanzong came to the same spot with a former maid of Lady Yang named Hongtao. He told her to sing the song "Verse from Liangzhou" by Lady Yang and accompanied her on a jade flute himself. At the end of the song they looked at each other with tears running down their cheeks. Xuanzong later expanded the song. Its present version is further developed from the original.

During the Zhide period (756-758), Xuanzong revisited Huaqing Palace with an entourage of officials and palace maids mostly new. He made Zhang Yehu play "Ringing Bells in the Rain." In the middle of the melody, Xuanzong raised his eyes and looked around. He was filled with grief and began weeping, bringing tears to the eyes of everyone around him. In the court there was a dancer named Xie Ahman from Xinfeng who had been Lady Yang's favorite. One day Xuanzong asked her to dance to the melody "Over the Waves" as before. After the performance, she took the opportunity to present Xuanzong with a gold-grained arm bracelet which was given to her by Lady Yang. His eyes brimming with tears, Xuanzong stammered, "This is one of the two treasures my grandfather Gaozong brought back after the conquest of Korea. One was the Violet Gold Belt, the other this pair of Red Jade Bracelets. I gave the former to Prince Qi when he presented me with his verse, 'Dragon Pond'; the latter was my present for Honored Consort. When the King of Korea learned about this, he sent me a memorandum complaining that his country had been suffering from natural disasters and popular disaffection ever since the loss of the two national treasures. I never saw much value in them and had the Violet Gold Belt sent back to him, but kept the bracelets. Now that you have got them from Honored Consort, the mere sight of them evokes in me sad reveries..." and tears covered his cheeks again.

In the first year of the Qianyuan period (758), He Huaizhi told Xuanzong, "One summer day, Your Majesty was playing chess with a prince while I was accompanying the game with a *pipa* guitar. Lady Yang was watching by the side. When Your Majesty was about to lose quite a few pieces, she set free her pug-dog which upset the chessboard, much to the relief of Your Majesty. Then a gust of wind blew up her silk scarf which caught on my turban and remained there for a while before it fell down. When I returned home that night, I found there was a sweet smell on me. So I untied the turban and kept it in a silk pack. Now I would like to present it to Your Majesty." Xuanzong untied the pack and said immediately, "It smells of the perfume Ruilongnao. I put a few drops of it on the marble sculptures of lotus flowers in the hot-spring pool and found the fragrance still lingering there when I returned next time. It certainly keeps better with silk." Saying this, he sighed in reminiscence again. From then on Xuanzong shut himself in gloom, repeating a verse to himself:

Gingerly I move as an old man,
With wrinkled face and white hair.
All is quiet when the party is over,
Life still goes on like a dream.

On learning about Xuanzong's yearning for his deceased concubine, a Taoist priest from Sichuan called Yang Tongyou claimed he had mastered the magic of Li Shaojun[1] and could do something about it. Xuanzong was more than pleased to hear this and asked him to bring Lady Yang's spirit back to him. The Taoist exerted all his magic power but failed to find her spirit. But he said his own spirit could transcend his body and search the sky and the earth. But that attempt failed too. Then his spirit explored all quarters, beyond the east over the sea, and even crossing the Penglai Fairyland until a high mountain came in sight. The mountain was studded with pavilions and towers. As he approached it he found on the west side a round gate facing east. The door was closed; above it was a sign saying, "Residence of the Jade Lady Taizhen." The priest knocked on the door with his hairpin, and a young girl with her hair tied in two buns answered. Before he was able to utter a word the girl turned back into the yard. Then a maid in green appeared and asked where he was from. The priest said he was the envoy of the Emperor in search of Lady Yang. The maid said, "I'm afraid she is asleep. Please wait a moment." After a while, she showed him in, and announced, "Jade lady is coming." Wearing a gold lotus crown and a violet gauze scarf

---

[1] Li Shaojun was a Taoist priest in the Han Dynasty, who claimed to have the power to prolong life indefinitely.

over her shoulders, Jade lady presented herself in red jade jewelry and a pair of slippers with phoenix heads, followed by seven or eight maids.

She bowed slightly to the priest and asked after Emperor Xuanzong's health and also the events in the country after the fourteenth year of the Tianbao period (755). As she spoke a cloud of melancholy passed over her brow. She told the maid to fetch her a gold jewelry box and gave half the contents to the envoy, saying, "Please thank the Emperor with this from me. It's a memento for our wonderful past together." The priest's eyes betrayed his discontent as he took the present to leave. Jade Lady asked him what more he had to say; on his knees, he answered, "To prove that I was here, pray tell me of some events shared only by you and the Emperor, unknown to others. Otherwise, the jewelry box alone won't be sufficient to prove that this is no fraud." Jade lady was taken aback by the request. As if lost in thought, she slowly said, "It happened in the tenth year of the Tianbao period. I went with the Emperor in a carriage to the Lishan Summer Palace. One summer night in the seventh month, when the Cowherd Star came close to the Weaver Star, the Emperor with his hand on my shoulder was watching the skies. Touched by the legend of the Cowherd and the Weaver, we made a vow from our hearts: 'We shall be man and wife in all our future lives.' After that, we both wept. This sacred vow is known only to us." Then she burst into tears, saying, "Since this thought has come to my mind again, I can no longer live here, and must fall into the world of mortals to resume our ties again. That will either be in Heaven or on earth, we shall meet again as we did in the past." Then she continued, "The Emperor does not have long to live. I wish he would take good care of himself and not torment himself too deeply."

When the priest returned to report his journey to Xuanzong, the Emperor Emeritus was shaken with grief. On moving back to the Ganlu (the nectar of gods) Hall in the palace, he pined for Lady Yang every day, and began to abstain from cereals and fall into endless meditation. He did not even touch the cherries and sugarcane juice Empress Zhang had prepared for him. He often played a violet jade flute. One day when he was playing the flute, a pair of cranes landed in the courtyard and walked around for a while and then left. Xuanzong said to his maid Gong'ai, "I have been ordained by God to become the Immortal 'Yuanshi Kongsheng', and so now I have hope that I may see Honored Consort again. Since you don't like this flute you can give it to Dashou (Prince Li Yu)." Then he told her to prepare a hot bath for him. After the bath, he said, "Don't disturb me after I've gone to sleep." Later the maid heard him gurgle in his sleep. Alarmed, she went close to have a look. He was dead.

On the day of Lady Yang's death, an old matron at Mawei picked up a silk sock she had left behind.

She made a fortune from passers-by who just wanted to touch or have a look at it.

It was a tragedy indeed that Xuanzong had been on the throne too long. He tired of his official duties and his officials had to beg him to rein in his own excesses. After he had made Li Linfu prime minister, he left everything to Li's care and set himself above all criticism, wallowing in food and drink, song and dance, and the company of pretty women and girls. This resulted in the fall of the capital and his flight, leaving his officials behind to become captives of the rebels, and in the mutiny of his troops and the death of his beloved Lady Yang and her family, the whole country was drowned in a sea of fire and brought to ruin. All this catastrophe arose from the misrule of the notorious Prime Minister Yang Guozhong he had appointed!

Li (rite) is a system that defines the classes and the rule of a country. If an emperor does not perform his duties, what good will he be to the country? If a father fails to do his duty, how can he run his family? A ruler who makes either of these errors is doomed to failure. By taking one fatal step, Emperor Xuanzong brought shame on his great country, which led to An Lushan's rebellion with the Yang family's notoriety as an excuse. I have written "The Story of Lady Yang" not merely for entertainment, but also to provide a historical lesson.

17. The Haunting Legend of the Grand Canal

Anonymous

Emperor Yangdi of the Sui Dynasty was one of the most notorious tyrants in Chinese history, and so many legends about him sprang up in the Song Dynasty (690-1279), such as Records of the Sui Dynasty, The Sui Emperor Yangdi Travesty and The Mystic Mansion. The Haunting Legend of the Grand Canal is one such strange tale, which includes the paranormal.

China's Grand Canal is one of the world's historic wonders, the artery of China's economic and cultural interflow between its North and South. However, this was not what Emperor Yangdi envisaged when he ordered people to dig this canal for a pleasure-cruise down south across the vast land! This immense project brought untold misery on the people who constructed it. One cannot read its history without indignation at the cruelty of the tyrant and compassion for the sufferings of the laborers. Fueled by his fantasy to vie with the First Emperor of Qin who had built the Great Wall, he

constructed the Grand Canal only to leave behind a name equal to Nero of Rome and countless tales of punishment and retribution meted out to the oppressors and exploiters who served him.

This legend is chosen from Vol. 44 of a Ming-Dynasty handwritten script compiled by Zhang Zhongxiang. The author is anonymous.

An aurora promising the birth of a great ruler within 500 years was observed in the sky at Suiyang and reported to Emperor Yangdi by the astrologer Geng Chunchen. But the Emperor, who had become fatuous and licentious, ignored it. Around that time he went to his Magnolia Garden and had his favorite singer Yuan Bao'er sing "The Song of the Willow." Suddenly his eyes were struck by the painting, "The Fabulous Yangzhou," which he stared at for ages, unable to move. Empress Xiao at his side asked why he was so deeply enthralled; the Emperor answered, "It's not that I like the picture. The city in it reminds me of a place I have been to before."

With his left hand on her shoulder, he pointed out with his right the hills, the river, the village and the temple in the painting as if he were seeing the real things before him. "They were with me day and night when I was still Prince Chen governing the city of Yangzhou. In those days, I regarded the misty vapor over the land as part of the scenery there and had no dreams of wealth and honor. Who would have thought that I would be on the throne overwhelmed by my duties day in and day out, with no time to enjoy the beauty of nature at all?" said he with a grimace.

"Since your heart is over there in Yangzhou, why not go there on a tour?" the empress suggested. So the Emperor made up his mind and the next day consulted with his officials on a plan to travel first by the Luo River, and down the Yellow River to the sea, and then turn back to the Huai River to reach Yangzhou. But the journey, the officials reckoned, would be about ten thousand li (five thousand kilometers), not to speak of the strong currents and rough sea which involved high risks. The Grand Master of Remonstrance Xiao Huaijing (the empress' brother) presented his proposal: "I hear that in the days of the First Emperor of Qin, a regal aurora was observed in Nanjing. The Emperor had a firm rock removed from the upper stream of the Yangtze River, and the aurora vanished. Now in Suiyang such an aurora has been reported again. Your Majesty wants to visit the southeast by water, but is worried about possible hazards at Mengjin. I know of an old waterway lying to the northwest of Daliang (Kaifeng). That is where General Wang Fen of Qin flooded the city of Daliang. I suggest that Your Majesty draft large contingents of troops and laborers to dig a channel from Daliang and bring the water from the Mengjin River at Heyin in the west to the canal until it reaches Huaikou in the east. The total distance will be only a thousand li (five hundred kilometers). Before the canal ends up in Yangzhou, it will pass Suiyang and cut off the aurora there."

The Emperor was more than pleased by the suggestion, while the rest of the court remained silent. Seeing this, the Emperor was furious and issued an edict: "Anyone in this court opposing this scheme will be put to death." He appointed the Chief of Staff of the Northern Expeditionary Army, Ma Shumou, as Director of the project and Rebellion Suppression General Li Yuan, Vice-Director. But Li excused himself claiming illness, and General Linghu Xinda of the Left Guard filled the post instead. The canal was named River Bian, and a special office was set up for its construction. Meanwhile, an enormous labor force was mobilized; all men between 15 and 50 must report for duty to the local project station on pain of death for the whole family to its third clans. Besides this, a man or woman, regardless of age, was drawn from every fifth family to serve as a cook for the work force. Fifty thousand vicious young soldiers were selected to be overseers. The entire work force amounted to over 5,430,000 men and women. Ma Shumou sent one third of them to Shangyuanyi to dig the canal westward to Heyin, where it would merge with the old waterway at Daliang, and go on to Chousitai, swinging finally to the north. The other two thirds started from Shangyuanyi, going east. The mammoth project commenced work early in the eighth lunar month in the fifth year of the Daye period, stretching over a thousand kilometers from east to west.

Barely five yards had been dug when an ancient underground vault was struck. It was large and well lit with lanterns inside, and the walls were decorated with elaborate designs of flowers, bamboo, dragons and spirits. At the center was a coffin, evidently for a member of an illustrious family. The discovery was immediately reported to the project director who ordered that the coffin be opened. Lying inside was a rather obese man with a complexion almost like that of a living person, his skin smooth and white like jade. His hair flowed down from his brow, covering his face, chest, abdomen and feet, and continuing back beneath the body up to the waist. A stone tablet was found inscribed with characters resembling the primary bird-and-insect types created by Cang Jie[1]. A man from Xiapi who was able to read such characters was discharged from his labor to interpret the mysterious inscription. It read: "I am the Great God of Gold, lying dead here for a thousand years. When the time comes, a stream will flow beneath my body. I will meet Ma Shumou who will bury me again on a plateau. After another thousand years,

---

[1] Cang Jie is believed to be the chronicler of Huang Di (Yellow Emperor) who created Chinese characters.

when my hair reaches my head again, I will ascend to heaven." Ma Shumou himself prepared a new coffin and reburied the man at the western corner of the city wall (where the Great Buddha Temple is today).

When the excavation reached Chenliu, the Emperor sent an Emissary to present a jade tablet inscribed with his blessing for the canal and a pair of white jade ornaments to the Marquis Liu Temple dedicated to the deified Zhang Liang [1]. At the end of the ceremony, a gust of wind burst out through the windows like shrapnel across the faces of those gathered there. The frightened emissary withdrew at once. Work resumed with a frantic speed that turned the worksite into a humming beehive. In a few days the excavation force reached Yongqiu.

A laborer from Zhongmou suffering from a bad back fell behind his team. He was walking alone in a clear moonlit night when suddenly he heard a stern voice ordering him to clear the way for an official. The man waited half-bent by the roadside. After a while, a procession of guards approached with a nobleman in the hat and costume of a marquis riding a white horse. He ordered the laborer be brought to him and instructed him, "Say this to your monarch, 'The day I return a pair of white jade ornaments to you, you will be dead.'" At

---

[1] Zhang Liang was the War Counsellor of Liu Bang, the First Emperor of the Han Dynasty.

that, he ordered his footman to give a pair of jade ornaments to the laborer who was on his knees. Then he rode on westward until he disappeared from sight. When the laborer returned to Yongqiu, he delivered the jade ornaments to Ma Shumou who examined them closely and was astonished to find they were the sacrificial present from the Emperor for Zhang Liang. He asked the laborer how they had come into his possession; the man told him the story. Prompted by greed, Ma kept the jade ornaments without comprehending their portent. He killed the laborer for fear that he might talk, and ordered the construction proceed from Yongqiu.

Then they came to a large forest in which there was a tiny temple. Ma Shumou questioned an old villager who told him it was called "The Hermit's Tomb" and that the spirit of the temple had magic power. Ma disregarded the warning and had the tomb explored. Digging a few feet down revealed a pit. The laborers peeped down and could see a dim light, but no one dared to go inside. The officer in command named Di Quxie volunteered to go in and have a look. Ma Sumou praised him for his bravery and ordered the men to tie a rope around his waist and lower him into the pit. After a hundred yards or so he touched ground. Then he set himself loose and walking about a hundred paces, found himself in a stone house. On both the east and north side of the house there were four stone pillars to which an animal the size of an ox was tied with double chains. A closer look showed the animal to be an enormous rat. Then a stone door on the west side swung open and a page-boy came out, asking, "Are you Di Quxie?"

"Yes," he replied.

"Huangfu Jun has been waiting for you," the boy said and showed him in. There a man dressed in red and wearing a casual cap was sitting on a high pedestal. Di bowed twice to him but received no response. A man in green took him to the steps on the west side. Then the man on the pedestal called out to the soldiers: "Bring Ah Mo (the childhood name of Emperor Yangdi) here." Several tough, burly warriors brought forth the huge rat by force. As an official of the court, Di knew "Ah Mo" was the Emperor's childhood name but failed to associate it with this monstrous rat. He just watched on holding his breath. "I ordered you to shed your fur and become ruler of a nation. Why, then, have you enslaved the people and become a tyrant? You have disobeyed the Law of Heaven." The rat just nodded, waving its tail. In a rage the man on the pedestal ordered his men to beat the rat over the head with a heavy club. Just one single blow produced a boom like a thunderclap, and the rat roared with pain. As the club was raised to strike again, an angel descended from heaven bearing a Taoist inscription. The man on the pedestal was startled and prostrated himself on the ground to listen to the announcement of the edict from heaven. The angel read: "Ah Mo's time on the throne is twelve years. Seven of these have now passed; in five years he should be strangled with a long scarf." Then the angel left. The man on the pedestal ordered the huge rat be chained to the stone pillars, and instructed Di, "Please say this to Ma Shumou, 'Thank you for not digging in my district. Next year I will present you with two gold swords. Please accept them in good grace.'" At these words, the man in green showed Di out through a side door.

After walking about ten li (five kilometers), Di found himself in a forest, making his way through the bushes. When he looked around, the man in green was gone. After going on three more li, he came upon a cottage with an old man sitting on a *kang*.[1] Di asked him the name of the area. "You are at the foot of Shaoshi Hill, in Songyang," the old man answered and asked him where he had been; Di told him his strange adventure. The old man explained the meaning of these events, and Di realized that EmperorYangdi was doomed. The old man further warned him, "The sooner you leave your office, the better it will be for your own life." As soon as Di stepped out of the house, it disappeared.

---

[1] The *kang* is a brick bed under which a fire is lit to heat the room in winter.

Meanwhile Ma Shumou had already reached Ningyang County. Di went to report his adventure to him.

It turned out that the vault had collapsed soon after Di had entered it, and he was considered dead. His return seemed like a miracle. Ma refused to believe his ghastly tale and said he had gone crazy, and this gave Di the excuse he needed to withdraw from office and live as a hermit in the Zhongnan Mountains. Strangely enough, at the very same time in the capital, Emperor Yangdi was seized by a violent headache which kept him from holding court for over a month. It was said that he had been hit on the head in a dream causing an ache that lasted a couple of days. This occurred on the very day when Di Quxie saw the big rat in the vault.

While Ma Shumou pushed on his project to Ningling County, he contracted a skin disease and could not even sit up. Yangdi sent the Imperial Doctor Chao Yuanfang to take care of him. Chao diagnosed: "An ill wind has got into the skin, and the disease manifests itself between the chest and abdomen. Take some herbs with steamed fat lamb about half a year old, and you'll be all right again." Ma Shumou did accordingly. Before the first prescription was finished, the disease was gone. From then on, he often ordered several lambs slaughtered and prepared with herbs and, tearing the meat apart with his hands, ate it like a wolf. He called it "Soft Chunks." Every day, thousands of people from surrounding counties and villages brought him lambs, and he compensated them well.

At Xiama Village in Ningling, there was a villain called Tao Lang'er who was the head of a well-to-do family. He and his brothers were all scoundrels. Fearing that the canal would come close to their ancestral tombs and expose them to robbery, they kidnapped a child, chopped off its head and feet, and served the meat steamed to Ma Shumou. Ma found the dish more delicious than usual and finished it with relish. He sent for Tao Lang'er and asked him for the recipe, and being drunk, Tao divulged the secret. When Tao had sobered up Ma sent him off with ten taels of gold, and ordered that a dyke be built around the Tao ancestral tomb to protect it from robbery. From then on, the Tao brothers frequently brought him kidnapped victims and made a fortune from it. Having heard this, other villains followed suit and were likewise rewarded. Thus hundreds of children disappeared in this way in Xiangcheng, Ningling and Suiyang, where heart-rending cries of distraught parents could be heard day and night. At that time, the Palace Guard General, Duan Da, was in charge of civil complaints to the Emperor. Ma sent his servant Huang Jinku to bribe the general with gold, and all the complaints about infant-eating were withheld. The complainants were flogged forty lashes and deported from the capital. Most of the deported never returned home alive.

At last Vice-Director Linghu Xinda heard of this and secretly had the bones of the eaten children collected. In a couple of days, the collection had filled a cart. Meanwhile in towns and villages, families with children made wooden chests strenghtened with iron strips, locked their children in at night and kept watch till dawn. The next morning they would open the chests and rejoice to find their children alive and kicking.

As the canal was approaching Suiyang, a village bailiff called Chen Bogong declared that if the canal were to continue on its present course, it would run through the city; if the canal were to bypass the city, special permission should first be obtained from the Emperor. At the word "bypass," Ma Shumou flew into a rage and ordered that Chen be chopped in two at the waist, but the vice-director pleaded mercy for the poor man. Meanwhile, in the City of Suiyang, there were one hundred and eighty influential families who feared that their homes and ancestral graves would be destroyed. They pooled together three thousand taels of gold to bribe Ma but failed to find a go-between for the task. By then the canal had proceeded into a forest and reached an ancient tomb dating back to the State of Song in the Spring and Autumn Period (770 B.C.—476 B.C.). The older generation believed it was the Tomb of Sima Huayuan. A stone chamber was found in it with lanterns, coffins and curtains which all turned to dust on exposure leaving only an inscribed stone tablet, which read: "Suiyang is a plateau, and the Bian River (the Canal) can be its moat. If the river refuses to bypass it, you will be given two broad swords." Ma Shumou dismissed it as nonsense and pushed onward.

That day Ma dreamt of an emissary who summoned him to a palace. There he saw a man in a red gauze robe and a black hat. Ma bowed to him and the man returned his courtesy, saying, "I am Duke Xiang of Song. The King of Heaven appointed me to guard this city and I have done so for two thousand years. If the General could be kind enough to bypass this city, all the residents would be grateful and sing your praise." Ma still refused to shift the course of the canal. Duke Xiang went on, "What I have said is not my personal wish but the will of Heaven, because within five hundred years a great ruler will be born here to establish an empire lasting ten thousand years. How can you destroy his promised glory just for a pleasure cruise?" Ma refused to give in. After a while, a messenger hurried in to announce the arrival of War Minister Sima Huayuan. The minister was shown in, wearing a violet robe and a black hat. After he showed his respects to the duke, the duke told him the problem of protecting Suiyang. Turning red, the man roared, "It is the will of the King of Heaven to protect the city. This Ma Shumou is a fool that defies the King of Heaven." He ordered that torture instruments be made ready. "What is the most painful torture?" Duke Xiang asked. The man in violet answered, "To pour molten copper down his throat. It will burn his stomach and intestines. This is the most painful." Duke Xiang ordered that this be done to Ma. Instantly Ma was stripped to the waist leaving only his underwear and tied to an iron post. He was scared out of his wits. The duke held back his men and asked him.

"Now, what about the city?"

"As you wish, as you wish," Ma repeated.

The duke ordered him released and given back his clothes. Before he could leave, the man in violet announced, "The King of Heaven grants Ma Shumou three thousand taels of gold, to be collected from the local people." The greedy Ma could not believe his ears and asked, "A grant of gold, what do you mean?" The emissary replied, "This will be delivered to you by the local people of Suiyang. What has been ordered in the nether world shall be carried out in the world of the living." At that, Ma woke up, his wits still scattered.

As promised, the people of Suiyang brought the bribe to Ma's servant Huang Jinku giving him the three thousand taels of gold for his master. As this conformed to his weird dream, Ma took it without a word. He summoned Chen Bogong and ordered him to dig to the west of Suiyang, sometimes going south sometimes north, zigzagging through the Liuzhao Village in the east and then coming back on course. Vice-Director Linghu learned of this and reported it to the Emperor several times, but the reports were withheld by Duan Da and never saw the light.

At Pengcheng the canal came to another forest, and here the canal diggers came upon the tomb of Prince Yan. The picks and shovels had only gone a few feet when the diggers struck a grave completely cast in copper and iron. They removed all the earth around it and revealed one stone side-door, securely locked, which they had to force open. This time Ma Shumou himself walked in, and after a hundred paces, he was met by two page-boys who told him that Prince Yan was expecting him. Ma followed them into a palace where a man wearing a tall crown and a red robe [1] was seated on a pedestal. Ma kowtowed to him and the prince responded respectfully, saying: "My grave is right on the course of the new river. I would like to present you with a jade treasure which will enable you to rule the whole country. In return, I would be grateful if my grave could be spared." Ma promised he would take care of everything. Prince Yan told his servant to present a jade seal to Ma, with the inscription "The Seal for the Emperor of a Hundred Generations." Ma Shumou was greatly pleased. The prince added, "Take good care of it. It forebodes

---

[1] The man in the red robe is supposed to be the King of Hell in control of human destiny.

the 'Double Swords'." At the same time in the capital, Emperor Yangdi suddenly discovered that he had lost his royal seal, and had the entire palace searched, but to no avail. There was nothing more that he could do except forbid news of the loss leaking out.

The Emperor drove forward the excavation with frantic haste. From Xuzhou onward, Ma Sumou had to work the canal diggers night and day, and the depletion of the labor force now reached one and a half million men. Dead bodies were strewn around the worksites.

One day Yangdi read of the construction of the Great Wall by the First Emperor of Qin in *Records of the Historian* in the Palace Library. "It has been a thousand years since the Qin Dynasty. I am afraid the Great Wall is crumbling," he said to Prime Minister Yuwen Shu. Knowing his mind, Yuwen said, "Your Majesty wants to emulate the First Emperor of Qin and carry on his immortal deeds for the good of posterity. The best thing to do is fortify the Wall and strengthen our defense." The flattering proposal was immediately accepted, and an edict was announced to appoint Duke He Ruobi as Director of the construction project and Grand Master of Remonstrance Gao Jiong as Vice-Director. Their duty was to gather a labor force of one million and two hundred thousand laborers from the Jiang, Huai, Wu, Chu, Xiang, Deng, Chen, Cai, Bing, Kai and Tuo prefectures. As soon as this was announced, He Ruobi objected: "I was told the construction of the ten-thousand-li (5000-km) Great Wall took countless numbers of lives. As a consequence, women could find no husbands, only widows and orphans were left in villages. Before the Wall was completed, the Qin Dynasty collapsed. If Your Majesty listens to such crazy ideas, and follows the steps of the First Emperor of Qin, you will end up the way the Qin Dynasty did." The Emperor was exasperated to hear this. Before he could utter a word, Yuwen Shu cut in and reprimanded He: "You are just a foolhardy soldier. What do you know about national affairs?" The duke's anger soared beyond control, and he struck Yuwen with an ivory tablet. The Emperor drove him out of court and put him under house arrest. That night the duke took poison and died. Gao also declined the commission. Yuwen Shu recommended Manager of Agriculture Yuwen Bin and Vice-Minister of Revenue Yuwen Kai to be the director and the vice-director instead.

While he was dredging the canal to make it deeper, Ma Shumou checked the labor force and found its depletion now totalled two and a half million. Even the guards, originally fifty thousand, were down to twenty-seven thousand. When the canal was finally completed, Ma reported to the Emperor. He was ordered to flood the Bian River (the Canal). As the Emperor himself was coming from Luoyang to the great canal, he ordered the building of five hundred dragon boats at top speed in the Jiang and Huai prefectures. Those families requisitioned to build a boat had to sell all they had to pay the cost. If the demand was not met, they would be chained and flogged, and their children would be sold to pay their debts.

When the dragon boats were launched, Emperor Yangdi cruised down the Huai River and docked at Daliang to have the boats elaborately decorated with "seven gems" and pavilion towers. Five hundred girls aged between 15 and 16 were recruited as "palace foot-girls" to haul the boats, ten to a boat , each with a colorful towline led by a goat. As it was the height of summer under a blazing sun, Yu Shiji, member of the Imperial Academy, pleaded that willow trees be planted along the banks of the canal. First, he reasoned, the roots of the trees would sprawl out and secure the soil of the dykes; secondly, the trees could provide shade for the foot-girls; thirdly, their leaves would provide fodder for the goats. The Emperor gladly accepted the proposal and promised a bolt of silk to any one who planted a willow tree on the bank. A folk song at that time had these two lines: "The Emperor planted the first willow, and the people followed on." When the planting was completed, Emperor Yangdi wrote two big characters, "yang" and "liu," the first being the imperial family name; the second the original Chinese name of willow. Hence the willow came to be called 'Yangliu' throughout China.

The spectacular procession of dragon boats extended, bow to stern, over a thousand li from Daliang to Huaikou without break. The silk sails passing by left a trail of fragrance far and wide. As the boats passed Yongqiu gradually into Ningling, the current grew strong, often holding up the procession, and the foot-girls were having a tough time. The convoy master, Imperial Guard General Xiangyu Juluo, reported that owing to the shallowness of the canal, progress was at a snail's pace. The Emperor asked Yu Shiji for solution. He replied, "Wooden geese made with iron webfeet, twelve feet long each, should be launched from the upper stream downward. Wherever they go aground will be the shoals." The solution worked—there were 129 shoals from Yongqiu to Guankou. The Emperor was enraged and checked the names of the officials in charge. He ordered the people on both sides of the canal where the wooden geese stopped be buried alive upside-down beneath the dykes. "Let them live as workers for the canal, and die as ghosts hugging sand!" he exclaimed. And so another fifty thousand lives were ended.

When the boats docked at Suiyang, Emperor Yangdi asked Ma Shumou, "How many streets, markets and residences have been pulled down on account of the excavation?"

"Suiyang is guarded by spirits who must not be disturbed. Any inroads upon the city would entail a catastrophe. I have made a detour to save this city."

Yangdi frowned and ordered Liu Cen to survey the crooked river course. Liu found it longer than the original course by twenty li. The Emperor was furious and ordered that Ma be thrown into jail. He sent for Linghu Xinda and asked the reason for the deviation.

Linghu reported: "From Ningling onward, Ma Shumou began to take the law into his own hands. Eating chopped lamb at first, he went on to eat infants, and encouraged thieves like Tao Lang'er to steal children for him to eat; he took bribes worth three thousand taels of gold to bypass Suiyang without permission."

Linghu showed the Emperor the bones of eaten children he had collected as proof.

"Why didn't you report on this earlier?" asked the Emperor.

"I did tender several reports to court but they were all held up by Duan Da and never reached Your Majesty," said Linghu.

The Emperor ordered Ma's luggage be searched, which revealed the bribe in gold he had taken from the people of Suiyang, the white jade ornaments returned by Marquis Zhang Liang, and the jade seal of the ordained monarch. The Emperor was astounded and said to Yuwen Shu, "The gold and the jade ornaments are nothing important. But how could he get my seal?"

Yuwen answered, "It must have been stolen by one of his thieves."

Yangdi was stunned, saying, "Today Ma Shumou could steal my seal; tomorrow he would steal my head!"

Linghu ventured further, "Since Ma sent Tao Lang'er to steal children, he probably used the same man to get that treasure seal."

Emperor Yangdi was angrier than ever. He set up a special commission with Duke Lai Hu'er, Court Aide Li Baiyao and Chamberlain for the Imperial Stud Yang Yichen to investigate the case. They first arrested Tao Lang'er and his family, and ordered him to confess how he had got into the palace and stolen the royal seal. Tao could not stand the torture and confessed to everything. The commission also punished Duan Da for suppressing Linghu Xinda's reports to the Emperor. A conclusion was made and reported to the Emperor. Yangdi consulted Yuwen Shu about the sentence. Yuwen said, "Ma Shumou is indicted for four crimes: cannibalism, bribery, theft of the national treasure and diverting the canal. He should be executed in the severest manner. As for his posterity, they are at the mercy of Your Majesty."

The Emperor decided: "Ma Shumou has committed most serious crimes, but he has also contributed to the canal. Let his children be spared." Ma was chopped into three at the waist on the bank of the canal.

Before Lai Hu'er arrived with the edict, Ma Shumou dreamt of an angel descending from heaven, announcing: "Duke Xiang of Song and Sima Huayuan have sent me here to thank the general for saving the city, and to present him with the promised two broad swords." Then he woke up and knew his days were numbered. Just then Lai Hu'er arrived, took him to the side of the canal and had him chopped into three. Tao Lang'er and his four brothers, together with Ma's servant Huang Jinku, were flogged to death. The Imperial Guard General Duan Da was spared his life but demoted to guard the city gate of Luoyang.

18. The Drifting Maple Leaf

Zhang Shi

Chinese emperors kept large numbers of beautiful women as maids in the palaces all their lives behind closely guarded walls. Unreconciled to such a languishing life in confinement, the maids yearned for their freedom and happiness, and this finds expression in stories like The Drifting Maple Leaf. *Such stories first appeared in the Tang Dynasty in works such as* Narrative Poetry *with simple plots. With the touch of a literary brush, Zhang Shi turned one of them into the romantic* Drifting Maple Leaf.

This poetic story gives praises and sympathy for palace maids' aspiration for freedom and happiness, which he attains through a series of happy coincidences:

A lonely scholar Yu You finds a maple leaf with a poem written on it drifting down a stream from the Imperial Palace; he becomes a dependant at Squire Han Yong's house;

Lady Han, a retired palace maid, comes to stay with the Squire's family as a relative, and she turns out to be the author of the poem on the maple leaf;

Yu You writes a poem in answer to Lady Han's, also on a leaf, and sends it back to the palace the way her poem came to him; Yu's poem is picked up by Lady Han;

With the blessing of Squire Han, they are happily married.

The dramatic plot, the romantic development and the happy ending are closely knit together with beautiful poetry.

The story is selected from Trivial Stories Retold, *first collection, Vol. 5. Nothing much is known about the author, Zhang Shi, alias Zijing, except that he lived in the middle of the Northern Song Dynasty (960-1127).* The Drifting Maple Leaf *is the only work of his that survives.*

During the reign of Emperor Xizong in the Tang Dynasty, there was a young scholar named Yu You. One late afternoon in autumn, he was taking a walk on a street near the Imperial Palace. The trees were rustling in the wind, as if bidding farewell to the setting sun. In a sombre nostalgic mood, Yu gazed at the fallen leaves drifting down the stream that flowed out from the palace. He bent down to wash his hands when a rather large maple leaf came in sight. The leaf appeared to be marked with ink, gently carrying, it seemed, a message from someone. Yu picked it up and found a poem on it:

> *Why so swift, little stream,*
> *The day's so dull in the palace?*

I send you, Maple Leaf, on a trip,
To the free world of my dream.

The leaf became Yu's treasure. He kept it in his bookcase and often mulled over the exquisite poem, wondering who the poet might be. It dawned upon him that the poet must be a maid in the palace from where the stream had carried the leaf. He treasured more than ever this precious leaf, which was often his topic in conversation with his enthusiastic friends. However, he became obsessed with it and began to fade away.

One day, a friend, meeting him in the street, asked why he looked so haggard. Yu said, "I haven't been able to eat or sleep for several months," and went on to tell his friend how he had found the maple leaf. His friend burst out laughing, saying, "How stupid you are! The poem was not meant particularly for you, it just came to you by chance. Why do you care so much about it? Besides, it came from the palace. What can you do about it? Fly into the palace? Even if you had wings you would not dare, would you? So stop making a fool of yourself!"

"Although God is high up in heaven, He will hear you," Yu argued. "As long as you are determined, God will grant your wish. I have heard about the story of Wang Xianke and Liu Wushuang who were separated by the palace walls, but they were united by a chivalrous bailiff's trick. You never can tell how things will end as long as you do not give up hope." So Yu kept on pining. He picked a maple leaf and wrote a couplet on it:

> *Having read the poem on a maple leaf,*
> *To whom shall I send my answer on this leaf?*

He dropped the leaf on the upper stream that flowed into the palace. Some people laughed at him; others praised him. But he received a couplet that said:

> *You owe much to that river*
> *That brought you the poem from the palace.*

Yu You took the civil service examination several times without success and gave up hope. He went to a rich squire named Han Yong in Hezhong, and took refuge in the squire's manor house. After a period, the squire sent for him to give him some good news, "Owing to some misconduct, some three thousand palace maids have been discharged and ordered to get married outside. Among these maids there is a kinswoman of my clan called Lady Han. She has left the palace and is now living with my family. You are a bachelor just over thirty, and I am sorry to say, living alone without fame or honor. Lady Han is bestowed with a handsome little fortune of well over a thousand strings of coppers. She comes from a good family and, now barely thirty, still looks very pretty. If you like, I can ask her to give you her hand. What do you say to that?"

Moved to tears, Yu You came down on his knees and said, "Sir, I am just a frustrated scholar, dependent on your kindness for food and lodging. I feel ashamed that I have nothing to offer in return for your benevolence. What you have told me is beyond my wildest dreams."

Han Yong sent for a matchmaker and had everything arranged forthwith for a full-ceremony wedding between the Yu and Han families. The wedding night was pure ecstasy for Yu You. The next morning he woke up to find his bride not only beautiful but well provided with a handsome dowry. He felt he was in a fairyland, soaring above the clouds in heaven....

A few days later, Lady Han was amazed to discover the maple leaf in Yu's bookcase. "This is my poem. How did it get here?" she asked. Yu told her the story. "I too found a maple leaf with a poem written on it like mine. Do you know who the author is?" Lady Han asked. She took the leaf she had found out of her trunk and Yu instantly recognized it. The new couple embraced each other, speechless with tears streaming down their cheeks. They firmly believed this must have been destined by fate; it could not possibly be merely a coincidence. Lady Han went on to tell him, "When I read your poem, I wrote another which is still in my trunk." She took it out and showed it to her husband. It read:

Walking alone alongside the stream,
A leaf I saw floating adrift.
Who can it be to have read
My poem speaking of my dream?

The poem received wide acclaim among Yu's friends when it was repeated to them.

One day Squire Han invited the newly weds to dinner. At the table, the squire said to them heartily, "I am glad to see you both so happy. You ought to thank your matchmaker now." With a sweet smile, Lady Han answered, "My union with Yu You was arranged by Heaven and not by any matchmaker." Surprised, Han asked why. Lady Han asked for a brush and wrote down a poem:

A poem floated down the stream,
Carrying my ten years' longing.
Today a couple happily married
Thanks to their matchmaker Maple Leaf.

Squire Han read it with a sigh, "So it was arranged by Heaven indeed! Nothing happens by chance, after all."

Later on, Emperor Xizong fled the capital to Sichuan due to a rebellion. Han Yong sent Yu You with a hundred footmen to be the vanguard for the Emperor's entourage. Since Lady Han had served in the palace, she was received by the Emperor in person. When she told His Majesty how she had married Yu You, the Emperor said, "So I have heard." He summoned Yu and said with a smile,

"You were once a guest of my house, weren't you?" Yu You fell on his knees to beg pardon for his impudence to have married a royal palace maid. When the Emperor returned to Chang'an, Yu You was given the post of Lieutenant of the Imperial Guards. Lady Han bore him five sons and three daughters. All their sons studied well and achieved high official posts, while all their daughters married into distinguished families. Lady Han was known for her excellent house keeping and won a title of the court for life. Their story was recorded in a poem by Prime Minister Zhang Jun:

A million families lived in Chang'an,
Where the palace moat flowed east day after
*   day.*
It carried a floating leaf bearing a poem one
*   day,*
To the hands of a lonely scholar.
He too wrote a poem on a leaf,
And sent it back the same way to the palace.
There were thousands of maids,
But the leaf went only to Lady Han.
Three thousand maids were discharged from the
*   palace,*
Lady Han was among them.
That to her was a great relief,
She thanked His Majesty in tears.
Then she went to a kinsman's house,
Where she met the man of her dreams.
How glorious was their wedding day,

How examplary a life they led.
Their many children prospered,
And distinguished themselves in society.
Such a legend has never been heard before,
It may well be passed down forever.

The author's comment:

A flowing stream and a maple leaf are without human sentiment, yet a sentimental lady set down her feelings on a leaf, something without sentiment, leaving it to float away; her message reached a sentimental man's hands and drew him eventually to her. Such a fanastic story has never been heard before. It proves that when Heaven has ordained it, even the poles can be brought together, otherwise even close neighbors may remain strangers all their lives. Those who congratulate themselves on getting married or frantically looking for a spouse may well draw a lesson from this story.

19. Black Garment Lane

Anonymous

Black Garment Lane *was originally a nostalgic poem by the great poet of the Tang Dynasty, Liu Yuxi. In the poem two large families named Wang and Xie are mentioned as both dressed in black. Inspired by imagination, the unknown author of the legend combines the two family names into the name of one person and relates the swallows' black feathers to the Black Garment Lane. The result is a story without much deep philosophy but well told from a single character's viewpoint, which creates a suspense of mystery.*

The hero, Wang Xie, after a shipwreck in a storm, comes to a small island where everybody, including the king, is dressed in black. His host and hostess, an old couple, keep calling him "master." Step by step, the reader follows the hero to solve the mystery, which is revealed at the end when he arrives home. The suspense draws him on like a magnet to finish the story at once, making it unique among the legends of the Song Dynasty.

The legend is selected from Trivial Stories Retold, *extra collection, Vol. 4 without an author's name. Judging from the style, it may well have been written by the compiler himself, although there is no evidence to prove this.*

In the Tang Dynasty, there was a rich shipping merchant by the name of Wang Xie who lived in Jinling (modern Nanjing). One day he set sail on a great ship bound for the Arabian Empire. After a month, he ran into a furious storm with raging winds and mountainous waves. Great whales, giant turtles and dragons burst out through the surface, adding to the violence of the waves. The storm grew fiercer, and the ship heaved and rolled like a toy, tossing everyone on board about ruthlessly until it struck a rock. The ship went down, and Wang Xie found himself alone, hugging a wooden board, floundering in the waves. Sea monsters with gaping mouths threatened to devour him. He closed his eyes, ready to die....

Three days later, he was carried by the waves to a small island. He let go of the board and clambered ashore. Walking about a hundred paces, he met an old couple both in their seventies, dressed in black. Seeing Wang, they exclaimed, "Why, this is our young master! How come you are here?" Wang told them about his terrible misfortune. The old couple took him to their home. When he was seated, they said, "Master must be hungry after such a terrible journey," and quickly laid out a table of sea food for him to eat.

It took Wang Xie a whole month to recover and regain his appetite. The old man said to him, "As a guest in this country, you must first see the king. As you were exhausted when you arrived, you could not do so; now I think you are strong enough to go." Wang agreed and went with the old man to the palace. After walking about three li, through a busy street and crossing a long bridge, they arrived at a sprawling palatial building. The guard at the entrance to the hall went in to announce their arrival. After a minute, a gorgeously attired lady emerged, saying, "His Majesty welcomes you."

The king sat in the hall attended only by females. Like his courtiers, he wore a black gown and a black crown. He said to Wang, "You are from the other side of the ocean, where you observe a different protocol, so you need not bend your knees."

"While I am in your country I must follow your rules," said Wang, kneeling down.

At this, the king bowed in response and invited him to join him and sit beside the throne. "We are in a remote corner of the world. What has brought you all the way here?" the king asked.

Wang Xie told him about the terrible storm and shipwreck and his landing on their island where he begged to take refuge.

"Where are you staying now?" the king asked.

"I am staying with an old man," Wang answered.

The king sent for the old man, who said to him, "He is my master in my home town. I will see to all he wants."

"Good. If you have any difficulty, do let me know," said the king. "He is now in your care." And the visit was over.

The old man had a pretty daughter who often looked boldly at Wang Xie while bringing him tea, or peeped at him through the curtains. One day, the old man asked Wang to have a drink together. When both were half drunk, Wang said appreciatively, "Being away from home, I rely on you for a living and feel quite at home with your family. Indeed I owe you a great deal. However, sometimes I just feel so lonely and helpless that I cannot eat or sleep well. I don't know what will happen if I fall ill."

"Don't worry, I am just coming to the point," the old man said. "I have a seventeen-year-old daughter who was born in your house. I will give her to you as your wife. I am sure she will make you happy. What do you say?"

"That's wonderful," Wang replied.

The old man chose an auspicious date and held the wedding ceremony in his house. Even the king sent wine and presents to the new couple with his blessing. After the wedding, Wang Xie had a good look at his wife—she had splendid eyes, a small waist, an oval face and black hair, and a charming lithe figure. When Wang Xie asked her the name of her country, she answered, "People call it Black Garment."

"But why does your father treat me as his young master? I didn't know him before; neither was he my servant. Why does he keep calling me master?" Wang asked.

"You will find out later,"was all his bride said.

However one night, when they were in bed, Wang's new wife suddenly burst into tears. When Wang asked why, she replied, "I am afraid we will soon have to part."

"What? Although I was carried to this island by the waves, since I had you as my wife, I have never thought of my home in my country again. Why do you talk of parting?" Wang asked anxiously.

"Everything is ordained by fate. You never can tell what lies ahead," said his wife in tears.

The day came when the king invited Wang Xie to a banquet in the Black Ink Hall where all the furniture, decorations and ornaments were all in black color, including the instruments used by the band. While they drank, the band played a quiet sweet melody which Wang could not name. The king proposed a toast to him with a black jade cup, saying, "You are only the second visitor to set foot on this island. Your predecessor was Mei Cheng of the Han Dynasty. I request you to kindly write down a verse for our children to sing in future." Wang gladly complied. A sheet of paper was spread before him and Wang raced across it with his brush:

My family prospered in shipping on high seas,
Often riding on the crest of sea waves on long
journeys.
But on a voyage this year, misfortune struck,
When our ship rocked and rolled on the sea.
Winds howled, and the clouds rolled dark,
Waves rose to the sky while lightning dazzled
the eyes.
And monsters crashed all around,
A deafening thunderclag, and the mast crashed
down.
The ship was sunk and only I survived,
Carried to an island on a plank when the storm
died down.
Though surrounded by royal favor,
I still feel lonely and helpless.
Now tears of yearning overflow my homesick
heart,
How much I envy the birds that can fly across
the sea.

"A marvellous poem indeed! But you are longing for home. All right, we will see about that. Even though you have no wings, you will fly above the clouds with the trade wind." At the end of the banquet, everyone wrote a verse in response to Wang's poem. Only his wife protested, "Why do you make fun of us in the last line of your poem?" Wang had no idea of what she meant.

When the monsoon was over, the sun was

brilliant and the sea calm. "You will soon be under way," said his wife, in tears. The king sent him word that it was time to say goodbye to his family. At the farewell dinner, his wife was weeping silently like a delicate flower in rain, a willow branch dripping with dew. Wang Xie was beside himself with grief. His wife handed him a farewell poem:

Happy parties are never too many,
But human feelings seldom last for ever.
Tonight the lone sail will set out,
My soul will fly with you on the home-bound wind.

"I will never fly north across the sea again," she said. "For I know when you see less than what you see today in me, you will turn your back on me; at the same time I will be filled with bitterness. So I would rather die here alone than fly north to visit you. You cannot take anything from here with you, though this is not because I am mean." She told her maid to bring her an elixir pill, saying, "This pill can call back a soul that has left the body for less than a month. The method is put a mirror on the chest of the dead person and the pill on his throat. Apply moxibustion over the pill with a burning mugwort strip, and the person will return to life. The pill is prepared by the Sea God, who forbids it to be carried across the sea except in a Kunlun Jade Box." She put the elixir in the specified box and tied the box onto Wang's left arm. She burst out crying and left him.

The king said to Wang Xie, "I have nothing but this little verse to give you":

On a great ship you came south,
Brought to my island by a storm.
We'll never meet again from now on,
Separated by endless sea and clouds.

Wang bade him farewell with a deep bow. The king ordered a Black Cloud Sedan be made ready and had Wang sit in. Then he called for the sedan to be sprinkled with water from the pond making feathers grow out across the sedan cover. He asked the old couple to escort Wang Xie home. "Just close your eyes and you will be home in a flash. If you open your eyes, you will fall into the sea!" the king warned him.

Wang closed his eyes and heard the howling wind and the distant sighs of the waves down below. When it became quiet, he opened his eyes and found himself alone in his old courtyard. There was no one about except a pair of swallows twittering on the beam, as if saying something. He looked up at them, and it dawned on him that the country he had visited was the Land of Swallows. Just then his whole family emerged, and they all embraced him.

"We were told you had been lost with the ship in a typhoon. How did you manage to survive and come back?" his folks asked. "I kept myself alive by clinging to a board of wood" was all he said, with no reference to the Land of Swallows.

Wang Xie had a son who was only three years old when he left. Finding his son absent, Wang looked for him, and was told the boy had died two weeks previously. He burst out crying, but suddenly remembered the elixir he had with him. He asked them to open the coffin and bring the body to him. He treated the boy the way his swallow-wife had told him, and the boy revived.

By fall the swallows on the beam twittered noisily as if saying farewell to him. Wang beckoned to them, and they fluttered down and landed on his arm. Wang Xie wrote a poem in tiny characters on a slip of paper and tied it to one of the bird's tails:

> By accident I came to dreamland,
> Where I took a pretty maiden's hand.
> There's no news of her since my return,
> Tears have flowed down my cheeks a hundred
>   times.

The two swallows returned in the next spring directly to Wang's arm, also tied with a tiny slip on the tails of one bird; it said:

> Long ago in love,
> Now separated afar.
> Much to write of our love,
> But no more swallows to deliver.

On reading it, Wang Xie was filled with pain

and remorse.

In the following spring, the swallows, being too old, did not come back. But the story had spread about the town, and Wang Xie's house became known as "Black Garment Lane." This story was confirmed by Liu Yuxi's poem of the same title in his collection "Five Verses of Jinling":

> *Wild flowers ablaze beside the scarlet bridge,*
> *The last sun ray shines into Black Garment Lane.*
> *The swallows used to visit Wang Xie's house,*
> *Now they build their nests under any eave.*

20. The Story of Li Shishi

Anonymous

Li Shishi, a courtesan famous in Chinese history, was celebrated in many literary works, including ballads and plays, in the Song Dynasty. The author of this story lays much emphasis upon her heroic patriotism. Toward the end of the story, she boldly stands with her patriotism and integrity in a sharp contrast to the traitors of the country like Zhang Bangchang. This was a popular subject in the literature of the Southern Song Dynasty (1127-1279).

There are several stages in the author's portrayal of the heroine: the first shows us how she differs from others in her childhood; the second describes her pride and taste through Emperor Huizong's first visit to her in disguise; the third stresses her serenity when she is told that her visitor was the Emperor; instead of panicking, she is sure on reflection that the emperor will not be angry with her; the fourth stage stresses the patriotism she displayed when the Jin Army invades the country and she donates everything the

Emperor has given her to support the Song Army;
finally, in face of the enemy commander and the
renegade Song officers, she scathingly berates the
traitors who sell their country and herself to the
enemy, and commits suicide, ending the story at its
climax.

The steady and intricate narration is vivid and
strongly persuasive, rendered in a crystal clear and
elegant style that does justice to the memorable
courtesan.

The story is selected from A Collection of Gems.
Lu Xun, a modern writer of highest repute,
classified it as a Song masterpiece in his Legends
of the Tang and Song Dynasties.

Li Shishi was the daughter of Wang Ying, a
craftsman at a dyeing works in the Yongqing
Quarters, Kaifeng, in the Song Dynasty. Her mother
died giving birth to her, and her father had to feed
her with soya milk to keep her alive. The baby
never cried. In those days, it was the local custom
for parents to send their children into a Buddhist
monastery for a period of time as a blessing. Wang
Ying also sent his little daughter to the Treasured
Light Temple. There the girl smiled for the first
time. "Welcome, little one," an old monk said to her.
"But do you know where your are?" Frightened,
she burst out crying. The old monk put his palm on
her head and she stopped crying immediately. "My
daughter really belongs here," Wang said to himself

with a smile. He named her "Shishi," meaning "a Buddhist disciple." When she was barely four years old, her father was thrown into prison and never came out alive. Shishi became an orphan, adopted by a prostitute called Madam Li. In Li's care, she grew up a well-trained beauty, unequalled in Li's profession across the capital.

Emperor Huizong ascended the throne. He soon proved to have extravagant and wasteful tasks, and a group of his ministers encouraged him to revive the old Grain Tax, which seemed to bring wealth and happiness to the capital. The wine tax alone brought in over ten thousand strings of coppers each day. For a time, the Treasury was filled with gold, silver, jewelry and silk. Courtiers like Tong Guan and Zhu Mian lured him with wine, women and songs, and pets like dogs and horses. They collected prize flowers and rare stones from all parts of the country and built a villa in the north of the city called Genyue, where the Emperor could abandon himself to sybaritic pleasures. However, Huizong grew bored with this, and wanted to seek more pleasure outside his palaces in disguise. He had a favorite eunuch named Zhang Di, who had been a regular visitor to the brothels in town before he was castrated. He knew Madam Li well, and so highly praised Shishi's beauty and art that the Emperor's heart was fluttering like a butterfly. The next day, Huizong sent him to give Madam Li a present of two bolts of velvet, two of glossy poplin, a pair of pearls and 30 *jin* (15 kilos) of silver under the name of a merchant Zhao Yi to express his wish for a visit. More than pleased with such a sumptuous gift, Madam Li gladly expressed her warm welcome.

That night, the Emperor changed into plain clothes and walked out among forty eunuchs through the Donghua Gate to Madam Li's house. He signaled his men to stop outside, and sauntered with Zhang Di into the shabby house. Madam Li came out, bowed and showed the guests in. Greeting them warmly, she served them several dishes of delicious fruit: frosted lotus-root, dates the size of an egg, etc. These had never been served before, even to court officials. The Emperor tasted one piece of each while Madam Li just sat by without showing Shishi to them. Zhang Di took the cue and left, then Madam Li took Huizong into a small chamber in which there was a desk by the window and several editions of classics on a shelf, while green bamboos rustled in the wind in the courtyard. The Emperor sat alone and made himself at home, wondering why Shishi had still not shown up.

After a while, Madam Li took him to a rear hall where a fine table of roast deer, wine-soaked chicken, fish fillet, mutton soup and fragrant rice was waiting for him. Huizong had a good appetite. After dinner, Madam Li had some conversation with him, but there was still no sign of Shishi. Madam Li invited him to take a hot bath, which at first he declined. Then Li whispered in his ear, "My child is very clean. Please do as she asked." Reluctantly, the Emperor followed Li to a small bathroom and took a bath. Then he was taken back to the rear hall where a new table was laid for him with food and drink. He could see that the cups and saucers were spotless. After pouring him a drink, Li disappeared and came back with a candle to show the Emperor to a bedroom. Pulling aside the door curtain, Huizong found only a dim light in it with no sign of Shishi.

The Emperor grew restless, and started to pace the floor beside the bed. After another long wait, the woman he had been waiting for emerged, attended by Madam Li. Only slightly made up, without rouge or powder, Shishi was in a white satin gown, fresh from a bath, like a gleaming lotus flower on a pond. With a cold skeptical glance at Huizong, she sat down without a word of greeting. "My child is rather spoilt. Please take no offense of her," Madam Li whispered in Huizong's ear. The Emperor took a good look at Shishi in the light, and was swept off his feet by her natural grace and aura and a pair of crystalline eyes. Huizong asked her age but got no reply. When he repeated the question, she simply moved away to another seat. "She likes to sit quietly. Please accept my apology," whispered Madam Li again. She let down the door curtain and retired.

Shishi left her seat, and taking off her short

black singlet, changed into an unlined white gown. With her right sleeve rolled up, she took down a zither and sat down primly to play "The Wild Geese Land on the Sand." The tune was slow and distant, gently soothing the Emperor until he forgot where he was. By the time she had played it three times, it was already daybreak. Huizong hastily left the room. Hearing him, Madam Li quickly got out of bed, and served him a cup of apricot milk, date cakes and some other pastries. The Emperor just swallowed the milk and left. His entourage, which had been waiting outside, escorted him back to the palace in a hurry. It was the seventeenth day of the eighth lunar month in the third year of the Daguan Period (1109).

Madam Li complained to Shishi, "Squire Zhao's gifts were generous enough. Why were you so cold to him?"

"He is only a filthy merchant. Why should I grovel at his feet?" Shishi retorted.

Madam Li laughed and said, "You are so upright you should be a censor someday." It did not take long for news of the Emperor's visit to Li's house to get around the whole town. Frightened out of her wits, Madam Li wept day and night. "If this is true, it will cost the heads of my whole clan," she said, wailing to Shishi.

"Don't panic, Mother. Since His Majesty was doting on me, how could he think of killing me? That night, he did not even lay a finger on me, which means that he loves me deeply. It is my fate to be in this nasty profession which has stained His Majesty's name. This might deserve capital punishment, but the Emperor can't just have people killed because of his own unscrupulous behavior. I am sure he will not go so far as that. So calm down and stop crying." Indeed nothing happened to Li's house.

The next first lunar month, Huizong sent Zhang Di to present Shishi with a Snake-belly Zither. It was an ancient instrument, and over time its color had turned deep brown with stripes like a snake's belly, and was regarded as a treasure of the palace. Zhang also gave her fifty taels of silver.

In the third lunar month, the Emperor paid another visit to Li's house, again dressed as a commoner. Shishi waited at the door on her knees, again, only lightly made up, and dressed in white. Evidently pleased, Huizong raised her to her feet. He found the entrance painted and redecorated, and the whole interior shining in splendor. However, no trace of its former grace was left. Madam Li dared not show her face. At Huizong's call, she came trembling all over like a leaf in the wind, forgetting her ritual greetings to a customer. A bit ruffled, the Emperor still amicably called her Mother and told her to be at ease and that they should treat each other like family. Li thanked His Majesty with a kowtow and showed him in.

As the house had just been renovated, Shishi

begged the Emperor on her knees to grant her a signboard inscribed by His Majesty. Seeing the blooming apricot flowers in front of the house, Huizong wrote down "The Intoxicating Apricot Pavilion." Then wine was served with Shishi standing aside and Madam Li, on her knees, passing the cup to the Emperor. Huizong told Shishi to sit down beside him and play the "Plum Flowers in Three Postures" on the Snake-belly Zither. Sipping the wine, the Emperor was full of praise for her performance. However, he noticed that the delicacies on the table were all shaped as dragons and phoenixes, just like those served to him in the palace. He asked why and was told they had been ordered from the palace by Madam Li. The Emperor was not at all pleased about this arrangement and told Madam Li that he preferred to be served as he had been before, and not extravagantly like this time. He left the table without finishing the dinner, and returned to the palace.

Huizong used to visit the art studios in the city, where he would give the painters motifs derived from poetry. Each year he would pick one or two of them to work for the court. In the ninth month that year, he gave Shishi a prize painting depicting "the horse neighing on the grass and its rider drunk in Apricot Flower Pavilion." Besides the painting, he also sent her ten of each type of fancy lanterns: the Lotus Silk, the Snow Warm, the Phoenix with

Pearls, etc., fancy crockery like Cormorant and Amber Cups, Crystal Saucers and the Squat Wrought Gold Teapot, one hundred catties of choice tea, several boxes of delicious pastries, and gold and silver, one thousand taels each. News of this fabulous present spread throughout the palace to Empress Zheng, who admonished Huizong for such folly. "Whores are cheap women," she said. "They should not be allowed to be so close to Your Majesty, and going out at night like that could be dangerous. Your Majesty should take better care of yourself." The Emperor nodded in agreement, and did not go out again for a year or two. His presents, however, continued to be sent.

In the second year of the Xuanhe Period (1120), Huizong went to visit Shishi again. He stood for some time in the Intoxicating Apricot Pavilion musing over a painting which he had sent as a gift, and when he turned around, he saw Shishi standing behind him. "How can a person in a painting come out into the real world?" he said jokingly. That day he gave her gold ornaments for her head, a pearl necklace, a bronze mirror carved with phoenixes on its back, and a gold incense burner. The following day more presents arrived: inkstones and inksticks, writing brushes with jade shafts and quality paper plus a hundred thousand strings of cash.

Zhang Di said in private to Huizong, " Your Majesty has to change clothes each time you wish to pay a visit to Li's house at night. This is inconvenient. There is a piece of land to the east of Genyue Palace about three li long leading straight to Li's house. If a covered passage were built accross this land, it would greatly facilitate Your Majesty's visits." "See to it," said the Emperor. So a memorandum by Zhang Di was presented to the Emperor, stating, "Since the Imperial Guards at present have to stay out in the open when they are off duty, we, the undersigned, will contribute money to build several hundred houses surrounded by a wall as dormitories for them." The Emperor granted their request, and the Guards could now patrol up to Madam Li's house. The area they covered became forbidden to others.

On the third day of the fourth lunar month the Emperor visited Li's house through the tunnel with gifts of games, including a jade chess-board with jade chess pieces, fans, colored and ornamental mats, bamboo curtains and colored coral hooks for the bed. That day, the Emperor lost two thousand taels of silver gambling with Shishi. On Shishi's birthday, he granted her a pair of gold ornaments for her hair, a pair of gold bracelets, a box of string pearls, several down kerchiefs, one hundred bolts of silk and one thousand taels of silver. To celebrate the victory over the Liao in 1123, the Emperor rewarded every minister and officer in court, and Shishi as well, with violet silk curtains, colorful tassels, silk quilts, dirt-free fur mattresses and one thousand taels of gold plus luxury sweet wines.

Madam Li was also given ten million coppers. The presents, all told, were worth one hundred million coppers.

At a royal banquet given by Huizong in the palace, Lady Wei, one of his concubines, quietly asked him, "What is so special about that Li Shishi Your Majesty is so fond of?"

"Nothing much, my dear. Except that among a hundred of you in simple clothes and without make-up, she alone will shine. Her natural grace and elegance surpasses mere good looks."

Not long after, Huizong gave the throne to his son, styled himself "Patriarch of Taoism" and moved into Taiyi Monastery, forsaking his former hedonistic life. "We have nothing to be happy about now, Mother," warned Shishi. "A calamity is awaiting us." "What shall we do, then?" Madam Li asked. "Leave everything to me," Shishi said.

By now, the Jin were invading North China, and the whole of Hebei was in peril. Shishi collected everything the Emperor had given her and sent them with a list to the Mayor of Kaifeng as a contribution to the Song Army. She bribed Zhang Di to beg Huizong to give her asylum in a Taoist convent as a nun. Her wish was granted and she moved into the Ciyun Convent in the north of the city. Then the capital fell. Looking for Shishi throughout the city, the Jin commander Talan declared: "The Emperor of Jin has heard of this woman, and must have her alive." Zhang Bangchang, the collaborating prime minister, tracked her down and turned her over to the Jin commander.

'Shishi said to Zhang Bangchang and his ilk, "I am only a despised whore once favored by the Song Emperor. I have no other wish but to die. You are a high officer well paid by the court to serve the country, but all you have done is to try by every means to destroy it. Now you grovel at the enemy's feet just to curry favor with your new master! You think I will be your tribute to them? Never!" She stabbed her own throat with a gold hairpin. Failing to kill herself, she broke the hairpin in two and swallowed it, and finally died in agony. Huizong, captured and confined in the town of Wuguo, could not restrain his tears when he heard how she had died.

This author finds it extraordinary that a prostitute like Li Shishi should be favored by the Emperor. But her loyalty and heroic death made her outstanding among all people. As for the prodigal licentious Emperor, he simply deserved to be captured by the enemy and perish in captivity.

21. A Bizzare Romance in Sichuan

Li Xianmin

Legends of love between a young man and a female fox were quite popular in the Tang Dynasty. "Ren the Fox Fairy" was one of these, but in that story the fox fairy retains some of the characteristics of an animal whereas in this story the heroine is more human. Song Yuan the fox-lady is not only very pretty but gifted in letters as well. She is loyal to her beloved and defies social prejudice and misunderstanding, willing to fight feudal morality in the free pursuit of happiness. In this respect, her character is a forerunner of fox fairies in the Qing Dynasty writer Pu Songling's fabulous tales.

Conspicuous for his absence in this story is the character Kong Changzong, who never appears in person. Although both he and Li Dadao are in love with fox fairies, Li, being decent and faithful, remains unhurt whereas Kong is changed into a beast and later decapitated. Why? Because Li does not flinch in pursuit of love at the risk of his life even when he knows Song is a fox, while Kong is hypocritical, being infatuated with lust but in deep remorse at the same time. In a word, Li's is love;

Kong's is sexual infatuation. The author exalts sublime love and condemns sheer lust. He delivers the story with a fine plot, in an elegant style making it a pleasure to read.

The story is taken from the collection Records from the Study of the Clouds. *Its author, Li Xianmin, alias Yanwen, was born in Yanjin County, Henan near Kaifeng. Nothing much of his credentials can be found except that his social standing was not high. His works* Records from the Study of the Clouds *amount to ten volumes, with thirteen legends in them. Most of them are records of popular tales of his time, written in a literary style and valuable for research.*

During the Shaoxing period (1131-1162) of the Southern Song Dynasty, an official named Li Bao, alias Shengyu, was appointed county magistrate to Danleng, Meizhou. As soon as he arrived, he announced all kinds of regulations and interviewed many people there to find out what they liked and disliked about the administration. Within a few months, he had won full support from the local people.

The magistrate had a garden at the back of his residence with a small pavilion called "Nine Thoughts." His son Li Dadao liked to take a break there while studying the classics. One day, sitting in his favorite haunt, the young scholar heard someone singing and clapping softly and was carried away by it. Following the sound, he found a girl, about fifteen years old. She moved gently, her hair arranged in two large loops, dangling slightly over her radiant face, which was like a fresh lotus flower, with two arched eyebrows like a pair of willow leaves. She seemed like a fairy on Penglai Island[1]. Dadao was taken aback. He retreated into the pavilion, debating with himself: "Maybe she's a prostitute. But she has too much bearing and charm, and she seems far too delicate for that. But, then, if she's a decent girl, why are there no housemaids attending her? And, anyway, there's no entrance to the garden, so how on earth did she get in?" As he was wondering, the girl stopped right in front of the pavilion. "Where are you from, young lady? Are you here alone?" Dadao asked.

"I am your neighbor called Song Yuan, the sixth child in my family. Just now I was taking a walk after a nap. It is such a beautiful day, that I got carried away and when I came to a low wall I jumped over it, finding myself alone in your garden. I am ashamed of my behavior," the girl apologized innocently.

"Your parents will be concerned when they find you missing for so long," warned Dadao archly.

"I lost my parents long ago, and also my elder

---

[1] Penglai, an island off the tip of the Shantong Peninsula, is home to fairies in Chinese mythology.

brother and sister-in-law. Now I am the eldest among the sisters," she replied.

"Do you have a family of your own?" Dadao asked, tentatively.

The girl blushed, somewhat confused. "I am not yet married. And you?"

"I am considering it, but I have no definite person in mind yet," he admitted frankly.

"Won't you consider me, poor and ugly as I am?" said Song with a sly smile.

"I am nobody myself. Come on, let's not joke about this," admonished Dadao.

"I am just a short ivy unable to reach a tall pine tree like you. How can I be joking with you?" the girl protested.

Encouraged by this, the young man took her to the western side of the pavilion, and tried to embrace her. "This is not the right time," she pleaded. "Please let me go now. I will come back in the evening. Wait here for me." And she left.

Li waited restlessly in the pavilion until dusk. At last the amber sun sank into the misty clouds in the west. The measured chimes of the deep evening bell rang out from the temple while the curtain of night descended slowly upon the distant towers and the ancient trees nearby, scattering a myriad of twinkling stars. Li caught a rich smell of sweet perfume, and turning around, found Song Yuan standing by. He took a step toward her and said,

"You came alone. Won't that cause you trouble with your maids?"

"No, no trouble at all," Song assured him.

Hand in hand, they entered Dadao's room. He laid out food and drink, and they sat talking, pouring out their feelings for each other at the table until it was quite late. Then they took off their clothes and enjoyed each other in bed to their hearts' content. At daybreak, Song said goodbye to Dadao and left quietly by herself. She returned every night for a month, each time leaving at dawn.

One day, feeling rather tired, Li Dadao fell asleep at his desk in the study. A servant came in with a note from someone called Scholar Li Er, asking for an interview. At the door, Dadao found the visitor to be a grand and imposing man. Having entered and sat down, the man said, "I am an acquaintance of your father and owe him much kindness. I am concerned that you are now under the spell of an evil spirit. Please allow me to get rid of your trouble."

"What do you mean?" Dadao asked.

"The girl you have been with is no human. Would you like to see what she really is?".

"All right," Dadao answered.

"Bring her in," the man ordered his attendant.

Soon Song Yuan was roughly brought in, her pretty face covered with tears, and her body writhing with shame. The man yelled at her, and she turned into a large fox, scurrying away with its tail between its legs. Startled, Dadao stood up to express his thanks. The man left him a magic incantation on the table, saying, "Wear it on you, and she will not come near you again. But I have a small request to ask of you. My house near the market is small and low. It is now out of repair and no longer habitable. If you could have it repaired and cleaned up, I would be very grateful to you."

"You have saved me from disaster. How could I refuse your request? I will see to it immediately," answered Dadao. The man bowed his farewell.

Dadao woke up in a sweat. Sitting up, he could recall every detail of his dream. Casting his eyes around, he saw the magic incantation lying on his desk: a derivation of the Taoist Eight Diagrams, and felt a chill run down his spine. He immediately told his father what had happened to him ever since he had met the girl, including the strong man's words in his dream. His father was astounded and explained to him, "The man in your dream must be the Guardian God Erlang whom I have worshipped many times."

The county magistrate went to the Erlang Temple himself, and finding both the hall and hallway had collapsed, he had them rebuilt. Dadao wore the incantation day and night, never being without it. He saw Song Yuan several times nearly, but she was unable to approach him and he said nothing to her. She could do nothing, but watch and cry.

For a fortnight nothing happened. One day, while taking a walk in the garden, Dadao found a dainty sheet of notepaper with a poem written on it. It was written by Song Yuan to the tune of "Butterfly Flirting with Flowers":

Dawn broke in through the windowpanes,
Alone in bed, my heart could not be solaced,
Rent by a painful lovesick longing,
So close was he yet I could not get near.
Do not walk away like a philanderer,
Do not sway with the wind of spring.
My heart is slashed a thousand times,
But you, cold and relentless, turn away.

Dadao repeated it many times with admiration of her talent and beauty. As he was struggling with himself, Song Yuan appeared again among the swaying willows, radiant, gentle and gorgeously dressed. Dadao sighed to himself: "What is most precious to a man in life is a beautiful woman. No one could be more precious to me than Song Yuan, so what else do I care? No one can tell what I shall be in the next life. Why must I give her up now?" He tore up the incantation and boldly embraced her. Song Yuan was certainly more than willing to be back in his arms again.

"You know everything about my origin," she said in tears. "I deserve to be cast away without any hope. But you do not turn your back on me, and keep longing for me. I will never forget this as long as I live."

Dadao assured her: "As long as you stay firm, my heart will never change." The couple were in love once again, sweeter than ever.

However, evidently Dadao was burning himself out with passion. Greatly alarmed, his parents sent for a witch-doctor to cure him but failed to rein him in. They confined him to a closed chamber to shut Song Yuan out. But the next day, the house was raided by hundreds of monkeys, which hopped around or hung themselves over the doors and windows, making a mess of everything. This exasperated Dadao's father. The old man shut himself in the study, but one day he saw a letter thrust in through the window. He quickly opened the door and rushed out. There was no one to be found. He opened the letter and read:

From: Kong Changzong, a successful imperial examination candidate of Kuizhou

To: Squire Li Bao

Dear Sir:

I have long admired your noble qualities and high integrity but regret to have failed to visit you.

I am a descendant of Confucius, the sage, now living in Sichuan. My ancestors were all distinguished scholars and court officials. I used to have great pride in my culture and talent as well as in my person, but have now fallen hopelessly under

*the charm of an evil spirit. A year ago they turned
me into an ugly animal.*

*I have learned that your son has had the same
misfortune. If he goes on like this, he will end up an
animal as I have. The spirit that was my wife is
Song Yuan's younger sister. They have both turned
themselves into beauties and bewitched many a
young man. It was a great pity that your son has
torn up the incantation against evil spirits and
chosen the path to his doom.*

*I have also learned that the fox spirits have sent
monkeys to your house and turned the place into a
shambles. You can easily dispel them by keeping a
few hawks and hounds on the premises. Now the
relationship between you and Dadao is father and
son, but between you and me it is one of human and
beast. Nevertheless I feel deeply sorry for all the
innocent victims and myself living with animals.
This is my sincere warning. You may take or leave it
at your own discretion.*

On reading the letter, Li Bao was deeply shaken.
He followed Kong's advice and brought a great
number of hawks and hounds to the house. The
monkeys did not come any more. But one night in a
dream, a man appeared and said to Li Bao, "I am
Kong Changzong who wrote you the letter before.
Because the letter had betrayed the secret of the fox
spirits, they killed me beside the West Creek. Not
being human when I was alive, my spirit cannot

rest with my animal body. I know you are generous and kind; I can only come to you for help. My body now is still rotting in the wilderness. I would be most indebted to you if you could have me buried." Li consented and woke up. He went to the West Creek to find Kong's body, but failed. He called upon a group of monks to give the lost spirit a service of redemption and burned an elegy written by himself for the dead, which read in part:

Life is abundant between heaven and earth, but who knows where it comes from? The Creator gives it a soul and a body. Nobody knows what he will be in his next life in the transmigration of his soul. So what is there in life to celebrate or to cry for? I am sorry you have had a most unfortunate life and have no one to tell it. On reading your letter to me, I see that you were a man of literary gift, but I must apologize for my failure to find your body as you requested. Since you did not care much for your animal body, why must you have it buried in a grave? Only Buddha can save your wandering soul. Please go on looking for redemption elsewhere and do not waste opportunities. I do not know where you are now in this desolate place. Can you hear my prayer for you?

A few days after the funeral service, the monkeys returned to Li's house despite the hawks and hounds. Li Bao could do nothing about it and gave up meddling in his son's affairs. The house was left in peace again.

Song Yuan and Dadao met regularly again, even more fervently than before. She gave her parents-in-law silk and woolen cloths as presents, which Li Bao accepted only for fear of offending her. Then Li's wife had a heart attack which almost took her life. Even the best doctors failed to cure her. Bringing a bunch of herbs, Song Yuan assured Dadao, saying, "Mother's illness is not really serious. Just have this herb boiled and make her drink the liquid; she will be all right again." Dadao was sceptical about the herb, which was just a bunch of circular-shaped leaves. Nevertheless, he boiled them as required and made his mother drink the liquid. In less than an hour, she had fully recovered. The whole family believed Song was a saint, and accepted her as one of them with no more bad feelings.

Late in spring that year, Dadao and Song Yuan were enjoying themselves in the back garden with a table laid out with food and drink. They played musical instruments and chatted heart to heart. Flushed with the drink, Song Yuan composed a poem on the spot:

> *The branches of the trees weave into a dark*
> *   curtain,*
> *The white flowers hang on them like falling*
> *   snow.*
> *Slowly the cheeks of the beauty burn crimson,*
> *She abandons all restraint.*

Amazed at her poetic talent, Dadao jokingly challenged her, "How about composing one with me?" looking at the budding peonies clustered with butterflies in the garden. "With pleasure," she nodded.

"Butterflies are fluttering over the peonies beside the railing," Dadao began.

"Orioles singing on the branches of the crabapple tree," Song chimed in.

"Willow branches swaying like silk in the wind," Dadao continued.

"Young bamboos shooting out like jade in green," Song wound up.

Dadao was overwhelmed by her swift mind and knowledge in rhymes. They went on in this way till dark. Some time later, Dadao had business to take care of in Meizhou. He promised to be back in ten days, but was detained there 20 days by his relatives and friends. "Why were you there so long?" asked Song. "Kept by my friends," Dadao explained.

"Darling, when you were away the days were so terribly long; only silence reigned in the house. I did not even bother with make-up. I wrote this poem about my love and hate during that time." It said:

The east wind is sending spring to its home,
Stirring the flowers in the garden.
The willow branches are playing with the
*   curtains,*

As if they were the skirts of dancers.
My hair is disheveled as I weep alone,
When will he be home, be home?
Life is like the flowers in spring,
How long can it last alone, alone?

Dadao bowed deep to apologize.

A famous teacher called Zhang Qixing came to town, giving lectures to a large audience in a monastery. Li Bao sent his son to attend the lectures there. In the evening Song Yuan crept into Dadao's room to spend the night together with him. All the other students heard about this and were anxious to see this legendary Song Yuan. She was not at all shy and would talk with pleasure to anyone. Sweet and intelligent, she soon left a wonderful impression on everyone. No one would dream of telling the teacher about her, and so she was able to continue her nightly visits.

A successful imperial examination candidate named Yang Biao heard of this, and begged to visit Song Yuan. She consented. When they met, Yang stood up and presented a gold ornament with exquisite workmanship to her, saying, "I got this before I left the capital. It is a work of art, something too beautiful for anyone in my hometown. I would like to give it to you in exchange for a poem by you." Song accepted it gracefully and complied with his request. She wrote:

Painting the world green,
The God of Spring brings the life-giving season.
Please don't give this gift to your sweetheart,
It will vex others when she's seen with it.

Yang left with the poem, more than satisfied.

Later on Song Yuan gave birth to a son. When the baby was about one year old, one night she knelt down before Dadao, wailing beyond control. Aghast, Dadao asked why; she just went on crying without a word. On repeated questioning, she slowly answered, "Our meeting was no accident, but destined by fate. Now our union is due to end and I must leave you." She pulled herself together and tidied herself for the last time. "I am so fortunate to love and be loved by you without any restraint that I would readily die for you. According to the *Book of Songs*, although the Cowherd and the Weaving Maid are allowed to meet only once a year, at least they have that. In the Tang Dynasty, although Lady Su expressed her grievance in a poem woven into a silk cloth, she yearned for reunion with her husband. Now our separation is imminent, but with no chance of any future reunion. We can only suffer in pain and anguish till the end of our days. How could I refrain from tears and sorrow?" Her tears ran down like rain, and so did Dadao's. "Kong Changzong slandered me with unfounded stories to your parents, but they did not doubt me. Instead they allowed me to be with you so that we have had a wonderful time together in these two years, far happier than ordinary human couples. How could I ever do any harm to you? Kong was merely a pedantic scholar. How could he understand me? You are still young; you should study hard for a bright future and bring honor to your parents and ancestors and fulfil your duty as a worthy son. You must look to the future and forget me completely...."

"But shall we ever meet again?" Dadao asked. Song Yuan took up a brush-pen and wrote down her answer:

After two years of life as man and wife,
Never to meet again, we must part.
Only in dreams can we reunite,
On a mountain beyond the clouds.

That night they talked very late before going to bed. Early the next morning, Dadao got up to say good morning to his parents as usual. When he returned to his room, Song Yuan and their son had disappeared. He could do nothing but sigh deeply. Every windy night when the moon shone in the sky, the image of his spouse Song Yuan would emerge in his mind's eye. But never did he hear from or about her again.

22. Injustice at Yuanzhou Court

Hong Mai

This story is about an unjust verdict at Yuanzhou Court passed on four innocent people who are wrongly put to death to cover up the appalling negligence of duty of a local official. What is more, the higher authorities know full well that the verdict is wrong but are afraid they may be held responsible for the misjudgement. They settled the case simply by executing the poor innocent people. The callousness, corruption and high-handed policy of feudal rule, which cared nothing about human life, are laid bare before the reader. In the story, the officials responsible for the case are each and all punished by God. This reflects the traditional belief in retribution and also the ancient Chinese idea of the afterlife.

The story is taken from Tales of Gods and Spirits *Vol. 6. Its author, Hong Mai (1123-1202), alias Jinglu and Yechu, was born in Boyang County, Jiangxi in the Song Dynasty. He was a successful candidate of the imperial examination and ended up an Imperial Scholar of High Order. He became a famous writer for his works,* Random Thoughts in the Rong Study *and* Stories about Gods and Spirits, *the latter being the largest collection of classic tales by one single author in China.*

Secretarial Officer Xiang Zichang was in charge of litigation in Yuanzhou Prefecture during the Yuanfu period (1098—1100) of the Song Dynasty. Together with Magistrate Huang of Xinchang County and Judge Zheng of Biezhou Prefecture, he conducted the imperial examination in Nan'an District. After the exam, he was going home when Judge Zheng, who had a sister married to an official in Yuanzhou, wanted to go with him. It happened that Magistrate Huang had been secretarial officer of Yuanzhou three years before, so both Xiang and Zheng invited Huang to go along with them. Huang declined. "Do you forget the nice ladies there in Yuanzhou?" asked Judge Zheng in jest. Magistrate Huang gave way, but most reluctantly. On arrival in Yuanzhou, Huang tried to find lodging outside the city, but was urged by Xiang to stay with him in his official residence.

When they arrived at the residence, Xiang asked them to sit down for a while and then showed them to their rooms. But he found Magistrate Huang in a trance, sitting like a stone despite repeated requests to move. Pointing at a brass tray, he asked abruptly, "How much is this? Can I buy it?" Glad to have a response, Xiang signaled to his servant to take it to Huang's room.

"That is something quite common; why are you so anxious to buy it?" asked Xiang.

"Put it in my coffin," Huang answered.

Xiang was alarmed at his extraordinary response. He took Huang by the hand and tried to put him down to rest. Huang did not move. Xiang called Zheng back to take a closer look at him. After a while Huang began to scream, obviously from great pain. Suddenly, his bowels opened, covering the floor with blood. The poor man scrambled up and down the bed, howling throughout the whole night.

Deeply worried, Xiang and Zheng solemnly asked him, "You are in a bad condition. Do you have anything urgent to tell us?" Huang nodded and begged to see his mother and his wife. Xiang immediately sent a letter to Huang's family in Xinchang County. He said to Huang, "You did not want to come at first, but came only at our request. Now you are in such a precarious condition; if anything should happen before your wife arrives, it would leave us two in a very awkward position. How could we explain it to your family? I hope you can hold on and tell us why you originally refused to come and the cause of your sudden illness." Huang listened, eyes wide open, and in spite of the pain, made the following confession.

When I was an official in this prefecture, the

Yichun county police chief sent three archers to buy provisions, such as chickens and pigs, in the countryside. But they failed to return after forty days, and their wives reported this to the government of the prefecture. As the governor was on good terms with the county police chief, he referred the matter to the latter. The police chief lied to him, saying, "There are a lot of bandits in that area and I sent three men to find their hideout. To keep their mission secret, they left with an order to buy provisions as cover. Till now they have not returned and are presumed dead. I ask permission to gather all policemen of the counties to wipe out the bandits." The governor granted his request and the police chief led the men to the mountains and stayed there for two weeks with no results.

The police chief found four poor, clumsy-looking peasants working in the fields. He sent for them through a clerk with twenty thousand coppers as a reward, and declared to them, "Three archers have been murdered by bandits who could not be found and brought to justice by the county police chief. He wants you to confess to the murder so that the case can be closed. The case would be brought to court and you would be sentenced to death, in name only. Actually, you would be clubbed a dozen times and set free. In return for this, you will get five thousand coppers each to care for your wives and children, with no harm or danger whatever to yourselves. When you are in court and asked whether you have committed murder, you must say yes. Then you will go to prison fully fed and soon be set free. So why not take up this offer?" The four men agreed. They were tied up and sent to the county seat. Since the position of the county magistrate was then vacant, the case was handled by the revenue officer. When the men were tried, they all admitted to the "crime" as they had been told. When the case was reviewed by me, the suspects still clung to their position as before, and so the case was closed with a death sentence passed on each of them.

Before the day of execution, I went to see the four men and found them not at all like vicious muderers, which made me doubt the veracity of the case and its verdict. So I sent away the warden and questioned them again on the details of the case; they still admitted their "guilt" in unison. I explained the relevant articles of the law to them and said, "Your heads will be cut off tomorrow if you have actually done what you have admitted to. You know that when your head is separated from your body, there is no way to join them together again." The four looked at one another and burst out crying, saying, "We thought that there would be an execution in name only, and that we would be released and receive a reward when we went home. We did not know we would really die for it!" They told me the whole truth. I was greatly astonished, and had them untied. The police chief got wind of this and secretly told the governor that the official in charge of the case, meaning me, had been bribed by the convicts and wanted to reverse the verdict. When I returned to the prefecture yamen and reported the case to the governor, he roared at me, saying, "This case was closed and approved by higher authorities already. Are you going to alter the case because you have taken bribes?" "I have found the case totally misjudged. How can I not argue for the wrongly accused?" I argued.

The governor turned the case over first to the administrative supervisor of the prefecture, and then to the county yamen, but no one would accept the task. According to normal procedure, it should have been sent to the provincial judicial department to be put on file and investigated again. However, the governor said, "If this were done, a lot of officials in this prefecture would be found negligent of duty. How can we revoke a sentence already passed?" Thus all the transfer proceedings were burned, and the case returned to our local judicial department with an order to carry out the sentence. I strongly argued against it on a moral basis for over a fortnight, but to no avail. It was reported to the governor, who made the revenue officer, the acting county magistrate, carry out the sentence. At last, before the execution, the governor wavered, being afraid that it would be entirely his own responsibility if I had not undersigned the order of execution. He begged me through a colleague, who said to me, "The convicts are irreversibly sentenced to death. Your stubbornness won't do any good. You had better undersign your name at the end of the file. After all, everybody knows it was the county police chief's fault." I put down my name against my will, and that was the end of the four poor men.

Two days later, an officer in a yellow uniform took two county officials with a heavy club to the judicial office and shouted to two clerks: "Take out the files immediately!" Before the clerks could object, the officer's blows rained on them. They all went into the archives and closed the door behind them, never to come out again. I went to the room myself and found it locked as it had been. But from the crack of the door, I could see the files all over the floor and the two clerks and two officials all dead inside. A few days later, the acting county magistrate died. The county police chief, who had been promoted for some merit, also died. The governor of the prefecture fell with a stroke of apoplexy. All in a string within forty days.

One day while I was eating, I saw the four convicts kneeling before me, saying, "We were wrongly put to death and appealed to the King of Heaven, who decided to redress the wrong. You were on the list for arrest, but we said to Him, 'Everything we needed to know in order to appeal to you, we learned from Huang. Now that those seven are dead, we consider ourselves avenged and beg Your Majesty to spare him. The King of Heaven said, 'If he had not signed his name you would not have died. The four of you were executed under his signature, so he should be the first to be condemned.' We kowtowed in tears for forty-nine days until finally your death was delayed for three years." They pulled up their trousers to show their bleeding knees as proof. "When it is time," they said, "we will come back for you." They kowtowed and diappeared. When I entered your house, I saw the four men again. They said they had been waiting for some time and there was not much time left for me. They urged me to send for my mother and my wife to say farewell to them. That is why I refused to come here at first. What more can I say?

"But where are the four men now?" asked Xiang Zichang. "There," said Huang, pointing a finger at one side of the room. "They are standing to attention." Xiang and Zheng had a table laid there and burned incense on it respectfully, praying: "It is clear to you that Mr. Huang is going to die without resistance. You have allowed him to say goodbye to his mother and his wife; why make him suffer such terrible pain?" No sooner had the prayer ended than Huang's pain was gone. He claimed that their prayer had worked; he felt no more pain but still looked exhausted.

About ten days later, Huang told his friend Xiang, "My mother has come. Please prepare a sedan for me to meet her."

"Why? The messenger is not back yet."

"The four men told me so," Huang answered. He went out and met his mother outside the courtyard. He had barely pulled aside the door curtain and bowed to her before he dropped dead.

图书在版编目(CIP)数据

中国传奇选:英文/(唐)元稹等撰. —北京:
外文出版社,1998
ISBN 7 – 119 – 02098 – 6

Ⅰ.中… Ⅱ.元… Ⅲ.①传奇小说–作品集–中国–唐代–英文
②传奇小说–作品集–中国–宋代–英文 Ⅳ.I242.1

中国版本图书馆 CIP 数据核字 (1997) 第 21491 号

责任编辑 吴灿飞
英文编辑 梁良兴
封面设计 王 志
插图绘制 李士伋

外文出版社网址:
　http://www.flp.com.cn
外文出版社电子信箱:
　info@flp.com.cn
　sales@flp.com.cn

中国传奇选
〔唐〕元稹等撰
杨宪益　戴乃迭　黄均　译
＊
©外文出版社
外文出版社出版
(中国北京百万庄大街 24 号)
邮政编码 100037
通县大中印刷厂印刷
中国国际图书贸易总公司发行
(中国北京车公庄西路 35 号)
北京邮政信箱第 399 号　邮政编码 100044
2001 年(36 开)第 1 版
2001 年第 1 版第 1 次印刷
(英)
ISBN 7 – 119 – 02098 – 6/I·464(外)
04000(平)
10 – E – 3229P